PENGUIN BOOKS

A GIRL CAN DREAM

T0333095

Books by Emily Barr

A GIRL CAN DREAM

EMILY BARR

PENGUIN BOOKS

PENGUIN BOOKS

UK | USA | Canada | Ireland | Australia
India | New Zealand | South Africa

Penguin Books is part of the Penguin Random House group of companies
whose addresses can be found at global.penguinrandomhouse.com

www.penguin.co.uk
www.puffin.co.uk
www.ladybird.co.uk

First published 2024

003

Set in 10.5/15.5pt Sabon LT Std
Typeset by Jouve (UK), Milton Keynes
Printed and bound in Great Britain by Clays Ltd, Elcograf S.p.A.

The authorized representative in the EEA is Penguin Random House Ireland,
Morrison Chambers, 32 Nassau Street, Dublin D02 YH68

A CIP catalogue record for this book is available from the British Library

ISBN: 978-0-241-64342-6

All correspondence to:
Penguin Books
Penguin Random House Children's
One Embassy Gardens, 8 Viaduct Gardens, London SW11 7BW

MIX
Paper | Supporting
responsible forestry
FSC
www.fsc.org
FSC® C018179

Penguin Random House is committed to a
sustainable future for our business, our readers
and our planet. This book is made from Forest
Stewardship Council® certified paper.

For Craig

1

Venice

As I stand at the window and look across the water, I feel myself waking up.

This is me. I move my hands. I yawn and sense the air hitting my lungs. I close my eyes and breathe slowly. *In . . . out . . . in . . . out . . . in.* When I open them, the view, the water, the boats are still there. I have no memory of arriving, but here I am.

Only one place looks like this. I am in the City of –

I speak out loud, testing my voice. 'Is Venice the City of . . . Love?' I don't expect an answer and when the voice comes from behind it makes me jump.

'No, babe,' it says. 'City of Love is Paris.'

I turn fast, and it's Phoebe. Phoebe! She's just standing there, looking at me. We're in a big room, an apartment. Why can't I remember how we got here? I must have blacked out or something. I walk over and hug her, and I've missed her so much. I'm so glad she's with me. It's not just her: Enzo is sitting on a sofa in a nest of sheets. Enzo! Our eyes meet over Phoebe's head and I can see that, in spite of everything, I'm forgiven. My heart swells with love.

'Venice should be the City of Love,' I say, because now I know what love is, and it's this, and I know what love isn't. I go back to the window and try to make sense of the fact that I'm here. The sun is shining on the canal. The water is light, the air watery. The elements are bleeding into one another.

Down below on the canal bank I see a man walking past. My heart quickens and I have to check it's not him. If I'm here, he could be too. It would be easy for him to follow me. In fact, that's exactly what he would do.

Anxiety blooms like the speeded-up film of a flower unfurling. Its tendrils reach out and colonize every bit of me.

Of course he's going to find me. He won't let me go this easily.

But then there's a hand on my shoulder and Phoebe is calming me. She always makes things make sense and I've missed her like crazy. I make an effort with my breathing. I am here, and he's not. I'm with my friends, my real friends: in spite of everything I've done, they were there when I needed them. And now we're safe.

'Venice is *La Serenissima*,' Enzo says, appearing beside us, hamming up his Italian accent. 'The most serene.'

I breathe deeply, look again at the man outside. He has disappeared into the crowd. It wasn't him.

The most serene. That is exactly what I need. It's why I'm here.

2

Somewhere across the water a bell is ringing: I can hear it chiming again and again, one single note. Boats are passing by, and people are walking around. Sunshine is sparkling across the canal and everything is beautiful. There is the gentlest mist on the horizon.

'This is like being in one of those paintings.' I lean my head and shoulders out of the window again. I stretch further and further until I feel my centre of gravity shifting, then pull back just before I fall, enjoying the adrenaline rush.

'Who am I thinking of?' I turn to Phoebe, who knows this stuff, stuff about art. I lean on the wall, feeling it hard against my shoulder blades. The tiled floor is cold under my bare feet.

'Canaletto,' she says. 'Yeah, I know what you mean.'

I nod and try to focus on Canaletto, practising being normal. A holiday in Venice with my friends: that's *not* actually a normal thing to do, but it's what I seem to be doing. How long did I black out for? What happened in that time? I have no memories of arriving at all.

I look at both of them and turn away when they catch me. I wonder when we're going to talk about it. Whether we're going to talk about it at all.

'Nominative determinism,' says Enzo, and it takes me a moment to catch up. 'Canaletto painted canals because his name was Mr Little-Canal.'

'Surely it was the other way round,' says Phoebe. 'I don't know much about him, but I bet his name was, like, Pedro Smith or whatever, and he got a nickname for being good at paintings of Venice. I'm guessing.'

'His name wasn't *Pedro*, you twat. That's Spanish.'

Enzo gets on his phone to check, while I am drawn back to the window. It's still Venice. I watch a boat being moored at the quay and see people getting off. They're wheeling suitcases: new arrivals. Stepping off the boat, dragging bags, shell-shocked to be here at last. To be in Venice. To arrive in the place you've dreamed of for years.

We did that last night. We must have done. I just can't remember it.

Anyway, I'm here.

My legs are trembling and then I'm sitting on the floor. Phoebe slides down next to me and puts an arm round my shoulders. I lean on her. She's shorter than me and more substantial. She didn't used to be.

'Hey,' she says. 'You're all shaky. Don't worry, Hazel. It's OK. We're here. It's good. You're doing great.'

I know I must look like shit, and I know it's going to take time, but here I am, in what I think must be Enzo's mum's studio apartment, wearing white pyjamas that I forgot I had,

4

and my friends are with me. I hold on to Phoebe for longer than I should, and then I look over her head at Enzo, who is making an 'awwww' face. When he sees me watching, he changes it into an eyeroll.

'Ladies,' he says, 'enough canoodling. Some of us are hungry.'

'We're not *canoodling*,' says Phoebe. 'Christ's sake, Enzo.'

They want breakfast, but I don't want to leave the apartment, and I haven't had breakfast for nearly a year. I'll just stay behind and look out of the window. I know there are thousands of tourists out there, all wanting to see the Bridge of Sighs and St Mark's Square, to go on a gondola and to find authentic Italian food at a place that's not a tourist trap, and I am not ready to be one of them. I just want to check that the door is locked, and look out of the window, and try to remember the things I've forgotten and to forget the things I don't want to have in my head.

Someone gripping the tops of my arms. Slapping my face.

Enzo, back in his nest of sheets on the sofa, is triumphant. Again, I have to focus to remember what we were talking about.

'Incorrect! He was called Giovanni Antonio Canal. That *was* his name. I wish I was called Giovanni Antonio Canal.'

'Change your name then,' says Phoebe.

'Maybe I will. Let's trial it.'

I can see my wheely suitcase spilling its contents across the room. I'm the only one who hasn't bothered to put things away, even though that would normally be Enzo. I start to pick up my clothes and fold them. If I'm not planning to leave this room, I should keep it presentable.

5

As I do it, however, I identify a strange feeling inside myself. It's been in the background for months, but I never let myself acknowledge it. This time I do.

'I'm . . . hungry,' I say. 'Actually. Because you mentioned breakfast, Enz. When you guys go out, could you bring something back for me?'

I sense the two of them looking at each other, and I don't want them to say that I have to go out with them so I spring into action, picking up a green satin dress from AllSaints that's too shiny to crease. Green. I decide to pair it with clumpy DM shoes and my spiky necklace, and head into the bathroom to shower and change, unilaterally deciding to go first. They can talk about me while I'm gone.

This bathroom is tiny, but it has the best shower ever. I stand under the water and it's like being poked by a thousand needles, in a good way. Like watery acupuncture. I turn my face up, feel it massaging my skin and making me new again. I stay there for ages, steam billowing round me. It washes off the bad stuff and leaves a new me behind. I hope it does. I need it to.

'Sorry.' I open the door and see them stop talking. 'I was ages and I used all the hot water.'

'You know you look gorgeous without that stuff,' says Phoebe, gesturing at my dress, my eyeliner flicks, my carefully messy clipped-up hair.

I shake my head. I'm not ready to lose my armour, even if I stay inside. If I don't create myself, I won't know who I am. I'm wearing green, and that's an unapproved colour, and it's a big step.

Phoebe showers quickly and coldly, swearing at me through the door. Enzo says that luckily for me he's already clean, so he just sprays himself with deodorant and cologne. Then they gather up bags and keys and stand in the doorway, looking at me.

'I'm staying here.' My words fall over each other. 'If you could get me a coffee and some ... food, that would be amazing. Thanks, guys.'

'Hazel,' says Phoebe.

'Mate,' says Enzo. 'No.'

They wait. I feel the tears pricking the backs of my eyes and tell them not to fall. Apart from the big stuff, I can't risk my eyeliner flicks. 'I can watch everything through the window. Baby steps. I don't need to go out. I don't think I *can* go out yet.'

Phoebe comes over and takes my hand. 'Haze. You can do this. It's Venice out there. Nothing bad. No one bad. Actual Venice. The place you've dreamed about.' She tries to pull me towards the door. I don't move.

'Come on,' says Enzo. 'We've wanted to do this since we were kids. There's no way I'm going out without you.'

Phoebe, small and determined, folds her arms.

'Same,' she says. 'If you stay here, we all do. I know you're scared, but you just have to face it. You can't hide from this. It's not scary out there. It's fabulous and you're coming. We're on holiday. It's going to be fun.'

I look away.

'Can we go somewhere nearby?' They nod.

I pick up my bag. 'You annoying bastards.'

7

3

I hold the handrail all the way down the five flights of stairs and the others keep having to wait on the landings for me to catch up.

'Ready for this?' Enzo is standing inside the heavy front door. I shrug. He opens it and, holding Phoebe's hand, I step out.

The watery smell and the sun hit me and I feel it around me, touching my skin, the hairs on my arms. It's on my face, under my feet, surrounding me. It's Venice. I'm not just looking at it: I'm in it. I'm a part of it. I'm here.

Enzo is chatting to a white-jacketed doorman at the hotel next door. There's a breakfast menu outside, in a silver frame. Stuck on the wall next to it are a bunch of posters for candlelit concerts, which I think would probably be quite nice. Sitting down, closing my eyes, letting music wash over me.

Enzo is trying to lead us into the hotel.

'How much is it?' I say. I must have spent *all* my savings getting here. I can't blow whatever's left on one breakfast.

Phoebe huffs. 'It's way too posh for us, Enz,' she says. 'Let's find a cafe. It's not as if there are no other options.'

'Nah, let's go here,' says Enzo. 'Hazel needs food now. Don't worry about the bill, ladies. My treat.' He nods to the doorman, and gives a rich-person signal of some kind that leads the man to magic up another waiter, who invites us to follow her to a table. 'Come on. Let's get you some food, Haze,' he says. 'You said it yourself – you're hungry. And you honestly look like you're about to keel over.'

'Serious?' Pheebs is sceptical, correctly. 'I mean, yeah, let's get Hazel a brilliant breakfast nearby, but not here, mate. She needs to be fed up, but if you forget you said you'll pay, we really will be *fed up*.'

She looks at me. We high-five at her weak pun. The normality makes my eyes prickle. They're not angry with me. They should be.

'I'm paying,' Enzo says. 'Promise.'

'We're supposed to be doing this cheaply,' I remind him. I don't remember that, but of course we are. 'And this is . . .' I check the menu as we walk past it, displayed in the frame like a work of art. 'Thirty! Thirty euros! Enz – what were you thinking?'

'Hey.' He nudges me, our shorthand for support. 'I'm thinking that we made you come out when you didn't want to. And this is the nearest place. I'm stoked you're here. And you're hungry. Please allow me to do something about that fact.'

A moment later we're seated by the window, at a table covered by a dark red tablecloth with a smaller white one over the top. The chairs are encased in fabric like the ones at our parents' embarrassingly elaborate wedding. The menus are hardback coffee-table books. I feel like an imposter, eating among the hotel guests who must be paying hundreds of euros a night to sleep in this building when we're staying next door for free. Enzo doesn't. He was born to this stuff. I came into it later, and I've never quite settled. I can remember when Mum and I were poor.

'Have whatever you fancy, ladies,' he says with a wave of his hand.

Phoebe attempts to order an iced oat chai latte and discovers that she can't, in fact, have whatever she fancies. We end up with regular coffee (black for me) from the tall pots, and fruit salad, and pastries. Enzo adds scrambled egg and bacon to his order, and makes sure we get fresh orange juice.

I look at the basket of pastries. I start with the fruit salad.

'This is how we do it,' says Enzo, sitting back, looking smug. 'In style.'

The people at the next table are our parents' age, and I can feel their glances sliding towards us and then away when I try to return them.

'I don't remember arriving,' I admit.

There. It's out in the world. I look at their faces and this seems OK. I must have been really out of it: they're not even surprised.

'I just have this big blank. I try to remember, but there's nothing. Was I weird?'

Phoebe puts her hand over mine. 'You were ... in a bit of a state,' she says. 'Don't worry. It's OK. You're here now, Haze. You're safe. You can relax and have fun.'

I look into her face. I've always been able to read Phoebe and I can see that she's sincere. After a while, I nod.

'Does Mum know we're here?'

They look at each other. 'Yes,' says Enzo. 'It's fine, Haze. Don't worry. Everything's sorted.'

'And it is Vittoria's apartment?'

'You know it. We finally made it.'

Then I feel my face doing a strange thing. The corners of my mouth rise up a bit.

I'm smiling.

Enzo is too. The thing we've been planning forever is actually happening. I can't believe I missed the start of it.

'Right,' he says, 'let the fun times commence. Holiday. We did it.'

I lean back. Being here is miraculous. I sip my coffee. I eat a grape. I think about the girl I used to be, and wonder whether I could ever be her again.

4

Kent

Nineteen months earlier

The music was pulsating through me. Somewhere along the way I'd lost my friends and now I was right at the front of the crowd. My hair was sticking to the back of my neck, and I was slick with sweat, surrounded by strangers, my red T-shirt clinging to me. All I could hear was music, and the drums seemed to be located inside my body, beating outwards. I yelled along with the song. Everything was amazing.

All the time I was staring at the drummer, jumping in time with her beats. I knew her name: Lina. I watched her sweating, pounding away, holding the whole thing together, and wondered whether I could ask for a drum kit. It was one of those comedy requests, a joke 'what I want for my birthday' item, but I suddenly really wanted one.

Her T-shirt was drenched with sweat. She was the coolest person I'd ever seen: throwing herself into it, using all her energy, lost in the music. I wanted her to look at me, but she didn't. She was concentrating completely.

I did feel eyes on me, though, and turned my gaze to the lead singer. He couldn't really have been looking at me, not out of everyone in this crowd, but it felt that way. When my eyes met his, he gave a little smile and nodded at me. Freddie Kennedy, the frontman, was one of those implausibly good-looking guys. Everyone fancied him. He had a perfect face, a smooth, deep voice, and I had to admit that he looked amazing in his jeans and sweaty T-shirt. I watched him drink from a bottle of water, saw his Adam's apple move as he swallowed. I felt his eyes on me the whole time.

I didn't break eye contact. He didn't either.

I heard a voice in my head saying, *Look away*.

I turned my eyes back to Lina the drummer.

Freddie was strutting round the stage again and the whole weird moment was over. I let the crowd move me around, and I yelled out some words because this band, Kennedy, did a mix of their own songs and covers. Right now it was the Pixies' 'Debaser', and all I wanted was to become the music. I wanted to transform myself into something that travelled in waves through time and space and made everyone feel joy.

Look away. That had been weird. I heard that voice in my head a lot, but it had never intruded this much before.

I stumbled on a discarded plastic cup and grabbed the person next to me. We were at the Old Bakery, a venue close to home, and it was hardly the Brixton Academy. This place only held a few hundred people, so nothing catastrophic was going to happen, but the guy turned and held me up.

'Hey!' he yelled into my ear. 'You OK?'

I nodded and he grinned. Then he leaned in again. 'Need some water?'

I shook my head because I knew better than to drink anything a strange man might hand me (Mum had drummed that into me). I felt his eyes on me as I went back into my music trance, my gaze firmly back on Lina the drummer. When the song ended, he was there again.

'You on your own?'

'Friends.' I waved a hand behind us.

'Need a break?' He motioned with his head, indicating getting out of the zone for a breather. I shook my head. Then I realized I was hot and thirsty and grabbed his arm to change my response to a nod. I followed him out of the crowd, to the bar at the back of the room.

This guy was a bit taller than me, gym-muscular, with very short hair and freckles. He seemed, I thought, nice enough. I looked back at the band, though I could hardly see them through the forest of heads. Freddie was yelling into the microphone again. Lina was hitting the drums, Ollie on guitar. I wondered whether Freddie and Lina were together. I knew that Ollie was his brother. Kennedy were local heroes, poised on the brink of megastardom. That was what everyone said. I'd told Mum this was what going to an early Radiohead gig would have been like for her, and she'd gone all misty-eyed and put on *The Bends*.

I turned to my new friend.

'What do you want?' he said. We still had to shout here, but we didn't actually have to yell until our throats hurt.

'Water, thanks.'

I watched the woman behind the bar hand him an intact bottle of water, watched him paying for it and handing it straight to me. I opened it and felt the seal break.

It slipped down my throat. The break from the intensity was actually nice, though I wanted to get back in soon.

He got himself a beer and tipped his bottle against mine.

'Thanks,' I said, smiling at him. Our arms touched as we leaned back.

'I'm Lewis.'

'Hazel.'

'Nice name. I don't know any Hazels.'

I wanted to say I didn't know any Lewises, but I couldn't because I knew loads. Instead I said, 'I don't know any Linas.'

Where had that come from? I cringed as I saw him take in what I'd said and frown slightly. 'But I know a few people called Lewis,' I added.

'Lina? The drummer?'

I nodded. I looked over at the stage. When the next song started, I said, 'Thanks for the water,' and headed back into the crowd and squeezed to the front again.

5
Venice

When we step outside the hotel, everything is perfect. There's a little breeze but the sky is clear. I stand still and breathe it in. This is real and I can't believe I'm here.

'You're right,' says Enzo. 'We're literally in a painting. One of Giovanni Antonio Canal's. You know, most places don't live up to the hype. I legit didn't think this would, but it does. You can practically see the brushstrokes.'

'How come you haven't been before?' asks Phoebe. We start walking, shuffling along with a lot of other people in what I guess is the direction of the main tourist stuff. 'If I had that studio, I'd live in it forever. I'd never go anywhere else.'

'Well, that'd be because I don't *have* it,' he says.

'It's your mum's.'

'Yeah. I knew some old dude had left her a place, but I never met him and you know perfectly well I don't exactly see her, so it's not been, like, *Oh great, my new home – I'll move here right now and be a digital nomad.*' He pauses. 'Now that I'm here, though, I might do that. There's a uni, you know. We should check it out.'

After Enzo and I watched that horror movie *Don't Look Now* inappropriately young, our takeaway, for some reason, was the fact that there were no roads in Venice, that people went everywhere by boat. Enzo called his mum to double-check that there really weren't any cars, and when she confirmed it we agreed that we would come here one day.

A place without cars feels like a haven, though I'm not quite sure why.

When Vittoria casually mentioned that she'd inherited an apartment, we thought we could go there for one of our birthdays, and then everything went wrong and now, somehow, here we are.

Vittoria is brittle, says *darling* a lot and lives in Milan. I remember her telling us, once, that if we used the apartment we should call in on her on our way home: I have no idea whether we're going to do that, and I'm relieved. I never want to make my own decisions ever again because when I do I fuck everything up.

'I might swim across the canal,' says Enzo.

'Go on then.' Phoebe gestures to the opaque water.

'Better let my breakfast settle or I'll get cramp.'

The path towards St Mark's Square is lined with souvenir sellers, their glass things and T-shirts spread out on stalls and rugs. I know it's tat, and that these glass trinkets are probably imported rather than handmade, and I walk past – until suddenly I don't.

Something hooks me: a glass bird, a green and yellow one. I almost feel it looking at me. Its glassy eye swivels round.

It doesn't. Of course it doesn't.

I check out the seller, who is sitting down beside the wares he's spread out on a mat. He's wearing a dark blue T-shirt with a Doctor Who logo (random) and jeans, and when our eyes meet my legs stop working. I stand there and stare at him, then the bird. It's not that I fancy him. I'm never going to fancy any man ever again. I feel I know him, even though we can't possibly have seen each other before. There's something in his eyes.

I look back at the bird, which is calling to me so hard that it's almost glowing. I reach down and pick it up, and even though it's glass it's hot in the palm of my hand. For a second I think it turns its smooth head to smile at me.

'*Quanto costa?*' I ask self-consciously, aware of my bilingual stepbrother at my side.

The stallholder gives me a long look. Then he nods and says, 'Five euros,' in English.

I open my purse, pleased to see I have some money in there. I hand him a five-euro note and close my hand round the bird. It's so small: it fits perfectly.

'Can't believe you paid five euros for that piece of crap,' says Enzo as we continue walking.

I ignore him. 'What's Italian for bird?'

'*Uccello.*'

'Then that's my bird's name. Cello for short.' I glance at him, then away. 'I know it's crap, but it's a symbol, Enz. You know? It's kinda – freedom and all that.'

He doesn't answer. He bumps me with his shoulder, and that's all I need. I put Uccello into the inside pocket of my tote bag.

We move with the flow of tourists. I note that I am out in the world, and managing. Then Phoebe touches my arm.

'Let's bail on following the crowd,' she says. 'I know there are things we want to see, but I'm sure we can find them this way.'

She leads me to a tiny alleyway and, as my plan is to make no decisions, I follow. Enzo's behind us.

'What's in here?' he says. 'Stinks!'

'No idea. That's the point.'

Phoebe sets off, heading away from the Riva degli Schiavoni. I walk fast to keep up and to get through the stench as quickly as possible. It smells of piss, basically, and of damp that comes up through paving stones and never dries out. The walls are high on either side of us. It's silent, apart from our footsteps, and for a second I think we could come out anywhere in the world.

But actually the alley leads us to a square with tall buildings and windows all around it. It's busy, but less so than where we were before.

Now that we know you can get away from the crowds by walking down a random path, we embrace it. I'm full of breakfast, fuller than I have been for over a year, and I find I have energy. I'm walking fast to burn it off, but also I'm walking fast because, for once, I can. My body is working. I can make it strong again.

We duck down the least likely path at every point, finding that some of them lead to dead ends, either in courtyards with no other exit or at the bank of a canal with no path.

The air is warm on my face and, even though the sun is hot, the breeze from the water makes it all perfect.

At one of our dead ends, there's a little boat just moored up to a post. I look at the side of it. It's called *Uccello*, like my bird. I reach into my bag and feel it smooth in my hand.

'Brilliant,' says Enzo, and he starts to climb in. 'Definitely a sign that it's for us since we've just been talking about *uccelli*.' It's a speedboat, and it does look tempting, but still.

'Nice,' says Phoebe, and she follows.

'You can't!' I move away. 'It's someone's *boat*! You can't just get in it.' I have no idea what they're doing. I take another step back, and then another.

'Chill, Haze,' says Enzo.

'They might be watching from one of those windows. They'll call the canal police! Please don't.'

'We won't steal it. We just want to sit in a boat, and this one is all tucked away,' says Phoebe, and I catch her giving Enzo a little look, the two of them commenting wordlessly on my anxiety. I sit down and hug my knees.

'We need to get a selfie,' says Enzo. 'Going in a boat was one of our things to do today.'

I look up. 'A gondola! Not someone's actual private boat. It's like getting into somebody's car parked on a street.'

I can't stop them, so retreat back into myself while they giggle in the boat, making it rock from side to side. They take a million selfies, pouting into the camera, the water behind them. I'm in the background of some until they tell me to move because I'm killing the vibe. Nobody shouts from a window. The canal police don't turn up.

I take Cello out of my bag and hold her in the palm of my hand. She comforts me: I miss my mum. I miss my dad. I only have a glass bird on my side.

I try to summon my dad's voice in my head. This doesn't often work any more, but maybe now it will.

Why have I forgotten the journey? I say. *Why can't I remember coming here?* He doesn't answer.

I shift up, away from them and look across the narrow canal. There's a blank wall there, creamish, with a watermark above the current water level. Higher up there's a little window. It's dark and blank.

Then it's not.

There are eyes looking back at me. A face.

It comes into focus. It's a girl, about my age, I think. She has short black hair and she's staring right at me.

Phoebe and Enzo are climbing out of the boat. I see them in my peripheral vision, but I don't turn my gaze away from the girl. It's like our eye contact is the only thing there is. She looks at me and I look at her, and then everything that's around me disappears.

Her face fades away.

There is only the blue of the sky, going darker, darker, darker and then pulsing.

My feet aren't on the ground any more. I'm somewhere else.

I hold Cello tightly. I try to breathe and count.

6

Venice has gone. I feel myself hanging in the air. Time stretches on and I can't stay like this, but here I am. Suspended.

An explosion? Did a bomb go off?

Have I fainted? If I've blacked out again, I hope the others catch me before I fall in the canal.

I hear my name, from far away. *Hazel?* Gentle. A new voice.

I don't know how the word can come from nowhere and everywhere.

I hang in the air, waiting for gravity to kick in. I look for the others, but I can't see them; everything around me is bright and blue and there's nothing. No shapes, no people, no heat, no sound. I can move my eyes, but not my head. I do my best to stretch out, but there's nothing solid. The air is almost tactile around me. I try to do the numbered breathing, but I don't think I'm breathing at all.

It lasts longer than it could possibly last.

Then there's a jolt and I'm back.

7

And we're walking with the crowds. The Grand Canal is over to our left, and everyone, including us, is shuffling towards where I guess the tourist stuff is located.

'What?' I stop and look around. I stretch out my hands. Close my eyes and open them. Cello was in my hand and now she's not. Where is she? I look down. She's not on the paving stones. I check my bag. Not there.

And anyway what are we doing here? Have I blacked out again? Why are we at the Grand Canal and not by the *Uccello* boat? There's Enzo, huffing next to me. There's Phoebe, looking around, probably for a place that serves iced oat latte.

Is it still morning? Afternoon? Is it the same day?

'What what?' asks Enzo, his voice lazy.

'I mean, what just happened?'

'Hey,' says Phoebe. 'You OK?' She pauses. 'We're in Venice, Haze. Remember? I know you had some memory gaps, but everything's fine.'

I look around, wanting this to make sense. I touch the back of my head, my bum, my legs, trying to work out whether I fell, but everything's dry. I didn't end up in the canal. Nothing is bruised or scraped. Nothing hurts at all.

'What time is it?'

I search my bag again, but Cello has definitely disappeared. I open my purse and see the five-euro note I used to buy her.

'Ten-ish,' says Enzo.

'Ten thirteen,' says Phoebe, checking.

'In the morning?'

Enzo makes a face. 'Duh.' He stops, looking at the purse in my hand. 'You didn't get robbed?'

'The opposite. I got money back.'

I stop and look around. The sun is high in the sky. The man who sold me the bird is up ahead. We haven't got there yet . . .

I haven't blacked out. I've gone back in time. *What?*

'Did I buy a glass bird?'

'What? What are you talking about, H?'

'I'm talking about . . . Oh, I don't know. Weren't we here before?'

'Oh,' says Phoebe. 'I get that sometimes. Déjà vu. You feel like you've bought a glass bird before? But actually you've just imagined doing it?'

'It's understandable if you feel a bit weird, Haze,' says Enzo. 'A lot has happened.'

I don't know how to explain, so I just pull the clip out of the back of my hair and let it loose. Did I do that before? No. I walk over to the same guy, who's wearing his Doctor Who T-shirt, and when he looks at me there's that recognition in his eyes again.

Phoebe is right: I'm experiencing déjà vu. It happens. I'm half mad anyway, so it shouldn't be surprising.

'Hello again,' he says. I shoot a look at Enzo and Phoebe, but they're talking about something and haven't heard.

I stare. Something shivers right through me.

No. He will have heard what we were just saying. He's heard Phoebe talking about déjà vu and he's playing along with it.

I hand him the same five-euro note, put the same bird in my pocket and let Phoebe take us down the same alleyway, rationalizing like crazy as I go. This is me cracking up. I thought I saw a girl through a window and then ... Anyway, I'm here.

I follow Phoebe and Enzo through the alleys again. Last time we took the narrowest path whenever there was a choice, but this time we pick one randomly. We stop in a square with a curvy-walled church in it. This is new. New to me but old.

'Where next?' Enzo is checking out the different exits. There are three, not counting the way we've just come. 'Haze – your turn.'

I look at the paths. I have no idea. I know I'm taking way too long to decide so I point at the middle one.

Half an hour later and we haven't come to the place with the boat, and nothing weird has happened. I'm starting to rationalize it, even to forget about it. Stress. Brains are weird. That kind of thing. It recedes. It was a moment and, like so many other things, it's over. There wasn't a girl at a window or a boat. There wasn't a blue pulsating sky. I *did* buy a glass bird. I bought it once. That's why I have one, not two.

My feet hurt. I'm a bit thirsty. I have a water bottle in my bag and so I take a huge swig from it.

We're sitting on a bench, looking out at a canal. There's washing strung across it, all bright white against the strip of pale blue sky. I can smell the water. It's not horrible, just intense. Water and old stone. Little motorboats keep coming past, and the people smile at us and sometimes wave.

I can't quite lose the image of Phoebe and Enzo messing around in that boat. Taking selfies. Making me move because I was scowling in the background. It feels as real as this does. I know it happened. They were mucking about and . . .

'Pheebs?' I say. 'Can I look at your phone?'

'Why?'

'I want to check out your photos.'

She gives me a bit of a look, but I don't care because I've just realized I can prove this, one way or another.

'Knock yourself out.' She hands it over.

Her most recent pictures are from the breakfast table. Enzo and me clinking our coffee cups. An aerial view of a croissant. The three of us leaning together for a selfie, the people at the table behind visibly disapproving. I scroll back from there, even though there's no point. Phoebe in the studio bathroom for some reason taking a photo to check her make-up rather than using the huge mirror. The view from the window, across the Grand Canal. Me and

Enzo sitting on the sofa, bright-eyed and excited. Venice as some distant lights in the dark. I don't remember the last two at all.

I hand the phone back. I don't want to see anything before that. 'Thanks.'

She takes a photo of me, and then one of Enzo, and then a selfie of the three of us, and puts the phone in her pocket.

'What time is acceptable for a gelato?'

'Any time,' says Enzo. 'It's holiday, and it's Italy. Both those things mean it's gelato whenever you want.'

'In that case,' I say, 'let's get one.' I force myself to enter into the conversation properly, to be normal. 'But, Pheebs, presumably you've found a particular place you want to go to, right?' She is the queen of research. 'The best one on Insta? We're not talking random ice cream, right?'

Phoebe is delighted. 'Yes! It's nearby too. Hazel – do you think you might have one?'

I nod, even though I don't want one at all. I need to get back into the holiday mood.

'I might,' I say. I get my own phone out, but there are no messages, thank God. I wonder, though, why Mum hasn't checked in. Why isn't there a barrage of messages from her, given we came here at such short notice?

I write her a quick text:

> Mum – everything's fine here.
> I'm in Italy with E & P and
> having a great time. Venice is
> gorgeous.

I attach a photo of a canal to prove that it's Venice because we both know how much I've lied about my location over the past year.

I take a few more photos of my own, so that if I have déjà vu or a weird blackout thing again, I'll be able to monitor it for myself. I photograph the three of us, together in Venice at last. The building behind us looks like a palace, but it's probably a house. Flat-fronted, old, its plasterwork stained, windows like rows of blank eyes watching us. For a second I think I see real eyes again, but, when I take a photo and zoom in, the window on the screen is blank.

The city enfolds me again. I find my worries drifting away and focus on walking. I want to be strong again. Alive. Vibrant.

We walk to the gelato place from Instagram. Phoebe buys a *Gianduiotto* chocolate ice cream because it's fancy, and Enzo spends ages choosing a dark chocolate with pistachio cream. I take a deep breath and ask for a strawberry sorbet because I like strawberries and partly, secretly, because sorbet is lighter than ice cream. There seems no point eating a load of double cream for no reason. Double cream. The idea suddenly makes me want to vomit.

I stop and frown at myself. Why? It's only ice cream. It's famous for being nice. That's its USP.

And, oh my God, I used to *love* ice cream. I'd have been trying the most exciting flavours. I'd have gone for anything with salt and sugar in it. For a second I'm back in the kitchen at home, eating salted-caramel ice cream from the tub with Enzo, the night of that first Kennedy gig.

I shake thoughts of that away and we sit on a red bench in a square and watch people going by. The strawberry is cold in my mouth and makes my teeth hurt. I let it melt on my tongue.

I sigh. I let her go, the imaginary stranger with the short black hair. It was nothing at all, something I conjured out of the dust and magic of this city. Italy is full of good-looking strangers and I don't need to engage with them. I have a boyfrien–

I wince. I *don't* have a boyfriend. That's the whole point. It's what all this is about.

8

Kent

Nineteen months earlier

We were among the last to leave the Kennedy gig because it took us so long to find each other.

'It was good,' said Phoebe. 'I mean, the singer's hilariously up himself. What a twat. I like the others, though.'

'He is not up himself!' I surprised myself at how defensive I was. I thought of him looking at me, giving me a half-smile. 'He's amazing.'

She patted my arm. 'All right there, Mrs Freddie Kennedy,' she said.

'Shut up.'

'Hazel's in love,' announced Enzo.

'Fuck off.'

Fatima came to the conversation late. 'That guy who bought you a drink? He looked fit. You gonna see him again?'

'No,' I said. 'I mean, yeah, he was nice. He got me a drink because I kind of fell over on him. I think he thought I was drunk.'

'But actually you were high on life,' said Enzo.

'High on Freddie Kennedy, more like,' said Phoebe, giving me a big grin. 'Come on, Haze. Let's get you home.'

'I tripped,' I said, 'and I'm not high on Freddie Kennedy.' They weren't listening.

I didn't want to tell Phoebe that if I was picking a member of Kennedy it would be Lina in a heartbeat. There were a lot of things I was discovering lately that I didn't quite understand about myself. One was the fact that I hadn't had a crush on a boy for ages. I loved art, my favourite subject at school, and I kept finding myself drawing girls.

We were standing on the pavement round the corner, our breath huffing into the November night, saying goodbye before we set off in different directions, when a door opened behind us and the band walked out. That was when we realized that we were accidentally waiting at the stage door.

There was actual Lina. Up close her white-blonde hair was dazzling. I stared at her in her tight jeans and sweatshirt and wished I looked like that. Hers were like normal clothes, but somehow more stylish. The cut of the sweatshirt, the way the denim clung to her legs, the boots she was wearing.

I glanced down at myself. We were almost rocking the same style, but she was cooler than anyone I'd ever seen.

I waited for her to look at me. She didn't.

'Brilliant gig, Lina!' said Enzo's mate Jack.

She gave us a huge smile. 'Cheers, guys. Thanks for coming. God, it's freezing, isn't it?'

'Freezing,' I echoed, too quietly.

Then Ollie Kennedy was there, beer bottle in one hand, guitar strung over his back. I half heard the others talking to him, heard him replying, but I wasn't really listening: I was watching Lina talking to Fatima. A van pulled up on the double yellow lines. A teenage girl, a bit older than us, jumped out and opened the sliding back door.

I felt a hand on my shoulder. It pressed down, light and heavy at the same time.

'Hey,' said a voice close to my ear. 'I saw you in the crowd tonight.'

Freddie Kennedy was talking to me, touching me, and somehow, even though Phoebe was right and he *was* up himself, he made my heart beat faster. I tried to think of something smart to say. I realized I was grinning like an idiot.

'Yeah.'

That was all I could manage. He was talking to *me*. Just me, up close. He remembered me. He made everything in my body feel different. It was a chemical thing, not a choice.

'Well, thanks for coming,' he said, and I pulled myself together and found my voice.

'The gig was amazing,' I told him. 'So cool. You guys are awesome.'

'That's very kind. Look, I don't know what you're up to right now, but do you guys fancy coming along to the –?'

Lina spoke sharply. 'Fred, they can't be more than sixteen.'

His eyes lingered on me and I felt myself change under the beam of his attention. 'Right, yeah. Thanks for coming tonight, guys. Means a lot to us to have support from a home crowd.' He turned to Lina and Ollie and patted himself down. 'Left my keys. Give me a sec.'

The girl who was waiting at the van said, 'Freddie?'

'One sec!' he called to her. She had long dark hair and a tight dress, and she climbed back inside the van.

We stood on the pavement while he dashed inside. I half wanted to tell him that I wasn't sixteen yet, that my birthday was still a few weeks away. I listened to my friends asking Lina and Ollie where they were playing next.

'Hoxton Underbelly in a couple of weeks,' said Ollie. 'If you fancy coming along, we could probably get you tickets.' He looked at Lina. 'Right?'

Freddie was back.

'Sure,' Lina said. 'Message Pete. Our manager. His number's on the website. Say I told you to.'

Freddie didn't look at me, but I felt his hand take mine. He put something in my palm and closed my fingers round it.

The thrill of the warmth of his hand on mine went through me, touching every cell inside my body, a warm electric shock. As soon as he'd moved away, I shoved the tiny piece of paper into my back pocket. The band climbed into the van and then they were gone.

When Enzo and I got home, all the lights were on and there was music playing. It was 'I Will Survive', and that meant one thing. 'I Will Survive' was Mum's break-up song. She had activated it often lately. The song was a cliché in the first place and now it had become the most stressful, unsettling sound in the world. Every note of it made me want to run and hide.

We stopped on the pavement and looked at each other.

My mum and Greg had been together since Enzo and I were ten. They were delighted when the two of us, both only children living with a single parent, slipped into a sibling relationship straight away: it turned out that each of us had always half wished for a twin, and we found everything we needed in each other. One of the first things I said to Enzo, as a nervous child who was sure this new boy was going to hate me, was, 'We both have a Z.' He'd grinned and fist-bumped me, which I'd misinterpreted, and so the Zed Club and its complex handshake had been born.

I felt I'd known Enzo all my life, as if we actually *were* twins and had been separated at birth. We even quizzed our parents about it, despite the two-month age gap, and they gave each other fond looks and told us not to be so silly, but that there were lots of different ways of having a family and this was one of them.

Mum and I had lived in a second-floor flat at the top of a Victorian house, with sloping ceilings and tiny rooms. Enzo and Greg had a huge town house, our current home, because Greg was a banker. Since both our parents were workaholics, Enzo and I had become inseparable almost at once. We made up our own little worlds, shorthands, in-jokes. Hazel and Enzo. Enzo and Hazel. The Zed Club soon had a 'logo':

E
N
HAZEL
O

We started with blanket dens and make-believe, and moved through TV, unsuitable movies, friends, crushes, rarely arguing and swiftly making up when we did. Enzo was closer to me than anyone in the world. Greg adopted me when he and Mum got married, so he was officially my dad too. We thought that made us half-siblings as well as step ones.

Greg, however, was not my dad.

My dad was Morris Angelopoulos. I heard his voice in my head, glimpsed him from the corner of my eye. I didn't entirely believe he wasn't still around somewhere. I saw him in crowds watching me from a distance. I mean, I knew he was dead, but a part of me still thought that one day I'd see him again.

Now Enzo and I were standing outside our house, listening for the sound of shouting voices, which weren't there unless you counted Gloria Gaynor's. We communicated by facial expression that we needed to go in and see what was happening, our breath huffing in the cold air. As we walked up to the front door, I was so nervous that I forgot about the fact that we were freezing, that we'd been to a gig, that Freddie Kennedy had handed me a piece of paper that was in my back pocket right now.

I unlocked the heavy door and we stepped in, closing it behind us. The house felt empty, but I knew it wasn't.

Mum and Greg had only had two or three happy years, or maybe even fewer than that. Now Enzo and I were desperate for them to stay together until we left home. They could literally stop us being brother and sister by getting divorced. We weren't going to parent-trap them (we had brainstormed it and failed to come up with a workable plan), but we needed them to stick it out for two and a half years until we left school.

The song finished and 'Gonna Get Along Without You Now' began; Mum was going through her playlist all right.

Enzo went into the empty living room and switched off the music, but that made the house too quiet. After a few seconds, I heard the beginning track of *This is Happening* by LCD Soundsystem. That was one of Enzo's favourite albums and, because he played it so much, it had become one of mine.

Then my mind did go back to the piece of paper in my pocket. I wondered when Kennedy's album was coming out. And I wondered why Freddie Kennedy had given this scrap of paper to me; why, out of all the adoring girls in the room, he had picked me, a girl who hadn't even been interested until I caught him looking.

We were in the basement kitchen, eating salted-caramel ice cream straight from the tub, when Mum came in. She was wearing her blue dressing gown and had her hair in a towel turban, and when she saw us she seemed to shrink.

'Oh hey, guys,' she said, fake-bright. 'Explains the music. Good gig?'

'Awesome,' said Enzo. 'Hazel fell over on someone and he bought her a drink.'

'Water!' I said because I knew where Mum went from here. 'It came in a bottle, and I took the lid off and broke the seal myself. Ice cream?'

She shook her head, but then got herself a spoon. 'Oh, why not?'

She pulled up a chair and dug in. For a few minutes the three of us just appreciated the joy that was a late-night sugar rush. Then Mum said, 'So, he bought you a drink of water? And then . . . ?'

I shrugged. The water-guy was a perfect distraction. Freddie's piece of paper was burning my bum, tattooing numbers I didn't know on to a part of me I couldn't see.

That's assuming he had given me his number. He might have handed me anything.

I knew, though. I was full of lava, brimming with something unexpected. I never had secrets from Enzo: we always told each other everything about our crushes. I looked at my brother now, the black hair that he was growing to make him look 'like Jesus', the heavy-framed glasses, the carefully constructed messy exterior hiding an anxious inside, and I loved him so much, and I knew that I couldn't tell him about Freddie because he would do his best to make me throw the number away.

He would point out that only a creep would give his number to a teenage girl. That Freddie was clearly a twat, and everyone knew it, that you could tell just by looking at him.

He would tell me not to be a groupie, that it would go badly for me. That I was worth more than that.

He would remind me that all my recent crushes were on girls and that actually it was Lina I liked.

And he'd be right, about all of it. I knew that, and it was why I couldn't tell him. Anyway, I was just intrigued.

'I doubt I'll see him again,' I said.

'Sure. Well, if you liked him, maybe you should.'

For once Mum didn't actually care. I didn't want to ask where Greg was, and, for all his usual bravado, Enzo clearly didn't either. Instead he switched on his Enzo-ness and entertained her with his story of the five of us accidentally hanging out at the stage door and the band thinking we were there to talk to them and offering us tickets for a London gig. I watched him carefully. I watched her.

Neither of them had a clue. Freddie had slipped me his piece of paper (number?) entirely under the radar.

'Do you think they meant it?' said Mum. 'About the Hoxton thing?'

'Doubt it. We'd be those twats trying to get free tickets off their management and looking like chancers.'

I couldn't bear it any longer. I fake yawned and said I was tired. I put my spoon in the dishwasher, inhaled a blast of comforting Mum-hug, then ran up the stairs to open my secret note.

Enzo and I had the whole top floor of this house. I went into our bathroom, which was looking good because the cleaner had been, and locked the door. I took the piece of paper out of my back pocket, put the toilet lid down and sat on it. My fingers shook as I unfolded the note.

Message me doll x

And there was a phone number.

I stared at it. He'd written it, with his own hands. For me. The frontman of the band had given me, a random from the audience, his number. He had put a line across the number seven. I decided it looked sophisticated, that I would adopt that from now on.

He had told me to message him.

The voice said, *Don't*. I told it to be quiet.

I couldn't send a message at half one in the morning anyway. I needed to wait until tomorrow. Today. Later today. I would craft the right message and I would send it, and I would do it without telling anyone and then I would see what happened next.

Every part of me knew that it had to be a secret. I was certain that everyone, including the sensible side of me, would think it was a bad idea. I felt the whisper of my dad's ghost around me. I often summoned him when I was alone, but now, for the first time, I shut him out.

I wasn't going to do anything. I was just intrigued.

9

Venice

The strawberry sorbet gives me energy again, and we set off for some more sightseeing.

We keep our phones in our pockets because we agree that it would be cheating to use maps, and follow yellow signs high up on walls until we find ourselves, finally, in Piazza San Marco – St Mark's Square. When we get there, it turns out to be exactly the way I wanted it to be.

A huge space stretches ahead of us, with colonnades, a basilica at the end with domes and curves, the pink and white of the Doge's Palace. There is the red-brick bell tower, pigeons, a band playing at one of the cafes.

It's precisely the way it should be. It feels almost too perfect. The curves and towers of the basilica make my eyes fill with tears. I blink them back.

The light is crystalline. The crosses at the top of the basilica are delicate against the sky. I see the statues of four horses up there, on the roof. The paved ground stretches on and on, its lines moving away like perspective lines. Normally famous things are smaller than you expect them to be, but this one is bigger. It takes my breath away.

It doesn't. I'm still breathing. In fact, the air feels different here. Breathing it in is making me better.

I imagine people from hundreds of years ago walking across these same stones. I can almost see them in the corners of my vision.

The crowds of tourists we dodged away from this morning (twice) seem to have ended up here: there are plenty of people, but somehow there's space for everyone.

'Fair play,' says Enzo. 'I thought this was meant to be one of those touristy hellholes.'

'It will be,' says Phoebe, 'in a couple of weeks, when it's the proper summer holidays. But yeah. It's so not.'

I stand and look at it.

For a moment I think everything stops. I think everyone is standing like a statue apart from me. But that's not real: it's in my head. They are moving. Nothing's wrong.

'He broke my mind,' I say.

Enzo is closest to me. 'Yeah,' he says, and he doesn't even look round. 'I knew he would.'

'Do you think I'm going to be OK, Enz?'

He turns to me then and we look at each other for a long time.

'Yes,' he says. 'You are, Hazel. We all are.'

Then I glimpse her across the square: I'm almost sure it's her. She's the girl who looked at me through the window, just before I glitched, or whatever the hell happened. She was a part of my déjà vu, though it wasn't déjà vu because it only happened once.

I shake my head to stop myself being weird. It's just a girl with short hair, in St Mark's Square. I take a deep breath and smile.

St Mark's Square flashes blue, and my own name rings in my ears.

Time passes, and I'm nowhere.

Then I'm back in my body, but somehow now I am somewhere else.

I'm sitting in a boat, but it's not a normal boat: it's long, made of shiny wood, and we're . . . and we're moving slowly. A gondola. I'm sitting on a comfortable white cushion. I blink and try to orientate myself. I adjust my silky dress.

Phoebe is next to me. Enzo is opposite us, and he's in full flow, talking Italian. When I turn to see who he's talking to, there's a man in a red-and-white striped T-shirt propelling us along.

I look around. We're passing under a bridge. The canal water smells like old stone. I lean over and try to make out my face in the water, to check that I'm really here, but it's opaque and I can't see anything.

Phoebe pulls me back to the present. 'Hazel?' she says.

I look at her. I nod. We are on a gondola, and since we haven't done this before I must have blacked out again. Another déjà vu or a time glitch or whatever it is has happened. I don't want to say anything because I'm sick of making everything about me.

I know that Phoebe and Enzo dropped everything to come here with me, to get me away, to bring me to his mum's apartment. To keep me safe. I know they have their own stuff going on, and the worst thing is that I realize that I have no idea what any of it is. I don't know because I've been the worst friend, the worst sister, in the world.

I've been entirely self-obsessed. I push away the panic about what is happening – what has happened – to my brain.

'Hey,' I say. 'Sorry I've been so – you know.'

Phoebe smiles. 'Stop saying sorry, babe. We're just glad we've got you back.'

'But what – I mean, it's June, isn't it?'

She nods.

'So you must have exams and all that?'

Phoebe looks away. Her expression is so intense that I think she's looking at something, but when I follow her gaze there's nothing strange there. Just a wide canal bank with cafe tables on it. People sitting there with their bright orange drinks. I wonder what I don't know.

'I mean, yeah,' she says. 'But it's OK. Don't worry. Honestly. Nothing was more important to us than getting you somewhere safe. And an unexpected holiday here in the City of . . . what was it?'

I remember Enzo this morning. 'Something serene?'

'Extremely serene?' she says.

Enzo hears us. '*La Serenissima*,' he says, breaking off from his conversation with the gondolier. 'The actual most serene of all.'

The gondolier joins in. I don't look round, but I hear his voice from behind me.

'The Most Serene Republic of Venice,' he says. 'It was a city state . . .' and I tune out from his history lesson, even though I'm sure it's interesting.

I won't tell them that I blacked out again. I must have been acting normally, to get into the gondola. I must have agreed that we'd do our ride. I must have climbed into this boat and sat here, next to Phoebe, probably paid my share. We must have collectively decided that Enzo would take the seat facing the gondolier. I've clearly lived this, then immediately forgotten it.

I hear a voice in my head. *Get away from me, Hazel. You're an embarrassment.*

I touch my hip. I feel the impact of a bruise. Where I landed on the ground. Shoved across the hallway.

I push the thought away, because Enzo and Phoebe don't seem to think I'm an embarrassment, and watch the impossible city drifting by. We go under bridges. Everything is beautiful. Everything is perfect. I am not an embarrassment, not here, not now.

I make a decision. I will live in the moment from now. I will not let weird brain-glitches and memory lapses get to me. I'll just go with the flow. I look round at the gondolier and wonder how much training you need to do this job, how easy it would be to drop the pole thing or tip up the boat, whether people ever fall in. I think of people punting in Cambridge, something I guess I've seen in films.

The thought of Cambridge makes me go cold.

I push it away. *Living in the now, remember, Hazel.*

I tip my head back and feel the sun on my face. The air is going into my lungs. My body's doing whatever it does with it, and then the carbon dioxide, or whatever it is, goes out. It's all working. Blood is pumping round my veins. Go with the flow. I can do this.

I open my eyes and find Phoebe looking at me with concern. When I smile, she gives me a grin.

'You look a bit better,' she says. I nod. I am a bit better.

'Don't worry about anything,' she says. 'OK?'

I watch a bird flying high above us. I grab my glass bird, and feel it again, cold and real in my fist. I don't know why it's important to me for this holiday, but it is.

Someone's watching us from a table on the canal bank. It's a man in his twenties, wearing a red T-shirt, and for a moment my heart stops.

He's here: he's found me. I scrabble around, look for a way out, even though I'm on a boat. I need to get away. I try to ask the gondolier to change direction, but no words come out.

Then we get closer and I see that this man is completely different. It's not him. He's not here. He watches us pass and his expression is ... nothing. He's looking at us, but not seeing us. He's talking.

He's talking because there's a woman at his table, and she has a baby on her lap. This man is a stranger. He leans over and takes the baby.

It's not him. I don't need to see him ever again. I'm free.

10

For the rest of the day I throw myself into being on holiday. The happy moments last longer and the weird moments don't bother me because I don't allow myself to freak out. More than once, my brain does glitchy things with time, and I go with it. It's not time: it's me. That's cheering.

I see the girl twice more: once, I go back about half an hour again and use the time to order a beer rather than a Coke (and even though I have no fake ID they serve me and I drink it slowly, enjoying it). The other time, I jump forward about twenty minutes and piece things together as best I can. On both occasions I cover it up. I don't let Phoebe or Enzo see because I want them to think I'm fine and normal again. I want them to enjoy their holiday.

In the evening, we go to an area called Canareggio. Phoebe directs us, telling us it's where we'll find the bars and cafes and non-tourist stuff. We cross a bridge and discover that she's not wrong.

The candlelit pavement tables, the moonlight on the canal, the warm night air on my arms – all of it is utterly perfect. There are people talking, people laughing, people with drinks in their hands. I look at my friends and I'm smiling.

'We need to begin with a crêpe,' says Phoebe.

'Eccentric choice,' says Enzo. 'Pancakes for dinner? Not gonna argue.'

'That place over there.' She points. 'Best crêpes in the world.'

I look over at it. It's a tiny little place, with a queue outside it and a wood sign in the window, with words carved into it: CREPES HOUSE BY PEPE. STREET FOOD.

'According to?' I say.

'Everyone on the internet.'

'Fair,' says Enzo. 'It'd be criminal to walk past.'

We join the queue, which moves quickly. When we get to the open glass door, I find myself standing in front of it, and I catch sight of my silhouette.

The girl in the reflection is not the *me* in my head. She has lost half her bodyweight. She has become terrified of the world. Her legs look weird, as if they can barely hold her up.

I touch my upper arms, and she does too. I used to be proud of my arm strength. Enzo and I would jump off the staircase that led to our top floor, and grab hold of the wooden railings and swing for as long as we could, and I could always do it for longer. I would hang there indefinitely. We only stopped doing it when the whole rail started to move and we realized we were pulling our house apart.

Shit. I look terrible. Not only that, but I had no idea. I remember a red dress, a zip that didn't do up, and I swallow hard.

Pancakes are so far beyond anything I would have contemplated.

I want to be someone who eats pancakes.

'*Nutella e banana, per favore*,' I say, and even though it's not really that straightforward – even though I know I won't actually finish it – even just saying the words, making my own choice, helps me think that one day my real self might come back.

We walk a bit further, eating our crêpes, and I let myself enjoy it. And I do enjoy it. I love it. I actually finish nearly all of mine and hand what's left to Enzo. Then we sit on the steps of a bridge with tiny bar snacks on paper plates, and bottles of beer that Enzo manages to buy for us. I ask them about college and gradually they tell me. We don't talk about me at all. I catch up, bit by bit, on their big news. Phoebe has been seeing someone.

'It's early days,' she says, 'but I like him.'

'Name?'

There's a pause, during which, luckily, no one comments on the fact that I don't know the name of my best friend's boyfriend. I'm sure we're all thinking it. I certainly am.

'Jakub,' she says, her voice gentle. *Yakub*.

'Good name.'

'Right? Early days but I like him so far.'

I look at her face, see that, for a moment, the strain has lifted. She looks like old Phoebe, happy Phoebe. Not the one who used to glance at me across a college corridor with disappointment and worry in her eyes, then look away.

'Can I meet him?'

She grins at that, and all her reserve melts away. 'Of course you can! He knows all about you. At first he was a bit starstruck because of – you know. The song and all that.'

It hangs in the air for a moment. I hold my breath. The moment stretches out. It stretches and stretches.

Then we snap back to normal.

'He had a steep learning curve. Now he's just glad we've got you.' She checks her phone and shows me a photo. I look at Phoebe, cheek to cheek with a boy I don't recognize at all. How can I never have seen him? He's handsome, dark, with short hair. He looks as if he's really into her.

'You look so happy.'

She nods. ''Fraid so.'

I put an arm round her shoulders and pull her close. Then I turn to Enzo. 'How about you? What else have I missed?'

'Nothing,' he says. 'You know me.'

I do know Enzo. He's theoretically gay, but in fact he never really wants to be with anyone. 'You've missed stuff with Dad, though,' he says. I hold up a hand.

'Nope,' I say. 'I am not here for that.'

He nods. 'Wise opinion.'

The next day it's warmer and I feel so much better that I dress carelessly, in a swirly skirt and a baggy T-shirt that ties in a knot at the waist. I spend five minutes arranging my hair into a casual ponytail, and spend a lot less time on my make-up. I can tell that the other two are pleased with me, and I'm almost convincing myself that my time freak-outs were just an understandable reaction to all the shit that's happened.

It felt real but it wasn't.

I've adopted that as my mantra. I say it in my head all the time. *It felt real but it wasn't. It felt real but it wasn't.*

Felt real, wasn't.

Felt, wasn't.

I'm in Venice, with my best friends. If I miss a bit, or do something twice, it's a small problem in the bigger picture. It doesn't even register. My brain will iron it all out soon.

We set off, today following the blue dot on Phoebe's map rather than wandering. I don't even care where we're going, though I know she wants to see a gallery and a church. I don't know which one we're going to first. I'm happy to be the passenger. Just feeling my body starting to become strong again is all the holiday I need. I'm living in the moment, like a bird, like the bird that is, today, in my skirt pocket.

It felt real but it wasn't. I pull my sunglasses on to my face and stride forward. This is Venice. That part is real.

Phoebe's walking ahead of us, pointing each time we need to take a turning. Enzo and I are a few paces behind her.

'When you're talking Italian,' I say, 'do you think in Italian?'

He shrugs. 'Kinda, I guess. You do know I'm not properly bilingual, right?'

'You *so* are.'

He shakes his head. 'I've never lived here. I speak it well, sure, because of my mother, but it's only the fact that you're so shit that makes you think I must be brilliant.'

'Fair enough.' I pause. 'I can sort of read it on paper, but when people are talking I literally don't get one single word.'

'Yeah. I noticed.'

I shove him. He shoves me back. By the time we come into the little square and find Phoebe waiting, we are in full sibling mode. It feels amazing, like everything I've missed happening all at once. I hang on to it. I love it.

'Hey, twinnies,' Phoebe says. 'Ready to go to church?'

Enzo looks at me. 'Coffee first, please. But then sure. Bit of absolution never did anyone any harm.'

I nod. I look away. The church in front of us is huge, but I don't think it has enough absolution inside it for the things I've done.

11

Kent

Nineteen months earlier

I spent way too long crafting the message, deleting-rewriting-deleting-rewriting to try to get it to sound casual. In the end, it read:

> Hi Freddie! It's Hazel from the
> gig last night. Thanks
> again – it was brilliant ✿

That was the best I could do and, pathetic as it was, I decided to stop messing with it. Either he'd reply or he wouldn't. I had planned to send it at midday, but then worried that messaging on the dot of twelve would look too obvious so I waited until seven minutes past, decided not to send it, and then sent it anyway.

Freddie Kennedy was making me feel weird. Why had someone so gorgeous and successful picked me? That was the part I didn't get. I hadn't been the most striking girl at the gig. He'd spotted me from the stage, but why when there were so many other girls? I wasn't being fake-modest: I knew I looked OK and I was comfortable with myself. But there had been girls at the gig in tiny vests and shorts looking amazing and he'd ignored them all in favour of me, in my jeans and T-shirt with sweaty hair all over the place.

I wanted to know why he'd done it, and if I didn't message him he wouldn't contact me because he didn't know my name, let alone my number. This was up to me.

I knew with a sharp feeling inside that this was a turning point.

He was twenty-six (I'd googled) and I was fifteen.

But I loved Kennedy, and he had given me his number.

And I was *nearly* sixteen.

I saved his number as 'Lily K' because I knew loads of people called Lily: if Enzo saw that name on my phone, he wouldn't ask why I had Freddie Kennedy's number.

The word 'delivered' appeared on the message.

Nothing happened.

I was desperate to tell Enzo, but he would say that Freddie was old. He would say that he lived in a world of music and drink and probably drugs, and that I was built for ice cream and movies. He would say that Freddie held all the power and experience, that he would be bad, bad, bad for me and that I should stick to listening to the music. I didn't want to think about these things so I didn't tell him. I didn't want to hear what the voice said either, so I made an effort to shut it out too. I should have done that years ago, probably. I knew it was weird.

After I sent the message, I knelt beside my bed and pulled out my box of special stuff because Freddie's note was going in there. Most of the other things in the box were photographs of tiny me with my actual dad, plus drawings I'd made from the photographs. This box contained everything that was just mine: I had never shown any of it to anyone else, not even Enzo, though he knew about it. I had a folder on my phone with all the photos from the old albums of my dad in it, but the pictures in here were real, on paper, mine. And the copies I'd drawn were mine too.

I looked at Morris's face. There he was, the man who hovered on the edge of my consciousness. I could only look him in the face in photographs, and I did it now. I looked at him, and I saw myself.

The voice belonged to Morris. Pathetically, there was a version of him that lived in my head, and I needed it to stop judging me.

I know I've probably just done something a bit silly, I said to him (in my head: I wasn't mad). *Just to see what happens next. I know it'll be fine and I need to do this on my own.*

It felt like a strange thing to say to my dad when I definitely wasn't telling Mum. But he was an imaginary dad so it didn't really count. I made his voice in my head say, *Just be careful.* Then I focused on switching it off.

He died when he, Mum and I were on holiday in Greece, but that was all I really knew as I'd been so young. Whenever I asked, she told me the same story: he'd been swimming and a freak current took him. There was nothing anyone could have done. She and I had been on the beach and we'd watched him struggle and then disappear. I'd heard it so many times that it had become almost comforting.

Until last year, when I'd heard her talking to Greg.

Greg had said: 'Hazel deserves to know the full story, Suze.'

And Mum said: 'She'd blame herself. I know she would. She doesn't need to know it at all.'

Since then, I'd had a dark feeling that it was my fault. I'd tried to cast myself back to a holiday I didn't remember, to relive a thing that I'd forgotten. A thing that was, in some way, my own fault.

I'd tried to get Mum to tell me since then, but she refused. She said the story she'd always told me was true. She said I must have misunderstood the overheard conversation, that they'd been talking about something else. Nothing I said would make her tell me.

I heard from the Greek side of Morris's family on my birthday and at Christmas, but I didn't really know them. He had a gravestone at the local cemetery in Kent, which I didn't visit because it didn't feel like he was there, and a memorial in his family church in Greece, and apparently we'd scattered some of his ashes on the beach at Margate (I couldn't even remember doing that) and the rest had gone into the sea where he died. So he really was dead: his ashes were all over the place, and he had two gravestones. Anyway, a man who would fake his own death to get away from his wife and child wouldn't have been much of a dad.

Mum had never been back to Greece since, and neither had I, though now I was old enough to go without her and maybe I would. Maybe, I thought, I would go with Enzo one day. Maybe my Greek family would tell me what had really happened, if they knew. Mum had got over it by moving on and never talking about her first husband at all, which seemed to work for her, but less so for me. In my core, I felt we had unfinished business. I longed to speak to him again, and so I did, often, in my head.

Meanwhile I did, of course, have a dad. Greg was unfailingly nice to me, and he always had been. He gave me pocket money and curfews and made a big show of cooking Sunday lunch. He treated me as his daughter, and I liked him. But I was, and always had been, obsessed by my missing father.

In the pictures, he had a black beard, and thick black hair like mine would have been if I didn't spend so much time and money dyeing and straightening it. I looked nothing like my mother: that was another reason why I missed him. She was tall and willowy and pale and I was an anomaly. I looked like Enzo's twin, and not at all like my mother's daughter.

I had missed him for twelve years. My precious memories involved my hand in his, walking in the rain, splashing in puddles in a pair of yellow wellies. Cuddling into his side while he read me a book. Holding my arms up for him to carry me. A smell, a glimpse, and then nothing forever and my mother's voice saying, 'She'd blame herself.'

What had I done?

There was a tap at the door and Enzo was there. I saw him looking at my box and, while his eyes were on the old photo of me and my dad, I shifted the other things so they covered Freddie's note.

'You OK?' he said. I watched him piece it together, incorrectly, but in a way that made a kind of sense. 'Oh, Haze. Greg'll be back, you know? We've been here before.'

I put the lid on the box and shoved it back under my bed.

'This one feels different. I don't want our family to change.'

I was surprised by how emotional it made me. It was shit that Mum and Greg appeared to have split up. Mum, as ever, wasn't talking about it. At least I wasn't on my own this time.

Enzo nodded. 'Me neither. Come here.'

We had a little hug and then he went off to the bathroom. A minute later I heard the shower starting.

I lay on my bed, reliving the moment when Freddie's fingers had brushed mine. The more I thought about it, the more magical it felt. My message must have been too boring. I regretted the stupid star emoji.

Just after the sounds of Enzo's shower stopped, my phone pinged.

Hazel! Hey doll.

That was it. He'd called me *doll* twice now. It was a weird endearment, but I'd take it. I waited for more and when it didn't come I checked the door to make sure it was closed, and messaged:

Hey yourself!

The reply was instant.

What you up to today?

Everything fizzed inside me. We were talking, just the two of us, in secret.

Not much. Things are a bit
weird at home so my brother
and I will prob go out for a bit.

Weird how?

Parents.

I looked at the word and regretted it. 'Parents' was a childish issue to have. Freddie wouldn't understand parent issues because he was closer to thirty than twenty.

Oh God. Tell me about it.

Oh. Apparently I was wrong. Even though I didn't know whether he actually meant it, I did tell him, bit by bit. He kept asking questions and I kept answering. I heard Enzo running downstairs. It felt strange and good to open up to someone new, someone who seemed genuinely interested in what I had to say.

So I've kind of got two dads, I wrote, after setting it all out. And I know Greg is the day to day one. He's the one who's here. So I feel kinda ungrateful.

That Greg guy isn't your dad though, he replied. Not really, and you know it.

I nodded. No one else had ever understood how ambiguous I felt about that. I asked about his family.

> Complicated. Very. Tell
> you when I see you.

When I see you? I knew where we were headed, but just when I was expecting him to suggest meeting up, he came in with:

> Do you like gaming?

I laughed. I really didn't.

> I'm rubbish. Never really
> done it. Honestly, I prefer
> drawing and reading.

> You're missing out! I'll
> show you sometime.

I sighed. I didn't want him to because it would be boring, but, while I was working out how to reply, he changed direction again.

So you're 16.

Yeah, I replied. Then I corrected myself.

Nearly.

when?

December 1.

While we were messaging, I was recast as someone who had heart-to-heart conversations with a rock star. A kind-of-rock nearly-star. I had never been this person before and I loved it.

After we'd been messaging for nearly an hour, I heard Mum shout for me up the stairs.

Got to go. Sorry! Family
calling.

I watched message after message drop in:

Sure. Look, do you fancy
getting a coffee sometime?

Only if you want to.

It's been nice chatting.

tbh I do give my number
to pretty girls sometimes

60

but you're a lot
younger and

listen to me! Babbling
like a twat! Sorry.

If you'd like to. No
pressure. I'm not that guy.

I beamed at the screen, loving his fragments of sentences. I concentrated hard as I typed the three words that would change my life.

I hesitated. A part of me knew I shouldn't do it. But he'd just owned it, he knew what this looked like, and he'd said straight out that it wasn't like that. That, I thought, made it fine.

I pressed send.

Regretted it.

Didn't.

I'd love to.

Delivered.

When Enzo came thundering upstairs to find me, I shoved my phone under the edge of the duvet, as if not having it in my hand would somehow make me appear less suspicious.

'Did you see the message from Greg?' His voice was strained. I hadn't because I'd been ignoring everything but

Freddie. While I retrieved the phone, Enzo crouched down and did a forward roll that took him over to my bed.

'Why the clowning?' I said when he stood up.

'Too much empty space.'

My room wasn't immaculate, but it was an IKEA showroom compared with his. He kept his stuff on the floor because, as he said, 'That's where there's most room.' There were generally several mugs of green mould, an array of plates with brittle toast crusts in unexpected places, around five cereal bowls with dried-on remnants. The cleaner refused to go into Enzo's room, but somehow he always walked out of there looking and smelling good.

He sat on the bed and looked over my shoulder as I opened Greg's message. He had set up a new group chat, without Mum in it. That was kind of horrible in itself. He'd called it 'Dad Stuff', though even Enzo, his own son, called him Greg. I thought of Morris, wished I could have my own Dad Stuff chat, but I knew it wasn't fair. That group would only have me in it. Me and a ghost, conversing one-sidedly.

Hey kids. You might (or might not!) have noticed that I'm not home. Don't worry – I'm going to be staying in the flat for a while but v much around. Hopefully things will be straightened out soon, but I wanted to reassure you that it's between me and Susie, and nothing either of you has done. How about a milkshake tomorrow? Burgers? Dad x

A message preview appeared at the top of the screen. For a second I thought the 'Lily K' disguise was so flimsy that Enzo was going to call me out, but of course he didn't. It said Perfect - so maybe we could

Enzo didn't react but my heart was racing. I was desperate to read the rest of it.

I looked at Greg's message again, and made myself focus. In spite of how awful everything was, I felt my lips twitching.

'Burgers and milkshake?' I said.

Enzo smiled too, and looked down at his lap, trying to hide it.

'This might be a good time to request a trip to Florida,' he said. 'Tap into that Disney dad energy while he has it.'

'Ask for the Beats headphones.'

He shook his head. 'Nah. I mean, yeah, course. But first I'm gonna mess with his head.' He reached for his own phone. As soon as he'd looked away from mine, I typed a quick sounds brilliant! back to Lily K, whose full message said Perfect - so maybe we could do something next weekend? and then locked the phone. When it vibrated, I read Enzo's response on 'Dad Stuff':

Can we go to McDonald's?

Greg was typing. His reply, when it came, said:

We can do better than that mate! I was thinking Gourmet Ethical Burgers.

Hazel and I want to go to McDonald's.

I looked up. 'I really don't.'

63

'I know. But you know he hates it. So it's fun.'

'Enz!' I said. 'Stop it!'

He sighed. 'I know. But this is weird. And he's, like, your dad too, right?'

I remembered what Freddie had said. '*That Greg guy isn't your dad . . . and you know it.*'

Sure, McDonald's would be fab, I wrote in solidarity. We exchanged tight smiles.

That week turned out to be a strange one. Greg didn't come back, and Lily K and I messaged every day. Enzo and I went to McDonald's with Greg and it was weird and tense and no one really knew what to say.

By the weekend, I was second-guessing everything. I was heading into London on Saturday to go for lunch at a pizza place in West Hampstead that Freddie knew. He didn't seem worried about being seen in public with a teenager, and that was because we were meeting as friends, to carry on the conversation we'd been having over messages. We'd both said that. It was a legitimate lunch with a new friend. Still, I half thought it was a practical joke, that somebody else was on the end of those messages. Was I being catfished? Should I let someone else know where I was going, just in case? Mum had drummed safety rules into me, and I knew you didn't just go and meet a stranger.

I decided I'd tell Phoebe. She was my best friend and it would have been too weird keeping this from her.

I called her late at night, making sure my door was closed.

'I'm going on a date on Saturday,' I said.

She shrieked. 'Go on! Who is she?'

'He,' I said.

'Who's he then?'

I hesitated. I didn't want to say his name, but I also did.

'He's a musician,' I said. 'A bit older. You know Kennedy? The band?'

Her voice changed. 'Oh God, Hazel. Tell me you're not going out with Freddie or Ollie Kennedy? Seriously, Haze? They'd be after a casual hook-up. You don't want that. It would be terrible for you.'

I backtracked. 'Nothing like that at all. Not from the actual band. Just a guy who looks like one of them.'

Her voice was suspicious. 'Who? And where are you meeting?'

I ended up telling her where I was going, but I made up a guy from the internet. I said I'd tell her everything afterwards. She was sceptical about the whole thing.

I worried I didn't know how to translate the closeness of our messaging into the real world. What if I froze and couldn't say anything? If I messed up, it would be over. Teachers noticed I wasn't focused. Friends complained I was staring into space. I just said sorry. I didn't explain. I hugged it all close to myself because it was a new, strange and exciting thing.

Enzo, of course, busted me. He was up earlier than usual on Saturday and when he caught me leaving the house, he looked me up and down with a smirk.

'Oh aye,' he said. That was something he'd taken to saying lately. It denoted scepticism.

'What?'

'You know *what*. I knew you were up to something. Who is it?'

'No one!'

'Where are you meeting this *no one*?'

'London.' London was just under an hour away and we went often.

'Where in London?'

'Yeah,' I said. 'I'm going to tell you that.'

I had promised to text Phoebe at four. I hoped Enzo wasn't going to compare notes with her in the meantime.

He stepped in front of me. 'I put it to you, Miss Angelopoulos, that you're heading out on a date. Evidence for the prosecution: styled hair with yellow flower hairclip. Your good jeans. Sexy vest and cute mustard cardy. Eyeliner flicks. Lipgloss like a casual movie star about town.' He sniffed the air. 'Perfume. Not trying too hard, but looking and smelling adorable. Plus, you've been doodling wedding dresses for a week.'

I had doodled a wedding dress once. I didn't know he'd seen it.

'Shut up! I have not been doodling wedding dresses, and I'm allowed to make an effort without it being for a guy.'

A date! Today! It kind of *was*. It radiated out from my stomach and warmed me all the way through. I was glad Enzo thought I looked good. *Casual movie star about town* was what I'd been going for.

'I know.' He grinned. 'It could be a girl.'

I nodded. 'Well, it's not.'

'I know. Because I have a pretty good idea who he is.'

I froze. I knew if I stayed quiet, he'd carry on talking, and he did. He pointed at me.

'That night we saw Kennedy? You've been smiling into your phone ever since. What was his name?'

I wanted to say *Freddie*. Every bit of me wanted to say that. I opened my mouth to do it.

I didn't.

I knew what Enzo would say. I could hear him echoing what Phoebe had said. '*Seriously, Haze? They'd be after a casual hook-up. You don't want that.*'

'Whose name?' I said.

'You know who, young lady! The guy you fell on in your little meet-cute. The one who bought you a bottle of water and didn't spike it. That gent.'

The guy had been nice enough. He would do. I reached for his name and tried to look coy.

'Lewis,' I said, looking at the ground. *Thank you, Lewis.* 'His name was Lewis. Now will you let me go?'

He stepped aside, smirking. 'Don't do anything I wouldn't do.'

'Plenty of scope!' I said over my shoulder, and I walked as fast as I could to the station.

12

Venice

The nearest cafe is right beside the church. We take an outside table. I feel the sun warming my arms and put on a bit more suncream. There are various types of croissants, and after looking at the list for ages I ask Enzo what *vuoto* means. He chuckles.

'Empty,' he says. 'A plain one, I'd guess.'

'OK. I am not ordering an empty croissant.' I pick one of the others, and the pastry that arrives is filled with something like Nutella: it's exactly the breakfast that five-year-old me would have chosen and I try to silence the nasty voice in my head as I pick it up.

This is good. I'm happy. I can eat a croissant for breakfast, like a normal person. This one, though, is a bit too much, like my crêpe from last night. It might make me sick.

I drink a frothy cappuccino and some water. I nibble at the edges of the croissant, and when Enzo notices me struggling he switches it with his almond one wordlessly and I eat it all.

I eat it all. That feels amazing. I sense its energy running through me.

'Why this church?' I say to Phoebe when I've finished. 'Out of all the hundreds of churches in the city.'

She's staring at it, jiggling her leg.

'Two monuments,' she says. 'Two artists are buried here. Well, one and a bit. There's Titian. Remember him? He's buried right in there. And Canova. He's a sculptor. You'd know his stuff. There's an epic monument to him inside.'

I only vaguely remember Titian from Phoebe's art history obsession and I'm pretty sure I've never heard of Canova. She showed me a painting that I think was by Titian at the National Gallery once and it was lovely. It had a blue starry sky and drunk people. If Phoebe wants to see Titian's grave, then that's fine by me. And that other guy's. I'd lost sight of the most basic things in life and now they fill me with joy. It's like that feeling when you've been ill and then you recover and promise you'll never take your health for granted again. I will never take my happiness for granted. I will never take relaxing around food, or choosing my own drink, or even the colours I wear, the things I do, the people I love, for granted. I have a long way to go, but I can see the path ahead and it's exhilarating.

I lean back in my chair and turn my face up to the sunshine. The church is a monolith beside us, Gothicky-looking and a bit forbidding. I tune out the others talking and look right up. I imagine it being built. Every one of those bricks arrived here on a boat. It's impossible. This whole city is impossible. They can't even have had scaffolding. Did they make wooden scaffolding? I have no idea. I turn to ask Phoebe, but she's laughing at something Enzo just said.

'High up, on wooden beams,' he says, continuing their conversation. 'All round the inside. You do mad jumps between beams.'

'I can't believe you know it from that,' says Phoebe.

'What's high up on wooden beams?' I ask.

'Ever played *Assassin's Creed*?' I can see from the expression on his face that Enzo's expecting me to say no. I try to arrange my face in a way that will make me look like someone who's barely heard of *Assassin's Creed*.

I don't want to talk about *Assassin's Creed*.

About video games.

Arguments

watching someone

playing

and being told off for not

concentrating.

It pushes in from all sides of my brain and I try to jump forward in time, to get out of this moment, but it doesn't work.

I pull myself back. 'Boring!' I say. My voice comes out tentative, and I try again. I feel myself wobbling, hold on to the edge of the table. 'Boring!' I say more fervently. Too fervently.

'Yeah. So, would you believe –' Phoebe stops mid-sentence. She blinks and looks around. When she speaks, her voice is different. It's small and scared. 'What the fuck was that?'

I watch her shake her head, take a deep breath. She looks at me, at Enzo, down at the plate. She touches the metal table with her fingertips, picks up the last piece of her croissant and puts it down. Looks into her coffee cup, and around, and up at the church.

'What the fuck what?' says Enzo, his voice languid.

She grabs my arm and her fingers dig into my flesh.

'What are we doing here? We were ...' She points over at the church. 'We were in there. Why are we here?'

She looks into my eyes. I look back into hers and I see it there. The same thing. The thing that has been happening to me. The thing I've rationalized as stress and trauma and breakdown, the thing I've decided just to go with. That's my issue: it can't have happened to Phoebe too. It cannot.

For some reason this is terrifying.

'Not the ... the déjà vu thing?' My voice comes out quieter than I expected, but she hears. 'Did time glitch for you?'

She gives a little nod, which turns into a shake of her head.

'Not really. Not déjà vu or a funny feeling or anything like that. It was real. Why are we here? We finished this breakfast. We went in there and we were looking at the tombs and talking about Titian and Canova and ...' She stares down at the table, frowning. 'I don't understand. Is this before or after?'

'Before,' I say. We haven't been in yet, so this must be before unless I've glitched too.

At the same time, Enzo says, 'What the heck are you on about?'

I can't help myself. 'Was there a girl? There was a flash and you were in the middle of nothing, kind of blue and bright, and then back here? Is that what happened?'

I shouldn't be prompting her, but the words come out fast, while my brain scrabbles around, trying to make any kind of sense out of this.

Enzo gives a sudden laugh. 'Excuse me? What am I missing, weirdos?'

Our eyes meet. She shakes her head.

'Not really,' she says. 'There wasn't a girl. No blue anything. It was dark and then light, like the sun was starting to rise. Something was about to happen. There was something stretched out in front of me and it didn't have an end. It was weird but it felt ... good. And then I was here. Back here, where I was before. I – no offence, but I kinda want to go back there.'

OK. So that was different, but it was the same thing. It wasn't just me. Something on the outside is doing this, and that's impossible, so it must be something in our heads.

Maybe this is how the next pandemic starts. It makes your brain do weird things. Maybe we've stumbled into some kind of time-glitchy weirdness. If that was a thing, which it's not. *Fuck's sake, Hazel.*

I shake myself and focus on the table in front of us. I'm still here. It's all OK.

Phoebe and I look at each other.

'How much time do you think it was?' I ask her. 'That you lived, I mean, before you pinged back here?'

She considers it, checks the time on her phone, looks at the church.

'Maybe twenty minutes,' she says. 'Can we go back in? Otherwise I just feel too weird.'

'You guys?' Enzo looks less sure of himself than usual. 'Straight up. Am I missing some big joke? Are you doing this to mess with me? Because, if you are, I'm afraid to say that it's working.'

'Oddly enough,' says Phoebe, 'this isn't about you, for once.'

There's a tension that wasn't there before. No one says anything. I do my best to smooth it over.

'Enz doesn't make everything about him,' I say. 'That's me, not him. It's fine.' I try to make it fine. 'Let's go in and look at Titian's grave, right? And other churchy stuff.'

Enzo huffs. 'Agreed. Just stop doing that, OK? Both of you.'

'Stop doing what?' A waiter comes over with a bill and a card machine, and I pay the bill, hoping there's money in my account. I'm terrible with money, particularly lately because every time I had any cash at all I ended up spending it, bailing him out. The payment goes through, and I'm relieved.

'Stop the fucking time travelling, or whatever the heck you two keep doing.'

'OK,' I say. 'Sure. We'll just stop it, right?'

My eyes meet Phoebe's. An infinity of things passes between us. Phoebe shrugs.

'Right,' she says. 'Good plan. Hadn't thought of that.' We wordlessly agree *we'll talk about this properly*.

Two euros later we're inside the church.

'Santa Maria Gloriosa dei Frari,' says Phoebe. 'Again.'

'*Santa Maria Gloriosa dei Frari*,' says Enzo, but in a proper Italian accent.

The ceiling is miles away. The floor is red and white diamond-checked tiles below our feet, the tiles scratched and smoothed by the years. Above us, the distant ceiling is vaulted, held up with pillars.

'Dei *Fra*ri,' I parrot, copying his intonation.

He shakes his head. '*Dei Frari.*'

'*Dei Frari.*'

He nods. 'That'll do.'

When I look up, it falls into place. That game. This church. I have flashes of an avatar jumping about high up above our heads, dressed in some kind of old Venetian outfit. Looting. I push it away and look around me at the real, non-pixellated place.

On our left is a huge triangular monument with 'CANOVA' engraved on it. It's a weird, modern-looking thing. The rest of the church is much more as you'd expect, though there are no pews, just empty space and a few folding chairs.

'Where's Titian? Not in there?'

Phoebe is twitchy. I know how weird she feels, doing this for the second time. I wonder whether I asked the same question when we were here before her time glitch.

She follows my eyes. 'No, that's Canova's tomb, like it says. Or not exactly his tomb.' She points to a more traditional one to our right. '*That* one's Titian's monument, but he's actually under our feet somewhere. He's not in there.'

I shudder. One of the greatest artists who ever lived and his bones are dust beneath our feet. I look at the other

74

tomb, which looks much more tomby. Then my eyes go back to the triangular one.

'So who's Canova?'

Phoebe smiles. 'You said that before. Philistine. *The Three Graces*? That's his biggest hit. You'd know it. Canova actually designed this tomb for Titian, but here it is, his.'

We walk over to the tomb together. It's huge, its point reaching up to the high window. There's a door in the triangle, with sculpted figures looking at it. Some are people. One is a lion. The whole thing makes me feel weird. I take half a step back.

Phoebe shakes her head. 'Isn't it magical? There's something so addictive about it. I want to jump the railings and explore.'

I lean over the metal fence that surrounds it. There are two doors. It's hard to make them out in the shadows, but one is slightly open and there's a greyish light shining out from inside.

'Is his body in there? Or is he under our feet too?'

She shakes her head. 'Most of his body is in his home village. It's not far from Venice.'

'Most of his body?' I remember her saying 'one and a bit' artists were buried in this church.

'In here,' she says, 'there's just his heart.'

She looks at me and grins, and for a second she doesn't seem like Phoebe at all. I look up and see an avatar, a pixellated Venetian, swinging away across the roof.

13

London

Nineteen months earlier

When Freddie saw me walking down the stairs, he pushed his dark glasses up on top of his head, and a flash of disappointment crossed his face. He hid it quickly but I saw.

I revisited that moment many times over the following year. I was wearing jeans and a yellow cardigan rather than something sexy. I had a stupid flower in my hair like a fucking bridesmaid.

I should have turned round and left right then, but instead I pushed it away and pretended I hadn't seen it because there were other feelings too and they were bigger and more compelling.

I'd looked at a million photos of him online, but the real him made me feel as if I'd walked through a wardrobe into Narnia. I was here with Freddie, a grown-up rock star, and I was completely intrigued and excited, and distracted, by the whole thing.

Enzo had made me feel good about myself, but now I felt unstylish and suburban. Stupid, with my hairclip.

I wanted to reach up and tug it out, but that would have looked weirder.

'Hazel! Look at you, you gorgeous girl.' He stood up and hugged me. The pizzeria was in a basement and his hair almost touched the ceiling. He kissed my cheek. I kissed the air next to his. He smelled good: some kind of cologne, plus Freddie Kennedy.

Freddie Kennedy.

My date.

I wanted to laugh at how ridiculous this was. How unexpected, how brilliant.

I wanted to reach out and stroke the tiny hairs on the back of his neck. Where had that come from? It was so random. I'd never wanted to stroke anyone's neck before. Freddie's cheekbones were sharp and he looked entirely like a rock star. He was wearing a striped T-shirt and jeans, with a denim jacket. *Double denim*, I thought. That was a rock-star kind of thing to do.

I looked at the other people, who didn't care about us at all because actually Kennedy were only famous among people who knew them, or people who were local to me. The band were from Kent, but now they lived in London because they were about to be big.

Freddie poured red wine from a carafe into two glasses and handed me one of them, and the menu.

'Hope you're hungry,' he said. 'They do the best pizzas. Next best thing to being in Italy. Order whatever you like.'

'Have you ordered?'

'Only the wine.'

'And have you been to Italy?'

He nodded. 'Yeah. Parents used to take me and Ollie every year, right from when I was a baby. Tuscany. Two parents, two kids, a villa where we would speak English loudly. Such a cliché.'

'My brother's Italian.'

'Yeah – Enzo? With a mum in Milan, right?'

He remembered from our texts. I started to relax.

I ordered a vegetable pizza. He got a seafood one and garlic bread and said, 'It's nice to see a girl eating properly. So boring when they just have the lettuce leaves.'

That made me feel a bit weird because it would never have occurred to me to order lettuce leaves when there was pizza, and I wondered who these boring girls were.

The wine went straight to my head and after a while I worried I was too drunk too fast and started taking fake sips, holding the glass to my lips and swallowing without drinking. Red wine was a new experience and I felt it heavy in my stomach, coating my tongue. I ran my tongue over my teeth, hoping the wine wasn't staining them pink.

Since we were from the same town, Freddie wanted to know exactly where I lived. I told him, and he went straight on to Google Maps.

'Nice street,' he said. 'What number?'

'Seventeen.'

He zoomed in and the thought of him scrutinizing the outside of our house was uncomfortable. All he said, though, was: 'You lucky bastards.'

I asked where he was from because I thought I should, but he just said, 'Nowhere like that, doll.'

I related the story of our painful McDonald's outing with Greg, trying to make Freddie laugh. Succeeding.

'How are things with the band?' I said. I couldn't believe that I'd become someone who could say a thing like this. I had been in the crowd as a fan, and now here I was, on a date with the lead singer.

Freddie sighed. 'Honestly, doll? Shit. We're meant to be recording our new album next month, but Ollie and I can't get it written. I mean, it's part written, but it's a pile of shite.'

He inhaled deeply and took a big gulp of wine. I saw his Adam's apple move as he swallowed and remembered him onstage.

'I have no idea what the fuck I'm doing. Everyone keeps promising we're on the brink of success, the next big thing. And it turns out that the thing that kills all my inspiration stone dead is being told that I'm the next big thing. That the only thing I have to do – the one tiny trivial step – is to write and record a brilliant album, with at least one banging song that Six Music will champion. I mean, how hard can *that* be, right?'

I knew what my line was here.

'You *are* brilliant, though,' I said. 'The other night – that was amazing. We all loved it. Me and my friends.'

'Yeah, sure, but there's, like, a world of difference between doing our old stuff and covers – we did covers! – in front of a friendly home crowd. Yeah, between that and pulling some wonderful new album out of my arse.'

He turned his gaze back to me and I tried to work out what I should say. Thanks to the wine, I tapped him on the knee.

'I believe in you, though,' I said.

Freddie grabbed my hand and looked at me for a long time. I stared back. I felt the air around me changing. I didn't look away, and he didn't either.

That was it: the moment when it all changed.

'I saw you in the crowd,' he said, his voice soft. 'Looking at me. You were the only good thing about that gig. A beautiful girl smiling at me. Gazing. Gazey girl. Gazey Hazy Hazel girl.' He seemed to pull himself back into the moment. 'And now here we are, with pizza.'

I had no idea how to react, or what he was asking. 'I bet you say that to all the girls.'

Freddie laughed. 'You have no idea.'

After the waitress took our plates away, he said, 'Out of interest, does anyone know you're with me today?'

'Nope. I mean, I told my mum I was meeting someone in town. She has a lot of safety rules. I have to text her at four.'

'But not who.'

'Not who.'

'And not exactly where?'

I shook my head, even though I had told her exactly where. I'd told Phoebe too. Mum wasn't going to turn up. Phoebe, however, might. My eyes kept darting to the stairs.

'Enzo saw me leaving dressed for a date, but he thinks it's someone else.'

He raised his eyebrows. 'This is dressing for a date?'

It hung there. A kick in the stomach. This was a new feeling: I'd always been quite happy with my style before. I'd never given it a massive amount of thought. I broke the silence by telling him about Enzo and Lewis. Freddie loved it and the atmosphere was happy again.

'Your birthday's next weekend,' he said.

I nodded. 'And you're twenty-six?'

'Not much older than you, in the scheme of things. I can already see you're more sensible than me, but this is – well, the kind of thing that families might not understand. And it sounds like your family have enough going on right now, so better not worry them by telling them you're hanging out in London with some musician. Just let them think it's a nice tame randomer.'

'Enzo and I normally tell each other everything.'

Freddie frowned. 'Not this, though,' he said. 'This time he thinks you're with Lewis. A discerning Kennedy fan. Cheers, Lewis.' He held up an empty wine glass. I clinked it with my full one. I passed it to him and he knocked it back in a couple of gulps.

'Cheers. So – how about we skip dessert and head to mine?'

I looked at him. He held my gaze again. His eyes were so dark.

'Where is it?' As if that was the thing that mattered.

'Kilburn. Ten minutes' walk.'

I didn't answer. I just gave a little nod because I could see he was waiting for it.

As we walked through streets of big terraced houses and mansion blocks, Freddie reached for my hand and hooked his little finger round mine.

'You're an artist?' he said. 'Right? You said that?'

'Oh God, not really. It's the thing I've always done to relax. I love it. Just picking up a pencil and doing a line drawing. I adore that. But I wouldn't call myself an artist.'

He squeezed my hand. 'Why not?' he said. 'You should. It's one of those things you become by saying it's what you are. When I started calling myself a musician, that was when everything changed.'

I didn't want to go to his flat. With every step, I wanted it less. I wanted to go home. I had come to meet him for fun, see what he was like in real life, not to go home with him.

What did he think would happen when we got there?

I knew really. I wasn't that naive. For Freddie this was a casual hook-up with a girl who caught his eye at a gig. His words rang in my head. *You have no idea*. He'd told me he gave his number to *pretty girls sometimes*. Was I a conquest? He knew when my birthday was: I supposed he thought I was close enough to sixteen for it to be OK.

Even though it was Freddie, even though I had been messaging him all week, I didn't want any of this. I felt the wine churning inside me, slowing me down, slowing my brain.

We walked past a woman who was maybe five years older than me. She was wearing denim shorts over ripped tights, a silky vest top and fishnet gloves. She looked amazing, and I thought Freddie should have been with someone like that, not a stupid child in jeans and a cardigan. He'd been hoping for a girl like her when I walked in: I knew he had.

He didn't want me to be his *girlfriend*. Of course he didn't! How pathetic of me to have imagined it, to have pictured us as boyfriend and girlfriend. He wasn't interested in seeing me again. All that eye contact and intensity was a technique that worked. He wanted a hook-up. I was a groupie. I was interesting to him because I was young.

I knew I couldn't do this.

I tried to speak a few times, but no words came. I tried harder. I really didn't want this.

'Freddie?'

He stopped. 'You OK?'

I nodded without looking at him. I looked at a blob of chewing gum on the pavement instead.

'What is it?'

'I'm – OK, I'm just going to say it.' I forced myself to be brave, so I took a deep breath and looked up into his perfect face. I felt my legs trembling, made myself say the words. 'So – I don't want a casual hook-up. I don't just want to be another groupie. I'm not – nearly as experienced as you probably think I am. Nowhere near. I don't think I can come to the flat, but thank you for asking me and thank you for lunch.'

I looked back down at the gum.

'Why did you think we were meeting, out of interest?' His voice was detached, different.

I addressed my words to the pavement.

'For lunch? I'll give you the money if you like.'

From the edge of my vision, I saw him nod.

'OK. Sure. Go on then. Give me the money. I'm so fucking sick of girls.'

I'd brought cash just in case. My hands trembled as I fumbled with two twenty-pound notes. He took them, folded them, put them in his back pocket. I blinked, trying to control the pricking behind my eyes. I was not going to cry. I mean, of course I was, but not until I was away from him.

'Go home. You're too young anyway. I'm a good guy so you weren't for me. And, Hazel? Wear red like at the gig. It looked way better on you than that yellow.'

I nearly changed my mind. What was I thinking? I had the opportunity to go home with a semi-famous musician, to kiss him, to have him always as my first. I could do that, couldn't I?

No.

'Sorry.' I turned and walked away.

I put the yellow hair flower into a bin outside the station, and gave the cardigan to a charity shop the next morning.

14

Venice

The faceless avatar melts away because of course he wasn't really there. Phoebe looks like herself again. I wander round the church, breathing in that churchy smell, calming myself down.

I see the candles next to altars. You light a candle to pray for someone, and praying can come in many forms. I find a two-euro coin in my purse and drop it into the coin box. I take a candle, light it from another one and put it in its place. When I stare at the flame, I see my dad's face.

I imagine his face all the time, but it's never been this intense before. I see him as I last remember him. I feel a breeze on my face, seawater on my legs. I hear him shouting my name.

Hazel!

The flame distorts the air above it. I don't know why I have the feeling of water on my legs. It feels so real that I have to look down to check.

I was three when he died. I think of Mum saying, 'You were so small.' I watched him being swept out to sea, but I don't remember it. I should remember it.

When I glance back at the pyramid, the doorway makes me catch my breath. There's something weird about it. Something wrong. I tell myself not to be stupid. It's an eye-catching tomb in a church, in a city filled with tombs and churches. But it has a doorway in it, and there's an old heart in there. Against all logic, I want to go inside.

I think of the girl watching me through the window. I think of the universe going weird. The jumps in time. Phoebe experiencing it too.

Enzo is talking to the security guy. No one's watching me. Maybe I could get in and out without anyone noticing. Perhaps it's something people do. There are two doors that meet in the middle, and one is open.

I imagine the open door glowing, like something in a video game alerting you to its possibilities. It pulls me forward, forward, forward. I look for Phoebe. She's not anywhere nearby.

The chapel next to the monument has a sign saying it's 'open for personal prayer'. I walk into it and, for form's sake, kneel on one of the cushions and say hi to my dad. His voice replies, loud and unexpected, echoing round the church, though only for me. It makes me jump. I haven't heard his voice in my head for ages and ages. I pushed him away.

'Hazel,' he says. 'You're close.'

Close to what?

No answer.

When I feel I've demonstrated 'personal prayer', I walk to the edge of the chapel, behind a little tree in a pot, and lean over the railing. There's a clear line from here to the pyramid doors, and it's almost entirely sheltered from view by a pillar and little trees in pots.

Why am I feeling I want to scramble over the fence and run in through the doors when I know there's a rotten heart in there? It's ridiculous. The feeling leaves me, with a whoosh. That was weird.

My heart is pounding and I drop back down on to one of the kneeling prayer places and wait for it to slow before I try to move.

Titian's tomb is a marble thing with pillars and more figures wearing draping clothes. I stand there and Phoebe walks fast down the aisle from the top of the church. I enjoy the huge cool space around us. I feel my heartbeat calming. I'm glad I didn't leap the fence and run into the tomb. What the fuck? I feel for my Cello. She's in my pocket, calming me.

'So Titian isn't actually in there?' I say randomly. My voice comes out quiet, but that's OK because we're in a church. I push my nausea down. All the weird stuff is in my head.

In Phoebe's too?

I see in her eyes how freaked out she is, but this isn't the moment for us to talk about it.

'He's in the building,' she says. 'He was really old when he died. Like, maybe nearly a hundred. And he's somewhere under the floor tiles.'

I glance over at the Canova monument. It's normal. Fine. I don't want to walk into it.

'No one puts the T-man in a box,' says Enzo, coming up behind us. 'Right? The other guy's heart, yeah, but not this guy.'

'Exactly.' Phoebe nods. 'They think he died of the plague, but because he wanted to be buried here everyone pretended he didn't. Plague victims had to be buried outside the city.'

I tune out and wander off. I walk past a carved wooden screen, through what I think are choir stalls, up to look at the altars at the top of the church.

'How are you doing?'

Phoebe has followed. We look at each other for a long time. I'm about to tell her about my weird, temporary compulsion to run into the tomb, to ask if it makes her feel strange too, when she starts speaking.

'Hazel – I'm so pleased you two let me come on your holiday. Thank you.'

That jolts me back to myself. I thought we were going to talk about what's happening here.

'What do you mean?' I guess this is easier but it's frustrating. 'You two let *me* come. In fact, you *made* me come.'

'But you and Enzo have been planning this since forever. I'm a late addition.'

I shake my head.

It plays in my head like a grainy video. Enzo and me watching that horror film. Enzo's mum finding herself the unexpected owner of a Venetian studio. A plan taking shape for a grand visit at some point, just the two of us. Phoebe's right: she wasn't part of that plan originally. They rescued me and then they brought me here because we had a haven to go to. Not for a holiday, but to get me out of danger.

'You weren't a late addition,' I say, 'because you were the one who arranged it, right?'

My mind is totally blank. There's so much I can't look at. So much in my brain is the wrong end of a magnet, repelling me every time I try to go near.

'Yeah, Enzo and I pulled the flights together fast, but it's still your thing. The Zed Club in Venice. Honestly – I wasn't sure how it would be, the three of us, because I know for sure that Enzo and I have both been thinking that once we had you back each of us would be your best friend again. He and I became close this last year because we had to, but I knew that when you came back I'd be the third wheel. You two have got all your in-jokes. All your shared history. You're practically twins. And you have that thing where you complete each other's thoughts just by raising an eyebrow. Anyway, who cares? I love you both, and I *get* Enzo now that we've, you know. Bonded.'

'You're not the third wheel,' I say. I think about it for a moment. 'And, even if you were, a tricycle is a lot more stable than a bike.' It sounds good in my head, but as the words leave my mouth I know it's just ridiculous. It's true, though. I smile. She giggles. I hug her.

I want to cling on to her forever.

'Thank you,' I say. 'I really, really mean it. I'll never forget what you've done for me.'

Will I? I'm forgetting all kinds of things right now: maybe I shouldn't make that promise.

'You're welcome.' She keeps hold of my hand as we step apart. Her hand is small and cool. 'That thing, though? The time thing? I'm kinda scared to go there, but what the fuck?'

I nod. We're looking into each other's faces. That little mole she has on her right cheek. I know her face better than my own.

I want to tell her that I've done it four times now. I open my mouth to say it, but then someone is walking across the tiles towards me and when I look it's that girl.

15

She's opening her mouth to speak, but before she can say anything

there's a blue flash, and everything disappears

again

and I DON'T WANT TO GO.

The world is deleted and I'm suspended over nothing. Not breathing, even though I'm trying. Not moving. Just me, in the void.

It lasts for longer this time. I think it does. It lasts minutes, hours, aeons. I flex my fingers and hold something, and although there's nothing there I can feel fabric. I hear my name. *Hazel.* The church has gone, but the voice is coming from above and all around me. A male voice. Is it my dad again?

It's not my dad.

It's *him.* I'm hearing his voice.

I think as hard as I can of the church. Its red and white tiles. Its tombs. My friends. Titian. I push myself back to it. If he is trying to pull me somewhere, I'm not going.

I'm staying.

I can't see anything but colour, and that colour is blue and it pulsates round me as if I'm in a living thing. I'm in the intestine of a blue creature.

Go back, go back, go back. Stay in the church.

And I do it.

I fly back to my body. I spread through it, jolting as the warmth spreads to my fingers and toes, inhabiting myself again.

I did it. I'm back in the real world. For the first time I controlled it.

16

I'm back in my body, but I'm not in the church. I'm sitting at a table.

I touch it with my fingertips. It's wooden. It feels like real wood. I close my eyes.

I was in the church. I saw the girl. I went to the blue place.

I was travelling through it

but I heard

his

voice

and I pulled myself away and now I'm here.

My heart is pounding so hard that I'm rocking on my chair in its rhythm. Am I meant to be here? What's happening?

I look around. Wooden table, indoors, small cafe. There's a drink in a big glass in front of me and it's bright orange, with an olive on a stick in it. This is an Aperol Spritz. I've never had one before, but I've seen them all over Venice. I pick it up and take a sip. Cold. The taste – sticky, sweet, like children's medicine – is not what I expected and it makes me wince, but then I think I like it.

My senses come back slowly, as if someone was switching me on bit by bit. I taste the drink again, but it takes a few seconds before I hear the voice.

'... for your trouble, young man,' Enzo says, and he starts laughing. It was clearly a punchline of some sort.

Cello. The little bird. There she is, in my pocket. I feel her. I take her out and put her on the table, next to my glass, and look into her little face. I know she's not wise because she's a piece of glass, but all the same she suddenly seems like the most reassuring thing in the world.

'Er, hello? No response at all?'

Enzo. He is totally at ease. We've obviously been here for a while. Why, though? How? Who was the *me* who came here? I check the time. It's midday. That'll be why we've got alcohol. Enzo would have decreed it was time to try a proper Venetian drink. I must have agreed. The staff must have served us without ID. There's a third drink on the table.

'Where's Phoebe?' I say.

He huffs out a massive sigh. 'Oh. Understood. You don't think it's funny at all? She's still in the church.'

I take another sip. Better not drink too much. It doesn't lead to anything good.

Enzo is annoyed with me. I tap his arm.

'Sorry,' I say. 'Sorry, Enz. I was a bit zoned out. I thought –' I decide to go as close to the truth as I can – 'I heard ... you know. A voice saying my name.' My voice drops to a whisper. '*His*. But it was only in my head.'

His head whips round. 'You sure?'

94

Enzo and I both look at every single person in the cafe.

I nod. I can't talk about the blue place because he doesn't get it. 'Yeah. Can you repeat what you were saying?'

After a few seconds, he happily launches into his story for the second time. It's a long-winded affair about how he gave some American tourists a tour of the church, making up stories, reproducing parts of things Phoebe had said, and reading church info. At the end, they gave him ten euros.

This time I burst out laughing. It feels good. It feels amazing.

'So you brought me straight over here and spent their money?'

'Yeah.' He looks at me, confused. 'And you were up for it, and we talked about having an Aperol for the first time. And we said cheers and took a sip and agreed that we need to get a bottle of this stuff to take home with us. Like, all that happened just now?'

'Sorry,' I say.

'Did he . . .' Enzo stops, and I see that he's preparing himself to say something big. 'H – sorry to ask, but did he ever hit you in the head? Because you're forgetting things, aren't you?'

I nod. Yes, I'm forgetting things. Yes, I think one of those things is the violence.

I change my nod to a shake. No, I don't want to go there.

The church is right outside the window. We're inside the cafe we sat outside for breakfast this morning. There's a coffee machine steaming, a row of bottles of bright orange Aperol. The window next to us is steamed up, and I lean over and write our names on it.

E
N
HAZEL
O

Enzo looks over at it. 'Zed Club forever.'

I think about what Phoebe said about being the third wheel and try to work out how to add her name. In the end, I make it work.

PHOEBE
N
HAZEL
O

Now when she joins us, she'll feel included. Enzo nods.

'Nice,' he says. 'Still Zed Club, though.'

I turn and give him our elaborate handshake. 'Always.'

We haven't done that for over a year.

Enzo says Phoebe is taking too long in the church, that we're going to go in and collect her if she doesn't turn up here soon.

'I'll go and get her,' I say. I start to get up. 'All the ice is melting in her drink.'

'In a moment.' He pushes me gently until I sit back down. 'Haze – I need to talk to you about something. Look: have you heard from Susie? Because I can't get hold of Greg. And I know we're on holiday and I don't want to be all, like . . .' He rubs his eyes and does some fake crying. '*Oh no! I want to talk to my daddy!* But it's a bit weird, considering that we came here in, y'know, quite a rush. Without really telling them what was going on.'

He stops and looks at me. I can feel him assessing my reaction. *Quite a rush.* I put my hand to my face.

'How does it feel?' He's peering at my cheek and I take my hand away.

'Fine,' I say. 'It feels fine. Honestly – it's fine!' I know it looks OK. I've seen it in the mirror.

'Sure?'

'Yeah.'

Running, running, running. A wooden room with a low ceiling. Sitting on a pavement. A hand round my arm pulling me up.

I gasp. I can't go there. I breathe in. Six. Out. Eight. In. Is that right? It will do.

One two three four five six.

One two three four five six seven eight.

The procession of numbers calms me. For a moment I'm a tiny child. Learning to count, chanting my numbers. With my parents? Are they there? For a second I feel them around.

Morris is there, in my head, and I let him in. *Listen to him*, he says. *Listen to Enzo. This is important.*

I nod. Breathe. *One two three four five six. One two three four five six seven eight.*

'OK,' I say to Enzo. 'Sorry. Yeah. I actually haven't heard from Mum. I texted her too. And she didn't answer.'

I take out the phone. Every time, I half expect a message from *him*, but there isn't one. Why hasn't Mum replied? Why hasn't she been frantic about us all jumping on a plane to Italy? She's the one with all the safety rules: why has she let all of this happen? I open our message thread, but there's only one message in it. It's from me, to her, and it's a draft. It says Mum – everything's fine here. I'm in Italy with E & P and having a great time. Venice is gorgeous. There's a picture of a canal attached.

I wrote that yesterday morning.

I press send. I watch the phone. An exclamation mark appears. Message not delivered.

Enzo nods. 'Same with my messages to Greg.'

'Weird.'

'Right?'

'I mean, Greg can be kinda distracted, but I thought Susie would be messaging you all the time.'

Have I been so monstrous that my own mother has given up on me? I tap her name, hold the phone to my ear. It just goes to a long tone. Unavailable.

I look at Enzo. 'What the hell? It's not ringing. Not going to voicemail. Just doing this –' I imitate the sound, then pass him the phone. He listens.

'What the heck?'

I cast around for an explanation. I find one.

'Brexit!'

'What?'

'Our phones! Don't we have to do a thing to get roaming before we go away now, or something? It's not them. It's us. Our phones don't work. Because we haven't set them up to work.'

I see relief flooding his face too.

'Of course,' he says. 'Of course that's it. It's us. Our phones.'

We smile at each other. I know it's a shaky explanation, but it works just enough.

'I mean,' says Enzo, 'it's way more likely than them both having no signal for an extended time.'

I think about it. 'I guess they could have got back together and gone on a second honeymoon. They could be on a – I don't know – plane to Australia?' I ask my dad, in my head. He doesn't reply. Maybe it's insensitive to ask your dead dad about your mum's second marriage. And anyway it's not that.

'They're not going to get back together, Haze.'

Something in his tone makes me snap to attention. 'How do you know?'

'Greg's got a girlfriend.'

Enzo's looking out of the window, through the Z of our logo to the church behind it, defined in the letters of our names, blurry beyond them. I'm not sure how to react, and then a man says something in Italian while trying to take Phoebe's chair from our table and for a second he is *him* and I gasp, but then he's not. Enzo says something back and the man takes one from somewhere else instead.

'Seriously?' I say. 'How long have you known? Who?'

He picks up a sachet of sugar and fiddles with it, sending the sugar down to the bottom, crunching it with his fingers, then turning it over and doing it again.

'Longer than I'd like,' he says. 'He didn't want me to tell you. I was going to yesterday, but you shut me down. Sorry for trying again.'

'And?'

'He asked me to go to Pizza Express to meet her, but I told him to go fuck himself. So I don't know her exactly, except that he's got mentionitis about her and so I can't help knowing quite a lot. Her name's Bella and she works at the bank. She's got a kid. A little boy called Milo, who's five. Bella, unlike Greg, is thirty-two.'

Mum is fifty. Greg is fifty-two. He's twenty years older than his new girlfriend. Not one decade but two. I feel sick, remembering how many times I rationalized the age gap between me and *him* by fast-forwarding it to a time when it would be less meaningful, because we would both have been proper adults. Turns out that all you have to do is wait, and then everything becomes fine.

'Does Mum know?'

'Doubt it.'

'Yeah.'

We sit in silence. I don't want to imagine this woman, but a picture arrives in my brain anyway of someone much younger than Mum, beautiful, gym-toned. I do some sums.

'Thirty-two is closer to our age than to his.' I remember *him* saying that the only people who cared about age gaps were jealous and bitter.

'Right? I said that to Greg. He started muttering about half your age plus seven, some equation that he claims means it's fine, even though I don't think even that works, and I told him to shut the fuck up.'

That equation makes me go cold. I push it away. I think of a little boy, a boy called Milo, and wonder whether he's going to come into our lives as a younger brother. No: my loyalty is to Mum, and my dad is Morris Angelopoulos. I don't want to talk or think about any of this, but Enzo is still going, and I can see how relieved he is to be getting it all out, so I let him.

'They met at work. I asked Dad if she's going to be our stepmum and he said it's early days, but then he kept banging on about how lovely and kind she is and how much she wants to meet us.'

I glug some Aperol and force a smile. 'I would imagine she really doesn't.'

'Right! You just know she's dreading it. He'll be reassuring her by pretending we're lovely.'

'Ha!'

'I told him he should have asked you to come for dough balls too, not that you would have eaten them.' I stare down at the table, self-conscious. 'But he told me not to be so stupid. Then he told me there's no need to say anything to you or Susie.'

I feel fiercely protective of my mother. When she finds this out, she's going to be gutted. I bet she's needed me over the past year, and I've been nothing but awful. I feel so sad for her that I want to get away from here and hug her.

I want to go back in time and do things differently. She was going through a horrible break-up and I did nothing to support her at all. I made it worse. I ran away to London, and then Cambridge.

Cambridge.

The word slices through me like an assassin's knife. It slides between my ribs and pierces my heart. I stand up. I can't do this. I can't face the thing that happened.

Morris is there, at the edge of my vision. He takes one of my arms and Enzo takes the other and they sit me back down.

Mum and Greg rushed into their marriage because of Enzo and me. They wanted our family to work so much that they ignored the fact that they didn't actually like each other that much. And now it's over, and it was never going to last forever anyway.

I look through our names at the church.

'We should go and find Phoebe,' I say.

We both knock back our drinks, and Enzo asks if we can have a takeaway cup for hers.

17

Kent

Nineteen months earlier

My horrible meeting with Freddie replayed in my head endlessly. I woke in the night, gasping. I wished I'd gone home with him. I wished I'd never met him. I snapped at Mum, ignored Enzo, couldn't focus on school. I went through my wardrobe and took out everything that had any yellow in it and got rid of it. Why had no one ever told me that yellow didn't suit me? I started wearing all my red stuff. I wished I was five years older. I wished I was stylish. I hated Freddie. I hated myself.

I drew dark pictures. Early one morning, I let my pencil do whatever it wanted and when I looked at the page there were waves, a storm out at sea. Lightning, a ship in trouble. A heavy-handed metaphor for how I was feeling. I decided to keep it and work it into a proper painting. I put it on the table and googled *Freddie Kennedy girlfriend* but didn't find much because he wasn't actually famous at all.

That night Enzo came into my room and said, 'Shall we try to get those free tickets for the Kennedy gig? In Hoxton?'

I shook my head. 'Don't fancy it,' I said.

'OK, sure.' If he'd pushed, I would have told him everything. He picked up my storm picture. 'Oooh, I like this one. Moody.'

In spite of myself, that made me happy. 'Do you? Thank you. I'm going to do it as a painting. It might not be too late to use it as coursework.'

I drafted messages to Freddie, apologizing, but didn't send them. I deleted his number, but I knew it by heart and just ended up resaving it: Lily K was back.

My dad's ghost didn't say anything and I was glad. This wasn't a thing you could share with your parents.

I'd never felt this lonely before. I hated it.

Luckily (kind of) things were so awful at home that my mood didn't attract much attention. I told Enzo that the date with Lewis had been crap and shook my head at all his follow-up questions. I told Phoebe the same thing about the date with the mystery guy, and hoped the two of them wouldn't compare notes. Mum sat around drinking coffee and playing break-up songs for a few days, then got her hair cut and joined the gym. When she wasn't doing that, she stayed at work all the time.

Greg cultivated a new jolly persona and finally managed to take us to the nice burger place. He asked Enzo if he wanted to move to the flat with him, and Enzo said no. Neither parent told us what had happened between them this time and we didn't ask. No one was happy. Everyone was pretending, all the time. The most fun thing in my life was getting my coursework done.

On Thursday I woke just before midnight because my phone, on the bedside table, was lighting up with messages.

> Hey doll!

> Sorry.

> I feel like a shmuck. is that how you spell it?

> You're so sweet.

> I don't deserve another chance

> but . . . ?

It was a dream. It had to be. I sat up in bed and looked again. I looked round. My real bedroom. Freddie was asking for another chance. His messages kept arriving.

> I guess I've lost sight of so many things.

> Can't quite get you out of my head.

Haven't been turned down for
a while!!! it stings.

It's making me do a bit of
self-reflection tbh.

You're so young and sweet.

And underage. Shit.

You haven't told anyone
right?

Would you meet me again?
just for a coffee, no
expectations on my part
promise. How about it? I want
to show you something.

That sounds sleazy.

Not in a sleazy way.

I'm such a mess, my hazy girl.

Fuck, fuck, fuck.

Oh happy birthday? today,
right??

> can I be the first to say happy
> birthday as of 8 minutes ago?

That was when it stopped. He was right: it was my sixteenth birthday and my first present was an apologetic stream of consciousness from a man who was now ten – not eleven – years older than I was.

I didn't reply because I didn't know what to say. I left him on read and slept fitfully until morning, falling asleep properly just before Enzo woke me up by leaping into the room and singing 'Happy Birthday' loudly, right into my ear.

I was feeling good.

Freddie had said sorry. I had made him reflect. He wanted to show me something. He had called me his *hazy girl*. It was a weird phrase but I'd take it. I went into my drafts and carefully deleted every message I'd filed there. Thank God I hadn't sent an apology of my own.

I wanted to reply, but decided not to do it until after school because I still had no idea what to say. It was enough, right now, to read his messages over and over. There was a spring in my step and a smile on my face, and Mum and Enzo thought it was because it was my birthday, as if I was a little kid.

I went to school and all my friends were nice to me. Phoebe, Fatima and Jack came over afterwards, and Phoebe produced a lemon meringue pie with candles just about staying upright in its crust, because she knew lemon meringue was my favourite. I told them all that I loved them. I put up my cards from my friends and family, including the one from my dad's family in Greece that said Χρόνια Πολλά! on it.

A huge bouquet arrived, red and pink roses, with a card saying 'Happy birthday doll. Love from Lewis xxxxx'.

I remembered him asking where we lived, zooming in on number 17. He had remembered.

I kept a rose, pressed between books, in my bedroom. When everyone had gone home, I finally replied to all his messages. I said thank you. I said yes.

On Saturday I turned down Pizza Express with Greg and told Enzo I was off to give Lewis one more chance after the birthday, and post-birthday flowers (more had come the next day with a note saying 'Happy birthday-boxing-day love Lewis xxxx'). Enzo said I should be dressing more sluttily and I thought he was probably right, but I was trying to strike a balance. I was wearing a short dress (dark red), opaque tights, DMs. I walked slowly to the station, second-guessing myself all the way.

I knew I shouldn't really be going to meet him again in secret, but I kept thinking of his eyes, his hair, his double denim, and I couldn't not. And he was sorry. He felt like a schmuck. I'd made him feel bad about himself and that was such a weird, weird, weird thing to happen. He was a musician whereas I went to school. I told Mum I was meeting someone called Lewis at St Pancras and she told me to be careful and have fun.

We were meeting at St Pancras station because it wasn't within walking distance of his flat and because it was where my train arrived and because he wanted to make it as easy for me as possible. He was on his best behaviour.

He was already there, sitting in the deli cafe with a coffee. He saw me coming, and grinned and waved, and as soon as I approached he jumped up, put his hands on my shoulders and kissed me on each cheek.

His lovely smell. Cologne with an undercurrent of Freddie Kennedy. My body reacted, even though I was trying to be so careful.

'What can I get you?'

'Cappuccino?' I said. 'Oat milk – thanks.'

I sat down and gazed at the people going by, some wheeling huge suitcases in the direction of the Eurostar, some dashing importantly towards who-knew-what. I watched a woman on a nearby table drinking a bottle of rosé on her own. I saw two girls, a bit older than me, holding hands as they walked towards the station exit. Something was happening and they were excited. Train announcements echoed. I didn't listen to the words. I was with Freddie. Was it going to be different this time?

'One oaty cappuccino for milady.'

That made me smile because it was something Enzo would have said.

'Thank you,' I said, and stopped. I had no idea what came next. He sat down.

'So how are things at home?' Freddie had got himself a black coffee and a glass that contained the kind of drink they had in old movies. I had no idea what those drinks even were. It was brown, with one big ice cube in it. Something like whisky or brandy.

'OK,' I said. 'I mean, kinda.'

'Is Greg back?'

I melted a little bit at the fact that he'd remembered to say *Greg* and not *your dad*.

'No. He's still in the flat. It's where Mum and I used to live, before they met. It's kinda nice of him to go there, rather than staying in his own home. I guess.'

'Yeah, at least you get the massive house. Break-ups are the worst. Oh – happy birthday again! Happy late birthday.'

'Thank you. And – thanks again for the flowers. They were totally gorgeous. All of them.'

He grinned. 'Don't thank me. Thank Lewis. But yeah, least I could do.'

'My mum thinks I'm seeing Lewis now.'

'Excellent.'

I took a sip of coffee, then wiped foam from my lip with a paper napkin. There might not have been any, but this way I knew there definitely wasn't. I wouldn't have to sit there thinking about my potential milk moustache.

He leaned forward and took my hand. I stretched out my fingers. His hand enclosed mine, warm and friendly.

'I'm so sorry,' he said. 'I don't know what's been going on with me. Thanks for giving me another chance, doll. You know I said I needed to show you something?'

I nodded.

'Well, it's what I've been doing since you sacked me off. And it's actually more like playing it than showing it. Is that OK?'

He took some big headphones out of his bag and leaned forward to put them on my head. They cut out all the sound around me. When the music started, I was in the middle of it. It was beside me, behind me, all around.

It was a home recording, with background noises. Freddie was playing the guitar and singing. He was singing to me.

He was singing *about* me.

Hazy girl. Gazey girl. You're too good for me.

Hazy, hazy gazey girl, you show me who I can be.

The tune was gentle and catchy. It was a gorgeous song. I swallowed hard. I didn't dare look at him.

Had Freddie Kennedy written a song for me?

For me?

I felt tears prickle at the back of my eyes. *Don't cry.* That would be pathetic.

I remembered his words: '*One banging song that Six Music will champion.*' I was sure this was it. It was one of those songs that instantly works, that you want to listen to again the moment it finishes.

I got to the end, then took the headphones off.

'Do you like it?'

I nodded but I couldn't speak. I hoped he couldn't see that I was in pieces.

'You made me feel so shit, you know? In a really positive way. Like I'd lost sight of myself and who I was. I'd become some shallow monster who had no idea how to treat a girl.'

The song had ended with extravagant promises: *I'll always treat you right. Please come back to me.* That kind of thing. I wondered if he meant that. Of course he did: he'd put it in a song.

'Sorry that I made you feel shit.'

'Hey!' He looked at me properly. 'Oh, Hazel. Oh darlin', don't cry. Come here.'

I blinked hard and, when he pulled me in close and hugged me and stroked my hair, I managed not to lose control completely. Still, I cried on his stripey T-shirt and he held me, then dashed off to the counter and came back with a pile of napkins. I forced myself back under control.

When I'd calmed down, he said, 'Sorry to upset you, doll. You held a mirror up to me and I didn't like what I saw. I don't want to be that guy any more.'

Any more. I silenced the alarm bell.

I wondered whether I had eye make-up all down my face. I scoured the area under each eye with a napkin just in case. 'It's a gorgeous song. Beautiful.' I breathed deeply. Where had all that emotion come from? 'Everyone's going to love it.'

'Thanks, doll! Ollie and Lina love it and I cannot *tell* you what a breakthrough that is. It's helped us crack our new album. Get the creative juices flowing. So you see? You *are* my muse.' He took a deep breath and gave me the world's most winning smile. 'Hazy girl – so that was an elaborate way of asking if you'll give me another chance?'

I spooned some chocolatey froth from the bottom of the mug into my mouth. My hand was shaking. I saw him notice it.

'Yes,' I said. 'Of course I will.'

18

Venice

Phoebe is right there, in the church. I'm so relieved that I want to cry. She's behind a pillar next to the Canova tomb, talking to someone I can't see, someone who slips away before I reach her.

I want to get Phoebe away from here, to go back to our normal carefree sightseeing. Enzo hands her the orange drink in a plastic cup that he carried into the church with a baseball cap on top of it: this seems to have been disguise enough.

'Oh hey,' she says when she sees us. She steps away from the railing and I'm glad. 'Sorry. I was about to come and find you. Seriously? What's that? You brought me an alcoholic drink in church?'

'Who were you talking to?' I say, but at the same time Enzo says: 'Think of it as communion wine.'

Phoebe takes the drink and sips it through the straw and nods.

'Ooh, that's nice. Thanks. They served you?'

'Clearly.'

'I did mean to come to the cafe. I was just looking at everything. The Titian altarpiece here is one of the greatest pieces of art in the whole Renaissance. But it's not that. It's more that I just can't quite step away from ...'

She looks back at the Canova monument. I do too. It's glowing again. It wants me to go there. I don't want to.

'I mean – sorry, Enz, I know you hate this weird stuff, but, Hazel, does it look weird to you? Is there a light coming out of it?'

I look away. 'Yes, and I don't like it.'

'What's it like?'

'It's kind of ... glowing.'

Enzo squints at it. 'It's really not, guys.'

'Right!' says Phoebe. 'It is. It's kind of going, "Look! Over here!" like it's in a video game. *Assassin's Creed* maybe? And it wants me to investigate. There's something there. I know there is. Something we need. There's this golden light coming out. Enz, can you really not see that?'

It's not golden when I look at it. I'm almost jealous.

There's a man walking towards us, who looks official, and so Phoebe takes the straw out of her drink, puts the cup to her lips and knocks back the whole lot before he can tell her to take it outside. He sees her, sighs and walks away.

'No, I cannot see golden light coming out of it! Fuck's sake. And didn't you say there's some guy's heart in there?'

I shudder. This is bad. I hate it, but I'm drawn to it in the weirdest way. And Phoebe, I can see, is even more drawn than I am. I need to get her out.

'Phoebe,' I say, 'don't even think about it. Nothing good would happen.'

She nods but doesn't look away. I take her arm and tug her towards the church door. We can get gelato, go on a boat, go back to the happy holiday vibes.

I have no idea what's going on. Why can't we contact anyone? Why is no one messaging us? I know in my heart that it's not because of our phones. Why is my own mother apparently ghosting me?

'Phoebe?' I touch her arm, try to lead her towards the sunshine. 'This is weird, but have you been in touch with anyone since you've been here? Jakub? You must have messaged each other, right?'

Her forehead wrinkles in a little frown as she's momentarily distracted. She moves away from the tomb.

'Actually, no. I guess he's stepping back to let me spend the time with you.'

'Have you messaged him?'

Her eyes snap back to the monument. 'I tried but it didn't go through. I guess reception's not great here. Four G or whatever.'

'We can use our phones on Maps easily enough.'

We stare at each other, and for a second I don't know anything. Where are we? What's going on? For a few seconds there's just me and Phoebe, staring at one another. I try to hang on to reality. I force myself back.

'Of course we can.' Enzo's disembodied voice makes me smile. 'Look, we've been in this old church long enough, ladies. Bored. Time for the next adventure.'

The surroundings come back.

Stop her.

It's Morris. His voice in my head. The hairs stand up on the back of my neck and I look round, and see that Phoebe has gone.

There's a movement over to the left and I realize she's doing the thing I didn't do. She's gone into the chapel next door, but unlike me she is climbing the metal fence in the spot that's hidden from view by the trees in pots.

I know what happens from here. Up the steps, over the lion, into the tomb.

I yell, 'Phoebe! No!'

She sprints up the tall marble steps, climbs over the lion, and runs into the glow.

There's a crack and a crash.

The whole place flashes red. It goes blank, and then it comes back. I'm climbing over the railing after her.

Hands grab me by the shoulders and pull me back. It's the man from the church and he's furious.

The door to the tomb slams shut.

I am ejected from the church.

I don't know where Enzo has gone.

And that is how we lose Phoebe.

19

Outside, the sun is warmer than it was before, reflecting on the stones. I can feel the heat coming off the ground as if it was a radiator. The sky is perfectly blue. I look up. There's a bird, and a plane, and they look the same.

Cello. I grab my bird and focus as hard as I can on getting myself back to the time before Phoebe ran into the tomb. I kind of controlled it on myself before. I look at the people walking through the square and want one of them to be the girl I've seen each time, the girl who makes time glitch, but none of them are her.

I cross the bridge and go to sit on the steps at the edge of the canal. I dangle my legs over and stare across the water. I think about the time before Phoebe vanished. I need to get there. The water is murky, and it's impossible to tell from here whether it's ten centimetres or infinitely deep. I remember the photos of these canals when there was a pandemic, when northern Italy was hit before we were. The water was clear because this murk is mud from the bottom, stirred up by boats. There were fish in here, visible when it was clear. I think there were even dolphins, though I could be making that up.

I wonder how often people drown. Imagine if the suddenly clear water had revealed all the bodies. It didn't, so I suppose that answers that. Or maybe it did, but it wasn't shown on the news at a time when there were already enough bodies.

From here, I can see everyone who walks over the bridge, and everyone who goes in and out of the church, and everybody who's in the square. I need one of them to be the glitching girl.

What's happening here, Dad? Is there something weird going on?

Dad. What's happened to Phoebe? Is this me cracking up? Or both of us?

Where is Phoebe?

Instead of his voice, for a second I hear hers.

I'm here, it says, so clearly that my head whips round, but she's not there at all.

'Where?' I say it out loud. She doesn't reply. Neither does he.

I look up at the sky and leave space for them to answer. This sometimes works with my dad: it's not that I think he's floating in the air next to me, listening to my thoughts and ready to whoosh into my ear with the answer. It's more that using him as my secret focal point leads me to find the answer in myself. I felt so grown up when I worked that out.

I kick my legs like a little child and wait.

Yes, darling, says the imaginary Morris-voice. *Of course there's something weird going on. Your phones don't work. You have huge memory lapses.*

I don't like my dad-voice, which is supposed to be the voice of reason, saying things like this, so I make him change tack and say: *You've been through a hard time. It's OK to find reality a bit of a struggle. Drink some water. You need to eat something because you've had alcohol for lunch and no food since breakfast.*

I jump up, cross the bridge again, and wander round the square. The paving stones are old and smooth under my feet, with weeds growing in a few of the cracks. I lean on a wall and get my phone out. There are no messages at all. I realize how much I'd hoped there would be something from Phoebe.

I'm just across the square, I write to the group chat. Come out.

With no one here to stop me, I go to open up my text thread with *him* because I'm strong enough to delete it now.

It's not there.

I must have already deleted it. I would have done it when I was on the way here. Deleting our messages was a big thing to do and I can't believe I've forgotten the moment I clicked it. I check WhatsApp and every other platform we were on, but there's nothing from him on any of them. There are no messages from unknown numbers. There's nothing hidden away.

I write *Lily K* in the name box, but nothing comes up. My phone tries to fill it in with all the other Lilys instead. I type an *F* but nothing comes up there either. I type in what I think is his number, though I've probably got it wrong. I write *hi* and press send. After a few moments, an exclamation mark appears.

Either the number was wrong or I've blocked him. Or he's blocked me. Or my phone isn't working internationally. I'm deeply into the settings, trying to work things out, when I look up.

The glitching girl is walking towards me. I'm so happy that she's going to take me back to a time when Phoebe was here that I run to her, opening my arms as I go.

I'm suddenly suspended in nothingness. I listen for someone shouting my name, but it's not there. Instead there's a screaming sound, above and below and all around me. It goes on and on and on, tearing my soul into pieces, and then there's a whoosh and I haven't gone anywhere at all.

20

London

Eighteen months earlier

On our third date we met at the South Bank. It was my idea, but as I fought through the London Eye crowds I regretted it. I was second-guessing myself with everything. As an out-of-towner, I'd clearly picked the most obvious part of London. I was embarrassed: I might as well have suggested meeting in Harrods.

The river was grey and solid-looking next to me, and the wind blew my hair round my face and whipped it into my eyes. I didn't want to tie it back because I needed a mirror if I was going to do that, so I just tucked it into my scarf and kept going.

Freddie grinned as he saw me approaching, by the skate park.

'Hey, gorgeous,' he said. 'Looking lovely, doll.'

I smiled. 'You too.'

I was wearing red, as he'd suggested. My scarf was red (it was from Primark, found in a frantic scouring of the shops after school) and my jumper was red, and I was wearing jeans and boots. Even my lipstick was red, which was a bit of a gamble.

Freddie was in jeans and a sloppy jumper with an old-looking coat. Somehow he made it all scream rock star.

'Sorry to have picked a really touristy part of town.'

'You kidding? I love it round here. You just stay away from that end of things. All the good stuff is this way.'

We started walking towards the good stuff, and then we were outside the BFI Southbank, and there was a Wes Anderson movie on, and Freddie was asking if I'd seen it. Leaves were blowing round our ankles. The air was freezing, the lights twinkling on the river. I felt like a girl in a movie.

I shook my head. I knew from Instagram that Wes Anderson films looked gorgeous.

'Me neither.' He gave me a huge, sincere grin. 'I love him. Been wanting to see this one. Do you fancy it?'

And so I became someone who would drop into the BFI Southbank to watch a Wes Anderson movie on the spur of the moment. Someone who didn't blink at paying twenty-six pounds for two tickets, though Freddie paid, not me. I remembered him taking the money from me for those pizzas, and didn't insist.

'If I got an under-sixteen ticket,' I said, looking at the prices, 'it would be much cheaper.'

'We're not doing that.' His mouth tensed up.

We sat in the back row, and Freddie got himself a whisky and me a Diet Coke, and I sat down feeling like a girl on a date in the olden days, wondering how this had happened so fast.

Freddie put his arm round the back of my chair and rested his hand on my shoulder, but he didn't push it any further than that and I was glad. A huge part of me wanted to kiss him but, in spite of what I'd said, in spite of the fact that he had written me a song and that he was clearly going through some kind of crisis and that I was weirdly helping him, I didn't want to do that yet. I held back. I actually watched, and loved, the movie.

After that, we walked, side by side, along the river, and talked about the film. We went all the way up to Tate Modern. I wanted to go in there. I hadn't told Freddie much about my art because it felt so stupid and schoolgirlish next to his music. He knew I liked drawing, but that was all. I wanted to tell him about my storm painting, but held back in case it was too amateurish.

'This has been really fun,' he said when we reached the gallery. 'Wholesome. The most wholesome day of my recent life. I feel like – I don't know. Like you gave me that wake-up call, and now there's something about you that makes me want to . . . I don't know. Incoming cliché alert, I guess. That OK?'

A river police boat sped past. That, I thought, must be a fun way to be in law enforcement. I wondered what kind of crimes they intercepted, whether you could flag them down if you needed them.

'Sure.'

'You make me want to be my best self. To watch movies and walk by the river. And you make me want to tell you something that I never actually talk about. This is a big thing for me to do. Is it OK with you?'

I had no idea what was coming, but made an encouraging noise.

He looked at the Tate. 'Can we go in there? Just to the free bits.'

'Of course!'

'I mean, you're the artist.'

I smiled. He had remembered.

'And it feels like the right place. I think I need to tell you my stuff. If I tell you my fucked-up life story, will you tell me all about you too?'

We started walking towards the gallery. 'You know about me.'

'There's more, though, isn't there? I want to know all of it, doll. Everything.'

In the huge space inside Tate Modern, we wandered round a sound-and-music installation, but I mainly listened to Freddie talking. My parent issues faded away because his story was so much worse than mine.

'Not many people know this,' he said, 'but – OK. Here goes.' He paused, blinked a few times. 'We had another brother. Me and Ollie. There were three of us. This is the bit you'll never read about in interviews. Harry and Ollie and me.' He pointed at himself. 'Youngest kid here. The naughty one. Harry was the bossy one, the sporty one. He didn't care for music at all. Yeah. So that was him. Four years older than me, two years older than Ollie. All very mathematical.'

'Right.'

I knew what was coming. He was talking in the past tense, so of course I did. I heard it in his voice, saw it in his face. I felt it.

'Yeah. I annoyed him all the time, but still Harry would look out for me. He was the only one who could talk me down when I was being a brat. And then, when we were all still kids –' He paused, took a couple of breaths. 'Well, he died. There one day, gone the next. And that's how I know how you feel about your dad, doll. I've been there. In a different way, but I get it.'

I felt sick. He did get it. He had been through worse. I wanted to know what had happened, but didn't like to ask.

'How old were you?'

'Seven. Harry was eleven. Just finished primary. I know you want to know what happened. This isn't healthy, but I still can't really talk about it. Car accident. That's all I can say. Because of the circumstances, Ollie and I couldn't deal. We still can't. It all goes into the art, if that's not too wanky a thing to say. Is it?'

I grabbed his hand. It was dry and warm. I squeezed it. He squeezed mine back and wiped his eyes with the back of his other hand.

'Of course it's not! I'm so sorry you've been through that.'

'Anyway. That's me. I have one photo of him. I keep it in my room, look at it when I need to. I'll show it to you sometime. You're in the inner circle now, doll. Tell me about you.'

And so, because he had been through something so much worse, and because he was actually interested, I told him everything. I didn't keep any of it back. I told him about Morris at the edges of my vision, as the guiding voice in my life. Guiding me when I drew. I told him all my thoughts, my feelings. I told him that I felt that I knew, from that eavesdropped conversation, that whatever had happened had in some way been my fault.

'Even if it was,' Freddie said, 'you were a bit too small to be held accountable, right? I mean, that's harsh.'

'It must be something terrible, though,' I said, 'or Mum would have told me.'

'Well, if you did, it was by mistake, right?'

I opened up completely in a way I had never done before, and when I'd finished he kissed me.

He kissed me in front of a painting by Ellsworth Kelly. I kissed him back. His lips were soft and gentle and he tasted of whisky, but I liked it.

'Promise we'll do this forever,' he muttered, leading me into a quiet corner.

Every nerve ending I had tingled.

'I promise,' I said, and he kissed me again, and again, and again.

21

Venice

I hear her voice.

'Hazel?'

'Phoebe!' I look all around but there's nothing. Just the billowing weird air. 'Where are you?'

Before I can get any more words out, I plummet.

It's before. I'm sitting next to Phoebe in the park. She's reading a book for coursework. It's called *Venetian Art: From Bellini to Titian.* I can feel the sun on my face. I think I remember this actually happening.

I feel myself being pulled away.

Then I'm in the school library and Phoebe's researching an art project. I'm writing a history essay. Phoebe huffs and taps my arm. 'Look at this!' she says. 'Look how freaky. These red cherubs.' I look over and see she's looking at a regular painting of Mary and baby Jesus, but that it has surreal-looking cherubs at the top, just faces and wings, all bright red. She starts to tell me about them.

*

Something pulls me away from the library and then I'm in the cafe. Our names are in the steam on the window, intersecting at the Z. I look down. There's a bright orange drink.

Enzo is next to me.

'Oh my God,' I say, 'what's going on, Enz? What's happening?' I'm crying, sobbing, and I don't care that we're in public. Now I've started, I can't stop.

'Haze?' He's frowning at me.

I stand up so quickly that the chair falls over behind me. There's a crack, and I'm back in the void.

I'm in the apartment, and it's yesterday morning. Phoebe says, 'Change your name then.'

Enzo says: 'Maybe I will. Let's trial it.'

I'm standing by the window. I open my arms and walk towards Phoebe. I need to hold her, to keep her safe.

I'm back in the void. I scream her name.

I'm outside the Frari church. I run in without paying and no one stops me. She's not looking at monuments or altarpieces. She's not sitting in a pew. She's not standing in the aisle, looking up at the distant ceiling. I don't know when this is, but she might be here. She might.

Then I see her in a choir stall on her own. She's beyond the altar, past a velvet rope and a 'no entry' sign in multiple languages.

'Phoebe!' I shout. I yell it so loudly that everyone must be looking at me. Phoebe glances over and gives me a little smile. I speed up, rushing towards her. There are footsteps approaching behind me and I turn to see the church guy coming for me.

Then, when I look back, she's gone.

She was there but now she's not.

I saw her sitting there but I didn't.

I'm standing on the side of a canal. There's Enzo. I look at the canal. It's a big one. Is it *the* big one? The grand one?

I wobble on my feet, but Enzo reaches over to steady me. He looks haunted.

'Shall we find a water taxi?' he says.

The sun is lower in the sky than it was before. Hours must have passed, if this is the same day. I focus on the details. This feels like something that hasn't happened yet. I just want to hang on to this. I need to keep it, to stay still, to stay in one time and one place for more than a few seconds because I've been bouncing around and I feel sick.

'No,' I say. 'I'm OK.'

There are tufts of grass between the paving stones. I grab the wall beside me and hold it with my fingertips as if that might keep me here. I watch a shiny beetle scuttling in the same direction we are and take care not to step on it. I walk next to Enzo. I guess we're heading back to the studio. I wait for the swooping feeling of going somewhere else, but it doesn't come. The ground is still there, beneath my feet. I count my breaths. I need to stay here.

'Enzo,' I say. 'Where's Phoebe?' I want to say more, but I don't have the words for it.

'Yeah. Time to go to the police,' he says as we walk. 'I'll do the talking.'

Enzo is more serious than I've ever seen him, apart from once.

'Have I been with you? Since we lost her? Because I just jumped here and . . .' I have no idea how to say this in a way that will be meaningful to him.

'You've been zoning in and out. I'm worried about you, Haze. You've been spiralling since she vanished. We massively overstepped, bringing you out here. We should have taken you home, or got you into some kind of . . . I don't know. Rehab.'

'Rehab.' All I can do is echo it. Do I need rehab? 'What for?'

Enzo's jaw is tight. I look out at the water. A police speedboat goes past. I watch the ripples it makes, hear them lapping against the bank. I see him start to raise his hand to summon it, and change his mind because it doesn't work that way.

For a moment I feel water on my legs, a sense of panic. I pull myself back. I'm not standing in water.

'I don't know,' he says. 'The food stuff. Support. Haze – I know you don't want to talk about it and I know that whatever the fuck has happened to Phoebe has messed things up. You've been blanking out all the time. Let's check if she's back at the apartment. And when we've found her then maybe we should just take you home, yeah? We can keep you safe there. This place is freaking me out.'

It's freaking me out too. It doesn't seem real. I suddenly feel that it's somewhere entirely different. Not the place it's pretending to be at all.

'Is it even Venice?' I say, and he snorts.

'Yeah. This place has canals. It has St Mark's Square. Gondolas. Loads and loads of bridges. Behold. Venice.'

We shuffle along. We pass people and I hardly register them. I don't look at the souvenir sellers, though I feel my little bird in my pocket and take some strength from her. I keep walking, keep breathing. I try to stay here, now, in this time and place. I try to anchor myself. *I am here, I am here, I am here.*

Don't fly away. Don't float off. Don't go to the void. Don't look for the girl.

'This was meant to be perfect!' His voice is loud and a pigeon flies away. He lowers his voice. 'We've been dreaming of this forever and I thought we'd done it. You know? Pheebs sorted it all while I was driving. Flights, tickets. Passports. Vittoria told me where to collect the key. Messages to the parents explaining we were all away together and that it was fine. Fielding the calls. She even got fucking travel insurance! Who even does that?'

He clearly wants an answer, so I say, 'Phoebe does. It's a Phoebe thing to do.'

'And yesterday was everything we'd needed it to be. You didn't even want to leave the apartment at first, and by the evening you were sitting on a bridge eating food. It was amazing. But now she's vanished without a trace, in a city where you can't exactly find a person easily. God knows where she went. And you've been tripping out all over the place – soz, H, but you're scaring me as much as she is.'

'I'm here.'

'Yeah, maybe, but you're not *here*, are you? You keep going blank, like a robot. I don't know why, but I know we've messed this up. We should have got you straight to a . . . a facility or something.'

He pauses and when he speaks again his voice is careful. 'You know we've hardly seen each other this year. You and me. I'm scared of whatever the things are that I don't know. From looking at you, I'm guessing it's an addiction thing? And I don't know why I didn't see it before.'

I can't look at him. It could have been. I think of how close I sailed to that particular iceberg.

'It's not,' I say. 'It's really not that.' I try to force a smile. 'I mean, I must look totally shit for you to think it, but I'm really not any kind of addict actually.'

He looks at me. I look him properly in the eye and feel him grounding me. I can't ping off through space and time. I have to stay here now. We stare at each other and I see him believing me, understanding that I'm really not addicted to coke or booze or anything else. I was addicted to an unworthy guy: that was all. We look at each other for so long that we nearly walk into the canal.

Then I remember Phoebe, and I go cold again.

'We did have a brilliant day yesterday,' I say after a while.

'Yes,' he says. 'And I thought that was it. I thought that was how it was going to be.'

'So we go back to the studio . . .'

'And if she's not there then police. You don't have to come if it's too much. You can wait in the apartment, and rest, and message me if she comes back. I'll report her missing. Should I call her family?'

I shake my head. 'Not yet.'

'You're right. Plus, our phones don't even work. Yeah. OK. We have a plan.'

We walk in silence for a long time. I start to feel that I'm standing still, walking on the spot, while the city moves beneath me. I'm a hamster on a wheel. I decide not to share the thought.

'You know when we arrived here,' says Enzo. 'Night before last?'

'Yeah.'

I stop. No. I don't.

'Actually,' I say, 'I don't remember arriving. I said that before and it's true. I just remember waking up yesterday morning and you were going to change your name.'

'Giovanni Antonio Canal,' he agrees.

'Did we come on a plane?'

'Well.' He runs his fingers through his hair. 'That's the thing. I didn't say this before, but I don't remember it either. And, with all this weird stuff, I'm guessing Phoebe doesn't.'

'What?'

'I mean, I know what our plan was, and we're here, so I guess we must have done it. Our flights were from Stansted to Marco Polo Airport. Then we were going to get the vaporetto across. Blue line to San Zaccaria B. It's near the studio. I know all that, but only because I remember Mum telling me on the phone.'

'But you don't remember us doing it?'

He looks round. I know he's looking for Phoebe.

'No.' His voice is quiet. 'I don't remember anything. I was sitting on the roof terrace, looking at the stars. It was the middle of the night. Phoebe was there. She knew the way back to the apartment, so we went, and you were there, tucked up in bed, fast asleep.'

I manage a quiet, 'Shit.'

'So I kind of spent ages rationalizing it. Phoebe and I didn't talk about it. You were the only one who did, and I just kinda took the role of being Mr Rational because . . .'

'It was less scary?'

'Yep. And then you started flipping out, and then Phoebe did, and I just kept scoffing at it because that way at least one of us was trying to keep things normal. I was waiting to start doing that glitchy thing myself tbh, but it hasn't happened. And now . . . Shit, Haze. I wish I could carry on being the voice of reason, but you know what? I fucking can't. I'm done. Where the hell is she? What's going on?'

We look at each other. I try to find something to say, but there's nothing.

'So . . . are we actually on holiday in Venice?'

Before he would have huffed at me for saying something like this – a few minutes ago, he did exactly that – but now, suddenly, he doesn't. Instead he gives a little shrug and takes my hand. We never walk hand in hand, but here we do, side by side, hanging on to the fact that, whatever is happening, at least we're together. We have each other.

We walk on. I breathe. I can feel myself breathing. It feels like breathing normally does. I force myself to be present. That is Enzo next to me. It looks like him, sounds like him, even smells like him (CK One, his retro love). And that, under my feet, is ... Venice? To my right, the canal. Above me, the sky.

'Sorry for telling you about Greg,' he says. 'The girlfriend business. I should have held it in a bit longer. That was the last thing you needed. It's shit for us, but it's hardly the first time that's happened to anyone, is it?'

I'd almost forgotten about what he'd told me about Greg and his new girlfriend, and I seize on the normality. 'Oh, that's fine,' I say. 'Promise. We kind of knew by now that they were done, right?'

'Yeah. Still, though. We didn't want any other partners on the scene because it complicates things, and Greg didn't get the memo.'

'Shame it's not up to us. I mean, honestly it's OK.'

This is better. This is a normal thing. Our eyes meet and I see that we're both thinking the same. *Talk about regular stuff.*

'At least we're seventeen. If they'd split when we were little, we might never have seen each other again, but that's not going to happen now. Really, Enz, I don't care about that. I mean, I do, but it's gonna be OK.'

He nudges me with his arm so hard that I almost fall in the canal. I push him back.

'It is,' he says. 'It is going to be OK. As soon as Phoebe comes back, everything will be dandy. She could have dropped her phone in a canal, right?'

'If she'd got mad at us, she would have lobbed it in.'

'She would.'

We're not far from the apartment. We walk along the Riva degli Schiavoni and I stop to look at the seller who sold me my glass bird yesterday. I'd forgotten about him.

He's wearing that Doctor Who T-shirt. It's making me think of something, but I don't know what or who.

'Hi,' I say. I reach into my pocket and my fingers close round Cello. The little bird has come with me through my blackouts, my weird mental gymnastics.

The man says, 'Hello, darling.'

It unnerves me. I hold Enzo more tightly and we walk away.

22

London

Eighteen months earlier

Our first kiss changed my life. I wanted to be with Freddie all the time. He was my drug. My everything. I felt myself falling entirely and utterly in love with him and I adored every moment of it.

It was the fact that he'd told me something so personal, so tragic, that he'd trusted me with his truth that did it. We didn't talk about Harry again for ages, not directly, but it was always there. His tragedy that mirrored mine.

When I was with him, I wanted to be right next to him, enveloped in him. When I was away from him, which was most of the time, I wanted to be talking to him. I wanted to be sending him photos and messages. I wanted to be gazing into space, thinking about him, remembering and imagining. I went to London the next weekend, and the one after. I felt like a girl in a story: I had got the guy and he wanted me forever. I told him how much I loved drawing, what an outlet it was for me, and he didn't laugh. He was interested. He wanted me to draw something for him.

I loved the fact that he never pushed me to take things further. He was happy to walk through the park with me, across the bridges, through the tourist places and the out-of-the-way spots. Three Saturdays after our first kiss we were back on the South Bank, fighting through the London Eye crowds, when Freddie stopped.

'I've never done that,' he said. 'Have you?'

'Once,' I said. 'When I was ten.'

He thought for a second. 'Let me guess: new family bonding?'

I squeezed his hand. I couldn't believe he knew my story so well, that he had immediately pieced that together.

'Yep. It was the first time I met Enzo. Our parents took us for freak shakes at a place called Maxwell's in Covent Garden, and then we came here.' I smiled, remembering how much I had resisted meeting *that boy*, and how it had changed instantly when I saw him. 'It was brilliant. There was a massive queue, but Greg got priority passes. Mum never did that kind of thing so I felt like the queen.'

'Right.' Freddie was looking around. He went up to a resolutely cheerful member of staff and said, 'Where do we get a priority pass, mate?'

Five minutes later we had wildly expensive tickets. Ten minutes after that we were stepping into a slow-moving capsule, having skipped the massive queue, and setting off.

'There we go,' he said as we rose slowly into the air. 'If that Greg guy can impress you with this, I can do it too.'

I looked over at him, surprised that he was competitive about it. I didn't like that. It was so unnecessary.

'Well,' I said, 'back then I was a little kid and I was so, so nervous about the fact that my mum had a new boyfriend and that she wanted me to meet his son. I'd met Greg before and I didn't like him just because I wouldn't have liked anyone. I totally didn't want to meet Enzo. I was certain I was going to hate him.'

'You should trust that first impression,' said Freddie. 'First impressions are when your lizard brain notices the things that your conscious brain doesn't.' He grinned. 'My first impression of you: gorgeous girl who had unaccountably paid money to hear us play.' He waited. I took the cue.

'My first impression of you: breathtakingly gorgeous rock star looking at me.'

He kissed the top of my head.

'Greg's really nice, though. I just didn't want someone else trying to be my dad. It had been Mum and me for ages and I didn't want that to change. So I went into it feeling grumpy, and the whole thing was a lovely surprise. And now,' I said, 'I'm here with you, and that's a million times better than anything else.' I stood on tiptoes to kiss him properly. I was hardly aware at all of the whole of London spread out in front of us, behind us, all around us.

He kissed me back, and I felt his hands on my waist. He kissed and kissed me, pulling me closer to him, stopping to tuck my hair behind my ear, starting again. When we emerged, we had passed the top part and were coming down the other side.

'I want to see your home,' he said. 'This huge house that the Greg guy gifted you. Invite me over when everyone's out.'

'I will,' I promised.

There were about twenty other people in the capsule. As far as I was concerned, they didn't exist because there was just me and Freddie in the universe, but when I walked over to the other side of the pod to look towards Kent, to wonder when I'd have a chance to invite Freddie over, I became vaguely aware of Freddie and a man in conversation. A Kennedy fan? I smiled at the thought. Probably not.

Then Freddie's voice was raised. He was angry.

'Mind your own fucking business, mate. How about that for an idea?'

The other voice was quieter. I took a few steps to my right, to hear what he was saying.

Up close the man looked like a tourist. He was wearing a blue T-shirt with 'We are' and a picture of a dolphin on it. He was a bit shorter than Freddie, but he looked tough.

'The thing is, pal, I wasn't talking to you.'

'No – you were talking to her.' Freddie was pointing to a woman who was standing next to the dolphin guy. '*About* me. About my girlfriend. Right in front of us.'

Girlfriend. That was new. I was alarmed, though. This was not sounding good.

The man shrugged. 'Didn't mean you to hear. Sorry.'

'She's nineteen.'

'Yeah? I'd have said fifteen or so.'

I was mildly affronted by this as I had dressed in black to look more sophisticated, with a red cardigan, and felt I was easily nailing eighteen. I felt myself yanked across the capsule as Freddie grabbed me by the wrist. It hurt, and I crashed into a small child, whose mother picked her up and said, 'Excuse *me*!' in an angry voice.

'Would you like to ask her? Hazel, please tell this busybody that you're nineteen.'

I looked up at Freddie. I looked at the dolphin man, who was huffing and clearly annoyed. Everyone else in the pod was now listening in. I felt Morris in among them. I'd pushed him away lately. My relationship with Freddie did not need parental supervision.

I gazed down at my feet. My DMs were a bit scuffed.

'I'm nineteen,' I said.

The man took half a step forward. 'It was a concern to my wife and me, that's all.'

I turned to his wife, and she gave me a little wave. She had very styled hair and a pink T-shirt.

I cleared my throat. I could feel the energy coming off Freddie and knew that he wanted to punch this man, and that we were in a confined space, and that it would be awful if the situation escalated.

I looked the man in the eye. 'I know I seem younger than I am. I always have. But honestly it's my nineteenth birthday today. I promise.'

I kept my eyes on him, then switched my gaze to his wife, channelling sincerity.

'Then I apologize,' he said. I could see that neither of them believed me.

'Happy birthday, honey,' said his wife.

I led Freddie away from them, but the trip was ruined. When we came to get off, the woman waited for me, and as I passed she muttered, 'Take care of yourself, sweetie.' Freddie twitched and I knew, again, that he wanted to punch someone.

I took his hand and walked him away as fast as I could. When we reached the Festival Hall, I saw a bar and led him into it.

'I can't buy you a drink,' I said. 'But if I could I'd get you one of those whisky ones.'

He glared, and then his face changed. He put his head in his hands, then went and bought himself a whisky-type drink, and handed me what I thought was a Coke until I sipped it, at which point I discovered that it also had alcohol in it.

'Cheers, doll,' he said, clinking glasses. 'Sorry you got caught up in that. What a wanker.'

'I know,' I said. 'And I'm sorry that kissing me in public can make a thing like that happen.' I shuffled up so I was close to him and put my hand on his back.

He said lots of sweary words about the American couple. I nodded and agreed, though deep down I knew they'd just been looking out for me. I caught a glimpse of Morris at the edge of my vision: he was hovering nearby and I spoke to him in my head.

I'm really happy. I'm having a brilliant time with Freddie.
He would have hit that man.

I know, but that's because he's protective of me. Of our relationship. He doesn't like other people judging it.

Hazel . . .

I pushed him out of my head.

142

I was a bit unsteady as we left the bar. We walked along the river again. Freddie had had three drinks and calmed down a bit.

'I guess PDAs are probably out,' he said, pulling his hand out of mine. 'If it's going to cause a scene. I s'pose I got a bit complacent. Shit. I wish you could come to mine. But it's your call.'

I wanted that too. I knew that if I said it, everything would change forever. I was still a bit nervous, though, so I didn't say anything.

'I mean, I'd love to tell the world about you. But we can't tell anyone until after the album. This is a terrible time to be outed as a guy with a teenage girlfriend.'

The word *girlfriend* sparkled in the air again. It sounded better this time, when he wasn't saying it in anger.

'Yeah. OK. It feels weird to be keeping you secret. I'm desperate to tell Enzo.'

'Right? Me too. Not Enzo but the world. But you have that Lewis as the perfect alibi, so let's hang on to him for now and keep things low-key in public.'

We crossed Waterloo Bridge. When we were halfway over, I tried to take Freddie's hand again and after a while he let me.

'The funny thing is,' he said as we passed a woman pushing a bicycle with a little dog in the basket, 'I don't feel you're younger than me at all. I can say things to you that I've never managed to say to anyone else. Mainly about – you know.'

'I know.' I said it gently, and he nodded and squeezed my hand.

'I've lived my life pretending Harry never existed,' he said. 'But now – well, I can see how the dynamic changed when he . . . went. My parents fell apart completely. Kind of like your mum's doing, but more dramatically. The worst thing in the world for them. Ollie stepped up to become the older brother because that's just Ollie, and I – well, I discovered speed at thirteen and never looked back.'

'Thirteen?'

'I know, doll. As soon as I found I could make everything feel better by being off my face, I was in. Drugs, booze, the lot. I can't quite believe I'm still here.'

'I'm glad you are.'

He stopped and looked at me. Time passed. A bird flew overhead.

Finally he spoke.

'Me too now. I wasn't that bothered before. But now I have you.'

23

Venice

The apartment is musty so I open all three windows. It's starting to get dark, and my legs ache. I lie on the bed and look at the ceiling.

Phoebe and I shared this bed, and now she's not here. It's a sturdy thing with a carved wooden headboard. For a second the ceiling flickers into something else. It becomes the night sky. There are stars and clouds and a strange light and I'm cold. It flashes blue, but I resist it with everything I have and force it back into a ceiling. I'm starting to control this stuff, just a tiny bit, but that doesn't count for much when everything else has gone to shit.

'I'm not completely losing it.'

I say it to convince myself. The ceiling is back in its place, white with a small crack in the paint. It's peeling a bit. It's not a crack in the actual plaster, and the ceiling isn't going to fall on top of me. There's no night sky up there. It's not even fully dark yet. I need to pull myself together.

This is real, and Phoebe is missing.

None of us can call anyone, and we don't remember how we got here.

I've never had anything like this happen to me before. Enzo has been jumping to conclusions based on what he knows about me, but the fact is this is different. I've struggled with anxiety. I've been crippled with worries that get out of control. Many times I've caught a glimpse of Morris in a crowd when I knew he couldn't actually be there (but I also felt that he could). I've stayed awake all night, crying about trivial things. I've doubted myself, questioned everything, but I've never seen the universe crack.

I've never watched a friend walk into an old tomb and vanish.

I've never found myself living through the same events twice, or skipping ahead to things that haven't happened yet.

I've never done anything like that. All of this is new.

'Are you going now?'

There's a fly up on the ceiling, walking around near the crack. I wonder whether it will speak to me.

'Yeah,' says Enzo. He's looking at his phone. 'There's a police station eight minutes' walk from here. Will you be OK?'

I'm safe here. If he was going to follow us, he would have done it by now. If the glitching girl comes, I'll ask her to take me back to this morning, and stop Phoebe even going into that stupid church in the first place.

'Yeah,' I say. 'I'll be fine. I'll lock the door.'

I think, for some reason, about Mum. As soon as she and Greg were together, our family stopped being me and her and a gap where Morris should have been, and we became a nuclear family. That term feels wrong. We became, I suppose, what looked like the ultimate traditional set-up. Two parents, a son and a daughter. And, even though we were patched together out of two different families, it worked, and Enzo and I even looked alike. Whenever we met anyone new, I'd see them jumping to that assumption. Mother, father, boy/girl twins. How lovely.

Having a brother changed me. Enzo has been the best thing that's ever happened to me.

'Before you go,' I say, 'can I say something without you laughing?'

'Can't guarantee.'

I see it in his eyes, though. He's freaking out at least as much as I am. He's been holding it all together too. I inhale deeply.

'You're the most important person I've ever met. You mean more than anyone. I've always missed my dad so much. Getting a brother is the best thing that's ever happened to me.'

Enzo doesn't laugh. He doesn't speak for ages. When he does, he says: 'Same, H. Same.'

He gathers his things together, preparing to go out. Then he turns and says: 'At least your dad didn't leave because he was bored of you. At least he wanted you. At least he loved you, you know?'

'Vittoria loves you.'

'Negative. She loves telling people she has a son. She loves me from a distance. She *likes* me, most of the time. She finds me amusing enough and I know how to be that guy. But,

Haze – she had a kid, decided motherhood was dull and that I was some leech who stopped her sleeping and wanted milk all the time, and so she handed me to my dad and fucked off to Milan, forever. When I was six months old. She gave me half a year and when I didn't measure up she bailed. So I know you feel shit and weird about your dad, and Susie's probably not told you the full story and tbh you should probably have some therapy or something, but from where I'm standing you have some positives there too.'

'Enz.' He's never said anything like this before.

'Yeah. I've never wanted to be, like, *poor little me* about it because I'm fine and, yeah, she's alive and I guess that's better really. But you know? At least you've got Susie, and she's been a bit all over the place, but that's because she's getting divorced and Greg's not been great either, but she loves you so much. She's been wildly worried about you.'

'Has she?'

'Hazel Angel. You lost most of your body weight. You practically left home. You came up with crap lies about where you were going and what you were doing, and any time anyone challenged you, you stormed off ... Have you really not noticed? She's been desperate. She tried to rope me in for an intervention, but I had to say I couldn't get through to you either, and it would just push you further away. Because it would have, right?' I nod. 'She's tried to confront you so many times. Once you just packed up a few things and said you were moving out, and that scared her so much she backed off. You're her world. And ...'

148

Enzo stops. I know he doesn't want to say the rest, but I can fill it in. He's not Vittoria's world. He's not really Greg's world either, not in the same way I'm Mum's.

'Love you,' I say.

'Love you too, H.'

I roll over on the bed and close my eyes, and everything just stops. It's the deepest sleep I've ever had.

When I wake, it's dark. I look across to Phoebe's side of the bed. Obviously she's not there. I check the sofa, but Enzo's not here either. I sit up, heart pounding. They can't both have gone. Enzo won't have walked into a tomb with a rotting heart. He just wouldn't do that, and anyway he was right here and he was going to the police.

He did go to the police.

I check the time. It's two o'clock. Two in the morning. The police station was an eight-minute walk away. He can't still be there. What if something happened to him on the way, or the way back? I reach for my phone, but it's not there.

I look out of the window. It's a clear night. Starry and moony, like the sky I saw for a few seconds when I was looking at the ceiling before. I can see the moon and one bright star next to it. Is that Mars? Venus? I can never remember.

I find my phone on the floor. Neither of them has messaged.

No one has messaged me at all.

I look more closely. Mum hasn't messaged me. My texts to her are undelivered. Lily K and his actual name have gone from my contacts. I look at the home screen: most of my apps have gone. All I have is text, Safari and photos. I look at the photos and they're all from the past two days.

It's as if this isn't really a phone.

I remember my conversation with Enzo. It's as if Venice isn't real at all.

The reason everything keeps going weird is because absolutely nothing here is what it appears to be.

I'm trying to keep the flood of bad feelings away as I find Enzo's number and try to call it. I hold my breath as it connects and I hear a faint ringing sound. Then the toilet flushes, and Enzo is there. He's frowning at the phone in his hand.

'Can't I go to the loo? You are one helluva control freak.'

'Oh my God!' I gasp. 'I thought you'd disappeared.'

He strides over to the kitchen and opens the fridge. 'Never. I'll never do that. I couldn't sleep because of, you know, Phoebe. Now you're awake, you can keep me company. Here we go!'

I yawn. Do I want to go back to sleep? Enzo's brandishing a bottle of wine. It's white, and that's fine by me. I don't think I'll ever drink red wine again. He opens a cupboard and takes out two stubby little tumblers, fills them both, passes me one.

'Did you go to the police? I think I've been in a really deep sleep.'

He nods and looks away. 'Yeah, you have. You just switched off – like one moment you were talking and the next you were out of it. I checked you were breathing, and then I went. I was relieved when you were still here, still breathing, when I got back. The police didn't care, H. They've got too much else going on. Told me to come back in twenty-four hours if we haven't heard from her.'

We look at each other.

'We need to call her family,' I say. I don't say that we can't do that because our phones don't work. Enzo doesn't either.

'Not at two in the morning,' he says instead.

I sip my drink. It's light, cold and just what I needed, even though it's the middle of the night and my mouth tastes sleepy.

'Fancy going up to the roof?' says Enzo.

24
Kent

January

And then I was all in.

I didn't see Freddie as much as I wanted over the Christmas holidays, and then, when we went back to school in January, everything changed.

I was walking to school in the first week of term, thinking about Freddie rather than my coursework, noting that I hadn't even really started on my storm painting, when I felt my phone vibrate in my pocket and I knew it was him because after much research I'd managed to set a vibration alert that signified one person only. It vibrated three times against my hip and I tuned out of a conversation that I'd barely been tuned into anyway. Enzo and Fatima were talking about their maths teacher because he'd been on a local website after rescuing someone from the sea.

I looked at my phone. The message preview said: Ready for some amazing news doll?

I opened it. There was nothing else. Freddie liked to make sure he had my attention before launching into conversations. He hated 'talking into the void', and he never did it any more. That barrage of self-criticism and apology on my birthday had never happened again.

Of course! I wrote back. Then the messages landed one after the other.

It's the album.

Obv barely exists yet but – this was actually Ollie's idea haha

We've got a title for it

Because they love my Hazy Girl song so much

Ollie was all like

'we could just call the album hazy'.

And I was like yeah, if you like

fake casual

What do you think?

Album named after you OK as a love gift doll?

I stared at the phone. Their album was named after me. And he'd said the word *love*. I let it fill me up, the warmth, the wonder, the fact that someone thought so much of me that he'd write a song and then an album with my name on it.

I was carried to school by angels. Enzo and Fatima didn't notice because we were nearly there. Later, when I passed Mr Musa in the corridor, I said, 'Well done, sir,' in passing.

He grinned and said, 'Thank you, Hazel.' Even he knew my name. For the first time I felt like someone. A person in the world. Someone people saw.

Going back to where we began here, I messaged from the train that weekend, but can we maybe go to yours today? It was a wintry day, and I knew our dates had become expensive and cold, could see that Freddie was getting bored of them. Being out in public all the time was impractical.

Also, everything was different now. I loved him. I wanted him to be my first, more than I'd ever wanted anything.

> OMG yes!!! Beware, it
> might not be the tidiest
> but YES PLEASE. I
> promise to be
> gentlemanly. Ollie and
> Lina might be about but
> don't mind them.

Do they know about us?

> Are you kidding? They play
> a song about you every
> day. Their next album has
> your name. They busted
> me instantly. They're
> always asking about the
> mysterious Hazel.

I wanted to ask: how come you're allowed to tell them, but I'm not allowed to tell *my* brother and best friend? Do they know I've got GCSEs this year? Are they assuming the Hazel in the song is some sophisticated twentysomething and will they be horrified when they meet me? Do I need to lie about my age? But I didn't ask: I supposed I'd find it all out soon enough.

I was scared of meeting them. Lina was still the cool woman who made jeans and a sweatshirt look amazing. Ollie was the one who scowled on stage, and the one, I now knew, who had shut off his feelings about his older brother and got on with being responsible, who disapproved of everything Freddie did and who I knew was therefore going to disapprove of me.

I let Apple Maps take me there from the station and was surprised when I found myself walking away from the warehouse apartments and classic mansion flats and mews houses with olive trees in pots. I was heading towards a place that was not at all what I'd expected. I had to stand outside and double-check the address, because of all the things I'd pictured Freddie's flat to be, this wasn't it.

It was a basement with a green stain down the front wall, and I had to hang on to the rail as I went down so I didn't slip on the frozen moss on the steps. At the bottom, I stood for a moment. I checked my reflection in the window, but then realized I wasn't looking at myself, but at Freddie's brother, who was peering out at me. He raised a hand. I wasn't sure whether he was mirroring what I'd been doing to my hair or waving.

Shit.

He opened the door and gave me a smile. It didn't feel particularly friendly.

I knew so much about him. I'd seen him onstage. And now here he was.

'The famous Hazel,' he said. He was taller than I'd remembered. Taller than Freddie. He stood back and ushered me in. 'Oh, I've seen you before. At the stage door. For fuck's sake, Hazel – how old are you?' His voice was deeper than Freddie's, and everything about him was more serious.

Freddie had definitely got the looks. Ollie was skinny and intense, with high cheekbones and something strange in his eyes. I was so worried about the fact that I wasn't allowed to mention their dead brother Harry that I was afraid I might be about to blurt his name out.

'Sixteen,' I said. Freddie hadn't told me to lie, so I didn't.

'You go to school, right?' I nodded. 'Are you really sixteen? Promise me Freddie hasn't got himself another underage girlfriend? I mean, clearly he has, but legally? Did he tell you to pretend to be sixteen because I would definitely ask?'

'I'm really sixteen.' The word *another* stayed in my head longer than I wanted it to. 'Do I have to show ID?'

'I mean, I can't check your driving licence because you're too young to have one.' He gave a big fake smile.

I didn't have anything to say to that. I was wearing flared jeans with a vintage woollen coat and my big red scarf. Clumpy boots. I'd thought I'd dressed older than sixteen.

Ollie looked at me for a while and I wondered whether I was meant to say something more, or if maybe I'd missed a cue to start enthusing about the band. He shouted, 'Fred!' over his shoulder. Then he turned back to me and leaned in. I could smell chewing gum. I leaned away.

'Hazel,' he said. 'For what it's worth, this is me – and Lina too – warning you off. I would love it if you turned round right now and went home. Please think about it. And if you don't, just bear this in mind: he's not going to do you any good. I can't believe he's tricked me into singing about a teenager. I should have fucking known.'

He turned and walked away, disappearing through a door in the dark hallway. I was pretty sure I wasn't meant to follow so I stayed where I was. After a minute or so, I took one step forward and closed the front door because I didn't want to let that freezing air in. Then I just stood there and waited.

The hallway smelled of damp and incense. The floorboards were sticky underfoot. Every inch of wall space was covered with paper, either posters for gigs or drawings in felt tip or song lyrics. I looked at a picture of an alien ship landing, done in green pen. Three aliens were walking off it, and the front one had a speech bubble that said, 'Greetings Earthlings! We come to see the band Kennedy.' It was quite good. I wanted to make an artwork of my own to stick on that wall.

Then there was an arm round my shoulders.

I leaned into Freddie and he kissed the top of my head. I allowed myself to relax a bit.

'Hey, gorgeous,' he said. 'Thanks for coming. Was Ollie OK?'

'Um . . . kinda.' *Another underage girlfriend.* The words echoed round my head. We'd never talked about exes. I knew I needed to ask Freddie.

He took my hand and led me into the flat. We passed through a living room in which Lina was doing a downward-facing dog. She said, 'Oh, hey,' from upside down, while Adriene on the TV screen said, 'Just stay here a minute and pedal it out.' I made an effort not to look at Lina's bum.

And then we were in Freddie's room.

Everything about it was half squalid and just-about-romantic, though I had to make quite an effort to get to that point. It made my room at home look like a little kid's bedroom. This was quite small and low-ceilinged. His bed was a mattress on the floor, and his table was piled high with books with titles like *Stoner* and *Nemesis*. There were black-and-white photos on the wall of what I thought was Kate Moss in the nineties. A guitar was leaning against the wall and music and notebooks and pens and clothes and candles and Freddie Freddie Freddieness.

I remembered that he'd told me he had a photo of his brother, Harry. I wondered whether it was in this room. I looked around in case it was on the wall.

I turned to smile at him, and forgot about everything else when he gave me a look that was somehow entirely and only about sex, and I stepped towards him and into his arms.

I pushed Ollie's warning out of my head. Ollie was damaged: I knew that. Ollie didn't know I knew, and he could only see me as a child, but I understood that he didn't want Freddie to be happy. I put his words from my mind.

It was time. I was ready. I wasn't underage, I was in love.

25
Venice

I find a pen and write a note on the back of a leaflet for the Galleria dell'Accademia.

Pheebs. We're on the roof. Come and find us xxx

I leave it right outside the apartment door, just in case. We both take our phones. We both message her again. Both messages are undelivered.

Enzo is right: the roof of this building is a magical place. It's flat, with reclining wooden sunloungers and a little table. Enzo goes to a plastic chest and takes out cushions and blankets. Soon we are sitting together on squashy cushions, glasses in our hands, looking across the Grand Canal and up at the stars while a breeze blows round us. It's the middle of the night, and the most magical thing.

'Phoebe?' I say it quietly. It suddenly feels as if she could be here. I whip round in case she's behind me.

The sky is so close I feel I could reach up and touch it. The stars are actually twinkling, like in the song. The air is warm on my face, and even from up here I can smell the

Venetian smell, the sun-warmed canal water. I try to convince myself that she'll be back. That at some point I'll go back in time, and when that happens I'll make sure she's OK. That's the only option I have. I know it's sketchy.

'Do you believe in the multiverse?' I don't look at him as I say it. I can't take my eyes off those stars.

'What?'

'You know. That there's a new universe for every single thing that could possibly happen. So everything's infinite and we just happen to be living in this one, but there's other versions of us living in other universes? Ones that are less ... freaky.'

Even without looking at him, I sense his affectionate frustration.

'I mean, maybe? I don't really care. Yeah, it's a nice thought, but we're never going to know, are we? Think that multiverses are real if you like. I'll tell you what's better, though. Don't you reckon it would be awesome to fly?'

That makes me turn my head and look at him. He is sitting up straight and his eyes are on the low wall that runs round the terrace.

We're five floors up. I know Enzo.

'No.' I say it as firmly as I can. 'No, I don't think it would be cool to fly. Not even in planes, actually, on principle, because of the fossil fuels. Even though I know we apparently did that to get here.'

'That's classic capitalism, though.' He is as easily distracted as I'd hoped. 'Shove all the guilt on to the consumer at the very last point in the chain, when it's a structural thing.' He pauses. 'But *anyway*. I'm talking about flying *without* fossil fuel. Without anything. Just jumping off and letting the air carry you. Second star to the right and straight on till morning. That kind of flying.'

He springs to his feet. Even though I'm happy here – even though I would love to spend the rest of the night right here, dozing under this blanket, beneath these stars – I follow him. Enzo is far too grounded and sensible, under that facade, to think he could fly after a glass of wine, but still. He's acting weirdly and it came on suddenly. It does feel strange up here. Kind of like the normal rules don't apply.

By the time I reach the edge of the flat roof, he's stepped up on to the wall. He sticks his arms out like a tightrope walker and takes a few steps.

I look over. It's a straight drop down, with nothing but a couple of geraniums on a lower window sill between him and the distant paving stones. My head spins. My stomach flips.

'Enzo!'

'Don't freak out. It's fine. If I was walking along a line this wide on the ground, you wouldn't think I'd step off it. So I won't here. If I can make it all the way round, you have to give me something, right?'

'No! Give you what?'

He takes a few more steps. I hold my breath.

'That bird,' he says. 'That tacky bird you've been holding all the time.'

'My bird?'

I'm still dressed. Cello is in my pocket. I touch her with my fingertips. I can't let her go. I feel that she's a part of me now. I cover the sides of her head with my finger and thumb, stopping her hearing this conversation.

'Yeah. I want it.'

'No.'

He stops and looks at me. 'Please?' He takes one foot off the wall and shakes it around, over the edge.

'I'll buy you one from the same guy, but you're not having mine.'

He puts his foot back down. I see from his grin that he's tricked me, and then I realize how. He's made me promise him a reward for doing something I don't want him to do. He's had wine and he's planning to walk round the top of a building, five floors up, in the middle of the night.

The roof is kind of rectangular, and the longest two sides are fine because they just adjoin the neighbouring roof terraces. The one he's standing on has the Riva degli Schiavoni and the Grand Canal five floors below. I'm not sure what's on the fourth side. It might be better. It can't be worse.

He sets off again and I don't speak because I can't startle him. If I try to grab him to bring him back, he might pull away and fall the wrong way. He looks at his feet, focusing, and I don't breathe until he makes it to the corner. While he's walking along the long side, the one with no serious drop, I say, 'Enzo, this is the stupidest thing you've ever done, and that's a crowded field. If you stumble, you die.'

'Not right now.' He does a comedy stumble for effect, and rights himself without dropping down.

'No. But please just walk up and down this bit. Please! Do it four times and that's more than the same distance.'

'Chill, Haze!'

The next side of the rectangle is just as dangerous as the first. It drops straight down between this building and the next on to a pathway. If he fell here, he *might* have a chance of grabbing something as he went.

Enzo doesn't do things like this. He's silly, all the time, but he doesn't do things to scare me. He doesn't do stupid things. He doesn't do anything dangerous, unless he has a very good reason, which he doesn't. In fact, under his confident facade he's the most sensible person I know.

I turn my back. I don't want to see it. The silence goes on, and I think he might have fallen without shouting so I turn back and see him reaching the second safe side.

He's almost done. It's going to be all right. He starts humming as he walks along the wall that separates our roof from that of the hotel next door. The tune begins to make sense, and I turn away again.

'Stop!' I say, my voice louder than I planned. 'Stop, Enzo. Why are you singing that?' I put my fingers in my ears. I can't bear to hear it.

He pauses. 'Oh God! Sorry. It's just "Hazy Girl" was everywhere, wasn't it? I forgot what it was. Sorry, H. I swear I'll erase it from my mind forever.'

And then he gets back to the dangerous side, and he walks to the point where he started, and, as I'm walking over to hug him and promise to buy him a glass bird of his own, he turns the other way and steps right off the roof.

26

I wake up cold, stiff, confused. I'm on the roof, lying on a wooden lounger, covered in a fleecy blanket. I'm still dressed. The air is fresh, the sky pale with a few clouds.

I gasp as I remember my dream. Enzo walking round the roof, stepping off.

Did he walk round the roof? Do I have to buy him a Cello of his own?

I look over to his lounger. He's not there.

I'm bolt upright. A half-empty wine bottle. Two little tumblers from the studio. There's a cushion and a blanket on his lounger and a tiny bit of wine in his glass. More in mine.

I was scared he had gone, last night, but he was just in the loo. It'll be something like that again: I'm just jumpy. I stand up and bundle the blankets and cushions back into the storage trunk, even though they're a bit damp and they'll probably go mouldy shut away in there.

I stand near the edge of the roof. The stars have faded away. I look down. There is no broken body on the pavement. Of course. It's time for me to work out what's going on here.

I pour the wine from the glasses into the gutter, and take them and the bottle back down to the apartment because Enzo must have gone there, and maybe Phoebe's here too. The door's unlocked, and the note I left has gone, and those things surely mean Enzo's already inside and perhaps Phoebe is too, and I'm so relieved that I want to cry, but I don't. I can still see him, humming that song, grinning, stepping off the wall. It was too real.

I push the door. It creaks a bit.

'Enz?'

The studio is empty. I phone him. Nothing happens. His phone doesn't ring. It doesn't make any sound at all, in my ear or in the apartment. There's just dead air. I call his name. I check every corner of the room. He's not in the bathroom. I look in the cupboards. I check behind the curtains. I know I'm not going to find my brother like this, but I have to do something.

I sit on the bed and close my eyes.

When I open them, this whole place might have faded away. I might be back to normal life. To something real. I will that to happen with all my strength. I focus on it with everything I have.

My bedroom at home.

Phoebe.

Enzo.

Normality.

I breathe deeply for a long time. The sounds around me change. The smell changes. Have I done it?

I open my eyes suddenly, expecting to find myself home in Kent.

It's not Kent, though.

It's Venice, but it feels different. It feels real.

Being on my own is a horrible thing for me: that's probably why I've conjured Morris to be with me at quiet moments, so I never feel I'm completely alone. I shut him out for over a year and now I need him again.

'Morris?' I say quietly. 'Dad?'

He's not there. The sounds outside are different now. I can hear the boats, the sounds of people talking on the street. It's all real.

I'm here.

I lean out of the window. It's not a painting: it's reality. I can't see the brushstrokes. It's a real place.

I open the cupboards. My stuff is all there – my clothes, my trainers, my flip-flops – but none of theirs. I run into the bathroom. One toothbrush. One tube of toothpaste. My make-up bag. My toiletries. No one else's.

None of this makes sense. *None of it.* I watched Phoebe walking into a tomb and Enzo stepping off a roof, but no one else saw either of those things. I live in the real world and things like that don't happen. If I stepped off a roof, I would die. If I'd followed Enzo, I'd have fallen five storeys and splatted on to the path. Or into the canal. If you land on water from a height, it's like hitting concrete. I'm sure I've read that. My mind is spiralling. I try to picture what it would have been like, and for a second I'm living it, heading towards the water at great speed, smashing into it like a wall.

Then I'm back, panting, gasping. My heart rate is so high that it feels like one continuous beat, that there's no pause between them, and although I know this must be bad for me it doesn't matter. I lean out of the window, as far as I can, much further than I should. I have to see the path below. I have to see if there's a bloodstain, a police officer, any sign that something bad has happened.

There's still no body. No cordoned-off area. No sign of blood. No police boat. Nothing.

Enzo can't have walked off the roof.

I saw him doing it, *but then I woke up*. I hold on to those facts.

The world this morning is different. If it was animated, it would be done in a different style.

If it was animated . . .

Am I an *avatar*? I think of Freddie, of the amount of time I spent trying to pretend I wanted to learn gaming, and then pretending it was fun to watch. Why did I do that? Why was it so important to try to be the girlfriend I thought he wanted?

If Freddie had found a way to trap me in his game, he would have done it.

Freddie.

This is the first time, since I got away, that I've said his name in my head.

Freddie. I look at it. I shrink away. I look at it again. I have a shower and try to find something to wear that isn't black. Most of my clothes are black now: I got rid of most of my coloured things because, as well as yellow, Freddie said blue didn't suit me either, and neither did pink or white.

'You should wear black, doll,' he said. 'Red too. Not every day, though.'

So that was what I did.

I find that green satin dress again and put it on, adding my barbed-wire necklace for protection. I remember that Enzo hated me wearing all black. He said I looked like a Victorian consumptive in mourning, or a ninja.

Where are my friends?

If they're not here, are they at home?

If they're not with me, what am I doing here?

I sit down on the floor and feel the weight of reality crushing me.

Half an hour later I stand up again. I think I've worked this out. I think I've made sense of it.

If Enzo and Phoebe weren't here at all, then it would explain why they both vanished in bizarre and impossible ways.

If I ran away on my own, without them (because I hadn't actually spoken to either of them properly for a long time), I would have come to Venice. I would have come here because I'd never mentioned it to Freddie, and because I knew that Vittoria would let me use her studio.

I scramble for my phone. Last time I looked, there was nothing on it from before two days ago, but now I find a WhatsApp chat with Vittoria.

Vittoria. Sorry to msg out of the blue but I'm desperate for somewhere to stay. Is your place in Venice free?

She had replied three minutes later.

Hazel! Darling girl. Enzo has been so worried. Of course, of course. You need to go to the hotel next door, the Gabrielli, and they'll give you the key. I'll let them know. When are you arriving? You must stay as long as you like.

I read down the conversation. I said I'd arrive that same evening, and it was – yes, three days ago.

Have I been here on my own for three days, hallucinating my friends? My imagination dispatching them (brutally) when I was strong enough to be on my own?

'It seems so,' I say to Cello. She doesn't reply because she's made of glass.

I'm shaky as I leave the apartment, trying to make sense of the tricks my brain has been playing on me. Then I decide not to, and push it all away. I know now that I'm here. I'm on my own. I have got away and I need to pull myself together.

I walk through a group of people to the edge of the water and sit there, my legs hanging down, and try not to think about how much I've been freaking out over the past few days. I hope I haven't done anything that anyone else would have noticed. I think it's all been internal, but I hope I haven't been going round having one-sided conversations with imaginary friends. I definitely might have tried to run into Canova's tomb after not-Phoebe. I'd better keep away from that church forever.

I turn and look up at the roof terrace.

It's so high. I can see the wall that I thought Enzo walked round. I can see the last place he stood before he stepped off. I was so scared, but I was scared because I realized I was on my own, rather than because my brother had actually flown into a starry sky and left me.

There are boats moored on either side of me, and a wooden jetty to my right. I take a deep breath, and another, and another. This is going to be OK. I came to Venice when I was utterly desperate, and on the brink of a breakdown, because I knew it would be my haven. I realize that my phone is working properly now, and, since Phoebe and Enzo weren't actually here, I can actually contact them and say all the things I need to tell them.

I guess Greg doesn't have a girlfriend called Bella and a potential stepson called Milo. I feel the tension leaving me as I let that go.

Mum! I can call Mum!

I grab my phone and press her name. I hear the ringing tone. It rings and rings and then goes to a robotic voicemail. I leave her a message, my words falling over themselves, talking faster and faster and faster.

'Mum! Mum, it's Hazel. I'm fine. I'm in Venice. I'm sorry, I think I came here in a bit of a state. A breakdown? Fugue state? I don't know what it's called, but I was having all kinds of hallucinations, and anyway now I'm feeling better. I'm OK. I'm staying in Enzo's mum's place. It's right on the Grand Canal. I guess I'll stay a few more days and then come home, but if you want to come out here then do! Please do! I can't wait to see you. I hope you're OK. I'm sorry I've been so crap, but I've got away. I did it, Mum. I love you.'

I hang up, then stare at the phone. I hope that made some kind of sense. Then I turn to the group chat that's called 'Coursework Chat' and write:

Guys! I'm sorry. How are you? You prob know I'm in Venice because Enz I guess V told you. I've been such a mess. I can't even begin to tell you. Honestly – you wouldn't believe it if I tried. Anyway I'm here. I got away and F is gone. When I get back I want to make it up to you, ok? So so sorry, H xxxxxx

The glass bird is in my pocket, and so I take her out and look at her.

'Hey, *Uccello*,' I say, and I give her a little smile. I guess I did pay a disconcerting man five euros for her.

I miss Phoebe and Enzo being here. I feel torn apart by the fact that I've spent the past few days bonding with them, apologizing to them, and allowing them to coax me, first of all out of the studio, and then to eat again, and then into a gondola, St Mark's Square, the church where Titian is buried, if that was even a real place. All that happened, but it wasn't real. I'm still not actually friends with them.

I look at the group chat. My message is grey ticked and they don't respond. I guess it's going to take longer in real life to get them to trust me again.

While I'm sitting here, with the sun on my face and the water lapping below my sandals, I decide to look at my old photos, to remind myself of the girl I could be again. If I go back to when I was fifteen, I can avoid Freddie, and I can look at my mum, the one person I know for sure loves me more than anyone else in the world. I hope she calls back soon.

I jump back two years and spend ages swiping through, surprised at how very different, how much younger I was. I look at me with Enzo, and see that he's different in real life from the version of him I summoned to keep me company here. The real Enzo is a bit less annoying, and he's taller and just . . . not the same. I manifested some kind of essence of him, and when I look at his nearly-two-years-ago reality I long for him. The real him. I see Phoebe, and realize how often her style has changed. She seems effortlessly cool.

When I'm more grounded, I'll try to call them. I can't do it now because I need to say the right things. *Sorry I said awful things to you when I had a boyfriend. Now we've broken up, will you be my friends again?* It's a hard sell. I gaze across the water and remember myself with imaginary Phoebe and Enzo, getting past the bit where I said sorry.

I scroll through my pictures and lose myself in a time when I was happy. Then I move on to the album that I hardly ever look at, the one buried deep in folders within folders: my photographs of the old pictures of my dad. Mum keeps the album at the bottom of her filing cabinet, hidden under a forest of upright files that all brush against it. She hid it from Greg, though surely Greg wouldn't have objected to her keeping pictures of her first husband. There are more of them in this album than the few I keep under my bed. Their whole life, and my first three years, is documented right here.

I don't often look at it. It can be too much when I try. I prefer the pictures in the box because there are only five of them. But I don't have that box. I have these ones, my origin story from the time I've almost forgotten.

There he is. Morris Angelopoulos holding his baby daughter. Me. He's holding me, cradling me, looking into my eyes. I'm looking back at him. We are happy. We both have masses of black hair. I look like a troll doll.

There's a picture of him pushing me in a buggy. I'm a bit bigger now, still trolly with hair sticking up all round my face, not long enough to be tamed by gravity. I have rosy cheeks and I'm grinning at the camera because Mum must have been behind it. I'm smiling at my mother. I don't think I've done that for a while.

My dad is giving her the exact same smile.

We look the same. I miss him with all my heart. I wait for him to speak into my ear, but he doesn't.

I scroll to the next picture. Now we're in the living room of a house I don't remember, because after he died Mum and I had to downscale due to his life insurance (lack of). I'm sitting on his knee in an armchair. He's wearing a dark blue T-shirt with writing that I can't make out because of a crease, and he's reading me a book: *Where the Wild Things Are*. He's pointing at something and I'm leaning in, serious-faced, studying it. Behind us there's a bookcase and a shelf of stuff. Pictures, an empty vase, a letter propped up. A few ornaments.

A glass bird.

I stop breathing. I zoom in further, further, further.

It's a small glass bird with green and yellow touches. It has a friendly face that makes it look as if it always knows what you're thinking. It is, in fact, the bird that's in my pocket right now. I take her out. I compare them.

This is Cello. Cello is in a photo of my dad from fifteen years ago.

And then I remember another thing. I remember a 'little glass ornament' going missing from the house. Mum mentioning it once, then never again.

I close the phone, stand up and start walking, breathing rapidly. I see myself reflected in the window of the Gabrielli Hotel and stop for a second. I should have some breakfast. The girl looking back at me is not in the least bit healthy. I run my fingers through my hair, tie it up with an elastic from my wrist and take a deep breath. Cello is in an old photo. Cello might have been in the house, with my mum's things. That is impossible. How have I run away here and bought something that used to belong to my dad? What is my brain doing now?

I tell myself that it's good. It shouldn't be weird or unsettling. It makes perfect sense. Maybe my parents visited

Venice before I was born and bought it here. Or even after. Actually the fact that I have her too makes me feel warm and golden inside. I'm here on my own and somehow my dad sent a glass bird to comfort me. A bird that was maybe lost, but that has found me again. I've snapped out of imaginary versions of people who, in real life, won't speak to me. I knew the bird was special and it is: it's a link to my actual dad.

I walk until I find the guy who sold it to me. He looks up and smiles.

'Hello again.' His voice is deeper than I remember it. I crouch down to look at the things he has spread on his rug. He has some birds there, but they don't have green and yellow on them. One has red and blue. One has silver. I take Cello out of my pocket and open my hand.

'You know you sold me this?' I hold her out to him and he nods.

'You're not happy?'

I close my hand round her. 'No, I'm very happy. I don't want to give her back.'

I know this man. I look at his T-shirt. I think of Morris in the old photographs. Was he wearing this top? No, he can't have been.

He kind of was, though.

'Do you have lots like this?'

He indicates the rest with a sweep of his arm. Then he reaches behind him and finds a green and yellow bird in his bag. He shows it to me. I'm not sure what to say, so I thank him and stand up. I almost buy a second one, but I'm not sure why I'd want two, so I don't.

'Where do you get the birds from?' I ask before I leave.

I'm not sure what he says because there's a sudden blast of a foghorn from a boat, but it sounds like 'from your photograph'. I'm so confused that I walk, and then run, away.

27

Kent

January

I was a different person after my first visit to Freddie's place. I'd had sex, and although it hadn't exactly been the way I'd imagined it, it had been OK (his extravagant promises about how he would make me feel were overstated, though I didn't tell him that). A fundamental thing had changed and I was amazed that I was able to hide it from everyone.

Actually I wasn't: Enzo saw it at once. He found me, the next morning, looked into my eyes and gave a little nod.

'Someone's been having fun,' he said. He gave me a little hug and said, 'You OK? I wish you'd let me meet this famous Lewis.'

'I will,' I said.

I'd promised Freddie I wouldn't tell anyone until after the album, which was going to be released at the end of June. But now that I'd met Lina and Ollie I felt it was really unfair that I wasn't allowed to tell Enzo and Phoebe. It nagged at me constantly: I was desperate to tell them everything, to share it all. In spite of Phoebe's reaction when I'd started to tell her, before our horrible first date, they would be nicer about it than Ollie. That was for sure.

Freddie had continued to call me his girlfriend, in our messages, and told me that he was going to stop dating other people (it hadn't occurred to me that he was, and when he saw my reaction he'd reassured me again and again that it was only hypothetical). I didn't want this to be a secret relationship. It didn't need to be anyway. Sixteen was old enough.

At lunchtime, I locked myself in the loos at school and messaged him.

> I promise you Enzo and Phoebe will understand. Please can I tell them? No one else. I hate keeping you secret when I want to tell the world! 🖤

He replied when I was halfway through chemistry. I read it under the table.

> Stop asking me doll. You know I can't have it getting out right now, so no. Can you come up Friday and stay over?? xxxx

I put the phone away before Miss Woodruff caught me, and spent the rest of the lesson daydreaming about Friday night. I could hold off for a few more weeks.

On Thursday, though, I was busted. I went home after school to catch up with all the work I hadn't been doing at the weekends, and I was halfway through an essay about *Pride and Prejudice* when my phone started to light up with messages.

The first was from Phoebe, and it said:

> H – what's going on?
> Who are you really
> seeing? Hope you're
> ok xxx

And Enzo's followed:

> Hazel Angel. We need to talk
> young lady.

I saw him typing and stopping, typing and stopping. Then his messages started pouring in, one after the other in a style that was unnervingly similar to Freddie's.

> So. Wtf H?

> Riddle me this.

Feebz and I just met the guy
you'd told us was your boyf in
town. Lewis? The guy who
sends birthday roses and takes
you to the movies and the art
galleries or whatever? Ring
bells? The guy who you've
been getting dewy-eyed and
down and dirty with?

He barely remembers you. He
was with his girlfriend when
we met him.

True things: he IS called
Lewis. He WAS at the
Kennedy gig, he DID buy you
a bottle of water.

Also true thing: you never even
swapped numbers. You have
never seen each other again.

Who the fuck are you going
off to meet?

Tell me. My mind is going
mad trying to work it out.

Is there a mystery man/
woman? You are BUSTED
so you have to tell us
everything.

I looked at it for a long time. I felt it in my stomach. My blood was going faster round my veins. I pictured the little blood cells racing each other to get to my heart first and make it beat more strongly. I pushed the essay away.

Finally, I could stop lying. The universe had sorted it for me.

I couldn't wait to write his name. I wrote the letters carefully, admired the way they looked.

I wrote:

Freddie

and then I wrote:

Kennedy

I looked at the words. I imagined being Hazel Kennedy. Hazel Kennedy sounded like someone who had a job, who got things done. She was a grown-up.

She wasn't me. I would never change my name anyway.

I looked at the words on the screen and I puffed out all my breath and deleted them.

OK. Tell you when I see you.

Enzo crashed into my room twelve minutes later with Phoebe just behind. I got up from the desk and time stood still.

Phoebe sat on the bed, back straight, looking at me. Her hair was shorter, in a pixie cut. I was going to mention it, then thought she might have done it a while ago and I just hadn't noticed.

I wasn't sure what to do, so sat back down and swivelled my chair round to face them. Enzo flung himself on to the bed next to Phoebe and scooted backwards to lean against the wall. The silence stretched on and on. Phoebe opened her mouth to say something and Enzo silenced her with a hand on her shoulder.

I couldn't bear it. I knew what they were doing and it was working. Seconds ticked by. They waited.

When I spoke, my voice was louder than I'd meant it to be.

'Freddie Kennedy,' I said.

I answered their main questions: twenty-six; because I knew you'd worry; yes, we have; last weekend. That, of course, led to more questions, and more and more and more, and in the end I cried and agreed to tell them the whole story in order, starting from the moment he slipped me his phone number.

'When we were all there?' said Phoebe. 'He gave you his number? In front of all your friends and both his bandmates? He put it into your hand and you didn't tell us?'

'Pervy twat,' said Enzo. 'Him not you.'

In spite of myself, I laughed through my tears. I'd missed telling them everything.

'I went to meet him the next weekend.' Phoebe passed me a tissue. 'Remember, Enz? You saw me leaving and accused me of seeing that guy Lewis, who I'd mainly forgotten about, so I just went with that. Pheebs, I started to tell you, but then you didn't like it so I changed the story. Sorry for lying. We went for pizza and wine in West Hampstead and then he asked if I wanted to go back to his place and I said yes.'

'Hazel!' Phoebe knew how far beyond my experience this would have taken me. She knew it was the last thing I'd have actually wanted or needed.

'I know. I didn't go. I said yes but I changed my mind and came home. He got annoyed. He was mad at me in fact. And I was angry too, but not to his face. With myself more than anything. I just felt like I'd been totally dumb and that I'd never see him again. And that he'd asked me to London for one reason, and I'd probably known that, but I went anyway because I was excited.'

'You were fifteen.' Phoebe's expression was deadly serious.

'And then?' said Enzo.

'He messaged. He was sorry. He'd been feeling guilty and he wrote a song for me. He sent flowers. The birthday roses. The birthday-boxing-day roses too.'

Enzo pointed at me. 'The card said they were from Lewis!'

I nodded. 'Alibi.'

Phoebe stood up. She walked over to me, pushed my school books aside and sat on the desk.

'Hazel. Face it: you didn't tell me and Enz because you knew we wouldn't like it. We both know that – you started telling me and then you realized it wasn't going to work. And you'd be right – I think he's a dick. I can't believe he invited a fifteen-year-old to meet him for sex. Well done for extricating yourself. But then you did it. You went back and you did it. Put aside all the rest of it: are you OK?'

I forced myself to meet her eyes and nodded. Was I OK? Yes, I was. I wanted to tell them about the things that connected us, but I couldn't break that confidence. And almost all the time I was more than OK.

We hadn't had this dynamic before. When I'd been out with boys, they'd always liked me more than I liked them. When I went out with girls . . . well, I'd never actually got that far. So I'd never been uncomfortable, never been out of my comfort zone.

I'd never fallen in love before. I'd been the one there for Phoebe when she was having dramas in her relationship with Alex. I'd been the straightforward one who never allowed any boy or girl to get close to me emotionally. I'd never come anywhere near caring before.

Now I did.

'I'm more than OK.' I was choosing my words carefully, trying to make them see that he wasn't sleazy.

'He's not like you think, Pheebs. Honestly, he's not. The thing you just said about me being fifteen – well, it was a wake-up call to him. He realized he didn't want to be that guy. He realized he cared about me. And since then it's been different.' I could feel my face changing. 'It's been

amazing! Oh my God, it really has. He's written a song . . .'
I paused. The album title and everything else was
confidential. 'I've been going on amazing dates. I'm really
happy and I'm glad you guys found out. I hated keeping it
secret.'

'Yeah, why did you?' said Enzo.

I felt tears in the back of my eyes. 'Because he asked me
to. Because of your reactions. It's not a great look for him
right now, when they've got an album coming out.'

'Seriously?' Enzo stood up and started pacing. 'I really
don't think anyone outside this house would give much of
a shit, babe. I can't imagine him being stalked by paps. But
whatever. I'm glad we know. Is he your *boyfriend*? Because,
honestly, I think maybe a short-term fling, but he's not
much of a long-term prospect, and if he . . . Well. Let's just
say if he messes you around he's going to have me to
answer to.' Enzo put his fists up and we all forced smiles.

I realized, in that moment, that actually Freddie wasn't
always the boyfriend Enzo and Phoebe would want for me.
He shut me down if I was annoying him. He told me what
to wear and what not to wear. There were things about this
relationship that I couldn't share with my friends. It was a
red flag, but I decided to ignore it. He was older. He was
lovely almost all the time.

'Can we meet him?' said Phoebe. 'I mean, you get to
meet your friend's boyfriend, right? That's a thing.'

I knew then that I shouldn't let this happen. I knew it
was a bad idea. Freddie would not appreciate the fact that
I'd told them everything, knowing he didn't want me to.

'Maybe.'

He hadn't wanted me to tell, but I hadn't told. They'd found me out. He would understand.

Enzo gave a tiny nod, and Phoebe said, 'Good. I'd like to make my own mind up.'

'Same,' said Enzo.

28

Venice

I stop in St Mark's Square. What should I do? I try to call Mum again, but it goes to voicemail and I leave her another stream-of-consciousness message. At its heart, it says I'm sorry and that I hope she's OK, but I keep saying the wrong words and accidentally telling her about Phoebe running into a tomb and Enzo stepping off the roof.

'Anyway,' I say, pulling myself together, 'I'm here, and I'm OK now, I promise. I'm going to come home. I can't wait to see you.'

Home! That's what I need to do. I need to go home. I look up flights on my phone. There's one tomorrow. I know I must have a return plane ticket, but I can't find it in my emails, or in my Apple wallet, or anywhere else. This new flight on a budget airline I haven't even heard of, for tomorrow, is just over a hundred pounds and so I decide to book it, but when I go to pay it turns out I don't have the funds.

Shit. I call Mum again. She doesn't answer again, and I hope she's OK. I start to get a bad feeling about her. While I've been here, lost and confused and hallucinating and broken, what has been happening to Mum? My poor mother, widowed, divorced, with her daughter putting her through hell. I hope she's with Enzo. I hope he's looking after her.

I buy a takeaway coffee and a croissant from a tiny cafe, relieved that I have enough cash, and walk randomly in the sun until I find myself beside a wooden bridge over the Grand Canal. I cross it, passing between tourists taking photos and selfies, and because everyone else is doing it I join in. I stand on the bridge, extend my arm and take a photo of myself against the sparkling backdrop of Venice, a coffee in my other hand. I look at the picture and see that I still look shit, but there's something new in my eyes. Something that wasn't there before, a thing that Freddie extinguished.

On the other side of the bridge I find the Accademia Gallery, and I remember that it was one of the places my fake-Phoebe wanted to visit, and so I bin my coffee cup and check how much it is. Free, thankfully, if you're under eighteen. They ask for ID, which makes me wonder where my passport is, but they're happy with the college card I find in my purse.

I set off, following the direction of the arrows.

The first doorway has a sign above it saying SOTTO SOTTO. I have no idea what that means, but I walk through it.

It's air-conditioned, and it smells like the National Gallery in London. Phoebe and I used to go there so she could show me the things she was studying for history of art. That's where I saw that Titian painting. That was real Phoebe. The memories make me cry, and I wipe under my eyes with a finger and try to hold it together. I pushed my friends away so much. I was the worst person, the worst friend ever. I walk past golden icon paintings without really seeing them, and I try to make sense of the last year of my life, though my memories are holey and as blurry as the world is currently as I look through tears that I seem unable to stop.

I totally hallucinated my friends being here because they won't speak to me in real life. That's pathetic. My brand-new bird is in an old photograph. I bought it because subliminally I knew my dad had had one the same. That's why I loved it the moment I saw it. Even though it doesn't make sense, it does. I keep her in my hand, inside my pocket, all the time. She gives me the only comfort I have.

Apart from the fact that I got away. I escaped, and ultimately that will be good, even if I can't remember doing it.

After a while, I realize I'm seeing the same people everywhere, which I guess makes sense as we're all wandering in the same direction, looking at the same things. There's a woman in a yellow dress. I recoil instinctively, then wonder whether actually a dress like that might look good on me, whether I could, in fact, now choose to wear yellow.

The thought is shocking. Horrifying. Could I? Of course I could. How could I not?

He only said it didn't suit me to put me down. I like yellow. I loved that yellow cardigan. It was mustardy and heavy, and I wish I hadn't given it away.

I take some numbered breaths and force myself to be calm. Yes, I can wear yellow. Yes, I will.

The woman in the yellow dress walks past again. Her dress is midi length and has huge gathered sleeves. I'd definitely like one like that.

I look at the paintings, which are mainly madonnas and babies. The sameness of it, the oldness, comforts me. I count my breaths and try not to cry, and just stare at the pictures, one after the other. I do my best to focus on bringing Phoebe back, even though she was never actually here.

The woman in the yellow dress walks past again, going the same way as before.

I realize that the background music is a Beethoven quartet, one of Mum's favourites.

The late quartets. Why hasn't Mum answered the phone or even tried to contact me? I realize that I can only hear the Beethoven background music and the squeaking of trainers on the wooden floor. Nobody is speaking. It's just music and footsteps.

And then a sound pulls me out of my head.

She's sitting in the corner, and if this was a Tate Modern exhibition I'd think she might be a piece of art, but instead she's clearly a person who is just a bit further than I am over the edge. She's crumpled up and has her head in her hands, and all I can see of her is a pair of purple harem pants that make me think of Lina, a pair of sequinned flip-flops and the back of her neck.

Everyone is ignoring her. What should I do? I watch for a while from a distance, then, because I can't walk past, I crouch down.

'Are you OK?' I wonder whether I should try it in Italian. I put a hand out and hover above her shoulder, wondering whether it's all right to touch a complete stranger. She twists away before I can try.

'No,' she says. 'Leave me alone.'

She speaks English, with an accent. South African? I don't know. I sit beside her, leaning on the white wall, and don't say anything. No one can cry like this indefinitely: I should know. I wait it out. No museum person comes along to chuck us out, though I'm half expecting that man from the Frari church to appear.

After a while, she starts hiccuping. Then she stops altogether. I want to pass her a tissue or something, but I don't have one, so I just watch her wiping her cheeks furiously with her fingers, then rubbing her eyes with the heels of her hands. She dries her face with the edge of her yellow T-shirt and takes some juddering breaths. I realize I know her. It's the girl. The one who was there every time I was glitching all over the place.

I risk a hand on her arm, and she jumps, then says, 'Shit! Are you still here?'

She has an angry energy about her and I'm not sure what to say. She doesn't seem to feel the need to say anything else, but she doesn't get up. In the end, I say, tentatively, 'I've seen you before, yeah?'

She folds her arms and turns her face away without speaking. Great. We sit there. I look around and my eye catches on a baby Jesus staring out at me from a golden frame. It's so weird to be in here, surrounded by virgin mothers and little godly babies with their willies out. Time goes by and people walk past, and I just stay there next to her. There's something a bit Zen about sitting on the floor of a gallery. We really could be an exhibit. *Two girls, not speaking*. After a while, I lean forward to look at her properly.

It's actually her.

This is the girl who made the universe break. The girl who, when I was in a state of, let's face it, madness, made me spin out of control, but now she's crumpled on the floor of an art gallery.

I've watched her looking at me through a window, have seen her in the Frari church, met her outside that church. And now she's here, and she's the one who looks broken.

She's about my age. And she's beautiful, with gorgeously cut hair and a long perfect neck. Her eyes are red and she looks furious, but still.

'I really have seen you before,' I say.

I wonder whether she's in the middle of some kind of breakdown, like me. Is seeing me making *her* universe break? Did I look like this when it was happening to me?

Is she spinning through time and space? It's a hard thing to articulate out loud, so I don't.

'Yeah. I've seen you too. Well done.'

'What's going on? Who are you? Do you remember?'

She sighs. 'I mean, I just can't do this. Go away.'

I don't want to leave her, so I just stay where I am and wait for something to happen.

29

London

I waited until Freddie and I were together before I told him that Enzo and Phoebe had busted me. I hoped that when I explained how the Lewis cover story had fallen apart he would understand.

He did not. He was so angry that I thought he'd dumped me.

'And you just caved and told them everything?' he shouted.

'I had to! They found out that I was lying about Lewis!'

'Just tell me you told them because you decided to.' His face was hard, his voice rising. We were in his flat on Friday evening. I was sitting on the mattress and he was standing up. He was so furious. I knew I'd got this entirely wrong.

'I'd respect you much more if you told the fucking truth. If you're lying about that, what else are you lying about?'

'I'm not lying.' This was, I was finding, a phrase that sounded less true the more you said it. 'I'm honestly not!' I heard my voice rising too, half crying, and pulled it back.

I blinked away the tears and tried to stay calm. 'Like I said, they saw the Lewis guy in town and he was on a date, so they went to talk to him because he was with another girl.'

'Right.'

'They did! And that's how they knew I wasn't seeing him.'

'And, even if that did happen, you decided to fess up to *everything*? You gave them my fucking name? You didn't even hesitate to do the thing that we'd specifically agreed you *weren't* going to do? To go directly against what you knew was important to me?'

I took a handful of tissues and wiped my eyes and blew my nose. If he dumped me now, what would I do? I couldn't bear it. I couldn't bear the way I'd messed this all up so much.

'Sorry. I'm so sorry. It was so brilliant to be able to talk about you and tell them how amazing you are, and I'd been caught out so I didn't think about anything else. I'm sorry, Freddie.'

He paced around, though the room was too small for that to be effective, and he ended up just standing by the door. 'Oh yeah, play the cute card.' He made his voice high-pitched and mocking. '*It was so brilliant to be able to talk about you*. If this goes round on TikTok or Snap or whatever . . . I hope you trust them as much as you say you do. Because now I have to trust them too. If this goes wrong, it is all. On. You.'

'Of course I trust them! Enzo's my brother.'

'He's not your brother.'

That stung.

'He *is* my brother.'

He huffed. 'He's just some guy whose dad was briefly married to your mum.'

'And I'd trust Phoebe with everything,' I said, betraying my brother totally. Who Enzo was, in Freddie's eyes, suddenly changed the way I thought of him too.

He sighed. 'Well, we're going to have to. Right. I'm getting a drink.' He softened a tiny bit and my heart leaped. 'Looks like you need one too, doll.'

He went to the kitchen and after a few moments I headed to the bathroom because I needed to do some serious patching up on my face. I was ugly and raw, make-up ruined, eyes swollen, cheeks puffy. I hated the fact that Freddie had seen me like this, even if his anger was the thing that had made it happen. Because I was the one who had made him angry, so it circled back to me.

The bathroom was opposite the kitchen and I froze on the threshold, hearing Ollie's voice.

Our paths had only crossed once since our first meeting, and he had been frosty. I'd tried to be nice and friendly, but he clearly hated me. I hadn't seen Lina at all since that moment of the downward-facing dog.

'She's a *child*, Fred.' I could hear him but couldn't see him. 'A fucking child. What's wrong with you? Yelling at a kid? And, as I've said a million times before, if you'd told me at the time that the song was about a schoolgirl who'd told you to sling your hook for sleazing, I wouldn't have done it. In fact, let's scrap it. I'm done with your shit. I don't want any part of this. I hate her being here. Hate everything about it. Just so we're clear. And that's not going to change.'

I felt the tears springing to my eyes again. He hated me. He hated me so much he was cancelling the song and the album that had my name on them.

'Haze thinks you hate *her*.'

'Julianna was bad enough, but this one's doing fucking GCSEs. She's a kid. It's not her fault. I warned her, the first time she came here, that she needs to get away from you for her own good.'

'Fuck off. She's over the age of con—'

'By what, five minutes? Am I meant to congratulate you for waiting until after her birthday?'

'You're jealous.'

I closed and locked the bathroom door, feeling sick. Julianna. I'd not heard that name before. Freddie had never alluded to her. He'd barely mentioned any previous girlfriends at all: when I'd asked, he'd brushed it off with a, '*No one like you, doll*.' Who the hell was Julianna?

I thought of the woman who'd been waiting for him in the van, after the gig. Was that her? I guessed that whoever Julianna was, she was older than me since Ollie seemed to feel that their relationship had been less 'bad'. The thought of Freddie bringing another teenage girl home, of Ollie disapproving of her too, made me feel uncomfortable. But I knew this was the most special relationship Freddie had been in. He'd told me. I tried to brush Julianna aside, but I didn't want there to be another girl, before or after me.

I looked at myself in the mirror. My face was horrific. I wanted to walk into the kitchen and defend Freddie. He was right: we had agreed I wouldn't tell anyone and I'd just gone ahead and done it. He was right to be angry. I couldn't believe it hadn't occurred to me to message him in the time between Enzo's string of messages and them coming into my room. There had been about fifteen minutes or so and I hadn't even considered it.

Freddie was right. I was wrong. I looked myself in the eye and promised to do better from now on. I had no idea what I'd do if he dumped me.

I used one of Lina's cotton-wool balls to clean my smeary face and borrowed her make-up to redo it. I sprayed on a bit of her Chanel perfume too and it made me feel less schoolgirly.

I looked at my arms and thought they were ugly. I had always had dark hairs on them because of my Greek heritage, and I'd never cared before, but now I covered both forearms with lather and shaved all the hairs off with a pink razor that I guessed was also Lina's. I rinsed it and washed the hairs down the sink.

I brushed my teeth with Freddie's toothbrush, then sprayed the bathroom with a Method spray that was there while I was at it, and put bleach down the loo, filling the time until my face went back to normal. I hated how furry and scummy this bathroom got. They had cleaning products, but they never seemed to use them.

When I felt more presentable, I left the room, ready to do whatever it took to make things right. Ollie was standing outside the bathroom door. I jumped when I saw him.

He looked me up and down with his flinty eyes and said, 'Bathroom smells nice. Certainly a sentence I've never said to my brother.'

'Ollie,' I said. I took a deep breath and hoped I looked calm. 'I heard what you were saying before and I just wanted to say it's not like that. Freddie's not taking advantage of me. I'm here because I want to be. I really like him and he was angry because I messed up. It wasn't his fault. It was mine.'

I forced myself to look at him. His gaze was so direct that I ended up turning away. I didn't like it.

'Go on then. What did you do that warranted that?'

'I – I told my brother and my best friend that I was seeing him, even though I knew he didn't want me to.'

He snorted. 'Right. And for that he yells at you until you're in pieces? Walk away, Hazel. Don't do this. Lina and I are very, very uncomfortable with this happening in our home. Of course he wants it to be secret. Get out while you can.'

He started to move past me. I couldn't let it end like this, so I said, 'It's really not like that. It was my fault. And I'm only ten years younger than Freddie. In a few years, it won't matter at all. And I know about Harry and –'

I hadn't meant to say that, but what the hell.

'You know about Harry?' He stared at me for a moment, then shrugged. 'OK, sure. But in a few years it will still matter very much indeed. Look, I can see you're smitten and all that, but don't say I didn't warn you. And this is coming from Lina too, OK? At least we've tried. Never say we didn't.'

Freddie handed me what I thought was a glass of water when I came back into his room. The energy was different and I felt the relief pounding through me.

'Sorry, doll,' he said. 'I went a little overboard there. I was just shocked. Here, drink up. You look pretty.'

I took the drink, and he tucked my hair behind my ears. 'And you smell like Lina! Jeez, that's weird.'

'I borrowed a little bit of her perfume.'

I took a gulp of water, and choked. It burned my mouth and made my throat close up. I gasped for air. Had he poisoned me? Had he handed me a glass of bleach?

Freddie laughed. 'Sorry, doll!'

'I thought it was water.'

'You looked like you needed a vodka. Have a water too if you like.'

I sipped it and it warmed me and made me start to feel different.

'That's OK,' I said. 'This is good.'

We made up, and everything was lovely again. After half a glass of neat vodka, I started talking about our age gap.

'I mean,' I said, 'when I'm twenty and you're thirty, no one will particularly care. And if we were forty and fifty it wouldn't matter at all. Forty and fifty are practically the same number.'

This was only going to be an issue for a couple more years and I was wishing those years away with every fibre of my being. I heard the intensity in my voice, wondered when I had become this person.

Freddie kissed me. 'God, you're brilliant when you're drunk and emotional. I should be mean to you and give you booze more often. So. We obviously need to deal with this issue. Why don't you fix up something for the weekend? I need to meet the famous Enzo and Phoebe. And, once we're friends, everything will be fine, doll. I promise it will.'

30

Venice

When the girl gets to her feet, I do too. She walks off without looking at me, and I follow. I barely even glance at the art: I just go where she goes, keeping my eyes on her so she can't slip away from me.

As I walk behind, I look at the way those harem pants hang off her hips and another part of me stirs. I hadn't expected anything like that to happen for a very long time, if ever, but I watch her walking and I feel things.

I lose my cool, however, when I follow her into a room with blue walls. There's a painting in there that makes me double-take. It looks like a standard mother-and-baby picture, except that above their heads there are six birds, except that they're not birds. They're bright red, and they are baby faces mounted on wings. I scream when I see them. Phoebe showed them to me, once, in a book.

The girl looks round. This time she is half amused.

'The cherubs?'

I nod, though if these are cherubs they're evil ones. I take hold of Cello. I'm breathing fast and my heart is going crazy. Remember: this is the real world. I've come back from the weirdness. I'm getting better.

'They freak me out,' I manage to say. The girl walks up to the painting.

'I mean,' she says, 'I freaking love them in this painting. Look at them, the little weirdos! On their little clouds. The baby's a bit perturbed, right?'

I smile. The word *perturbed* sounds brilliant in her accent, which I now think is Australian.

I'm calming down, right up until she says: 'It's when you see them out in the wild that they're nasty bastards.'

I follow her out of the gallery, and without speaking we go to the nearest cafe, which is right outside. I'd been going to get a tote from the giftshop to prove that I was here, but I can always go back for it.

'What do you want?' I think of my barely functioning bank card.

She shrugs. 'Lemonade?'

I come back with two glasses. It's home-made and cloudy, with bits in it, poured from a giant jug. I'm pleased with it. This is classy lemonade.

She takes the drink and sips it. She spits it out, spraying it all over the table.

'Oh my God,' she says. 'I was thinking of 7UP. What the hell is this shit?'

I can't help laughing. When she looks at me, I realize I'd been afraid that if our eyes met the universe would break again. That doesn't happen. Phew.

'This is proper lemonade. I like it.'

'Tastes like sucking an actual lemon. Gross.'

'It's the kind of lemonade you're supposed to make when life gives you lemons.'

'In that case,' she says, and she takes four sachets of sugar from the bowl on the table and tears them open, all at once, and tips the contents into her drink and stirs it vigorously. I sip mine through the straw. It's sour and cold.

We're sitting on high white stools by a window. The air conditioning is making the hairs stand up on my arms. I dangle my legs and feel like a child.

The girl gives a half-smile and lifts her glass in the most half-hearted of toasts.

'Thanks,' she says. 'You should have left me alone. I wish I could be nicer. But I'm all out of energy.'

I try a platitude. 'Hey,' I say, 'we're in Venice. The sun's shining. You're drinking lemonade. That has to be good, right?'

She huffs all her breath out and turns away from me. I look at the other people in this cafe. There are five, and the woman in the yellow dress I kept seeing in the gallery is one of them, drinking from an espresso cup.

This girl is hard work. I should leave her alone because she's mean and rude. I could go and talk to the woman in yellow instead. I could tell her I love her dress.

But here in front of me is the girl who broke my universe. The sight of her did something to me. Also, she's gorgeous and I don't want to walk away because she's making me feel things that I hadn't expected to feel ever again.

'I'm Hazel,' I say.

She doesn't say anything. I wait, but she doesn't tell me her name. We sit in silence and when I finish my drink I stand up. 'OK.' My voice wobbles a bit because I've been trying really hard and she won't let me in.

I think of Phoebe and Enzo, of my last year. Of what it's actually like to try to help someone who won't engage. 'I'll leave you to it.'

I walk over to the woman in yellow. '*Scusi?*' I say. She looks up. 'I like your dress. *Mi piace tu . . . vestito?*'

She nods and looks away. Fine. This place is just full of rude people and I wish again I was with my actual friends. I walk out of the little cafe into the warm air and set off back over the wooden bridge.

There are fast footsteps behind me.

'Sorry,' says a voice. I look round and it's her, the grumpy girl.

I keep walking.

She keeps up.

'I was having a moment. I was super rude. I *am* super rude. I didn't used to be, but that seems to be who I am now. It's complicated. But . . . sorry? Can we start over?'

I keep walking. 'If you want.'

'You said you're Hazel, right?' I nod. 'I'm Kamila. I can't believe I didn't tell you my name. That's so crap. You were being nice and I was a twat.'

I turn round. 'Yeah. You kinda were.' Her eyes are still red and because I can see how difficult this is for her I soften a bit. I know what it's like. I don't really, of course: I have no idea at all what's going on with her, and I hope nothing really terrible has happened. But I do know what it's like to be in a mess and not to let anyone help.

'Kamila,' I say. 'Hi.'

She nods. 'With a K and one l,' she says.

'Cute.' We walk in silence. On the other side of the bridge, I stop.

'Where were you going?' she says. I look at her face. I massively fancy her. It's such a strange, straightforward feeling. I'd never expected to fancy anyone ever again. Can I go with it? I can try to stick with her at least.

'Dunno,' I say. 'What about you?'

'Honestly? When I get in a state like this, I go to Torcello. Have you been?'

'Torcello?' It makes me think of Uccello, the bird, and I grab her in my hand. 'Where's that?'

She starts walking. 'An island. Past Murano and Burano. Come on. I'll show you. We can swap stories.'

The boat is a tourist one, but we're the only people on it apart from the driver, who doesn't speak to us and doesn't appear to want us to buy a ticket, but just waves us on. It wobbles as we climb on board. We sit side by side on a bench around the deck, and as soon as we're seated the engine starts. The breeze is warm in my face as we pull away from the dock.

We haven't spoken on the walk, but she appears not to hate me.

'Sorry to bang on,' I say, 'but have you seen me before?'

'You're not banging on,' she says. 'And yeah. I've seen you.'

We smile at each other. Every part of me sags with relief. A few other parts of me start to tingle. She's nothing like Freddie. Freddie would hate her. She's not skinny; she's allowed to be moody. She's cool.

Kamila sighs. 'Things get on top of me. Sometimes it's too hard. But yeah, I remember you,' she says. 'I saw you through a window once. Then I think I saw you in one of those churches. I forget which. There's so many of the bastards.'

'The Frari,' I say. 'Santa Maria Glorioso dei Frari. I think I spent ages in there. I was in a bit of a . . . weird state. I saw you too.'

I still don't ask her whether I made her universe break because I imagine I didn't, so instead I go with a boring question: 'How long have you been here?'

She turns her face up to the sunshine.

'Well, Hazel,' she says, and the wind carries her words out across the water, 'that is indeed quite the question. I can tell you that I came here in 2023.' Her face changes. 'I was travelling, in Europe, on my own. I was having the best time, and I came because it's freaking Venice, you know? Then something happened. I think I took a wrong turning somewhere and I haven't managed to leave.' She starts to say something else, then sags again. 'How about you?'

'What do you mean?' I say. I have a bad feeling. A very bad feeling. My stomach lurches as if I was in a plummeting lift. 'What do you mean, you haven't managed to leave? What's happened? Did something terrible happen to you? Why were you crying in the gallery?'

She shakes her head. 'Tell me about you.'

'You've been here since 2023? You live here, then?'

She looks at me. 'What year is it?'

'It's 2024.'

She sighs. 'Could be worse.'

I'm not sure where to start with that, so we lapse back into silence. We're speeding across the water now, and I lean back on the edge of the boat and look up to the sky. It's pale blue, almost cloudless. I watch three birds high above.

Minutes pass. Then she says, 'Do you know how long you've been here?'

'Yeah. Three nights.'

'Oh. Shit. You're brand new. Sorry.' I turn to look at her face, but she's bolt upright, staring back across the water to Venice. 'No wonder you're perky,' she says, so quietly I can hardly hear.

I laugh, though it's not really funny. 'Perky? I am not in the least bit perky.'

'You'll be one of the ones who doesn't stay for long.'

'Well,' I say, 'yeah. I'm not staying indefinitely. Probably a couple more days. I looked up a flight, but I couldn't pay for it. When I can get hold of my mum, she'll send me the money and I'll go back.'

'You haven't realized?'

'What?'

'Oh, Hazel. Shit. I'm sorry to be the one to do this. I can't even remember what it was like, being like you. None

208

of this is what you think it is. This isn't Venice. You walked under a sign? Sotto Sotto. Do you remember?'

I nod. It was at the gallery.

'It means underneath. This is stuff that happens under the real world. I call it the Deep Down. Not sure why. It's all a lie. Hazel – nothing here is real.'

31

London

February

I stayed at Freddie's on Friday night, telling Mum, who hardly seemed to hear me, that I was at Phoebe's. On Saturday morning I woke at eight, feeling weird waking up in a new place, had a shower, fixed my hair and make-up, and put a coffee beside a sleeping Freddie. I cleaned the bathroom again and did the considerable amount of washing up, while everyone else in the flat slept. We were meeting Phoebe and Enzo at half eleven and I was extremely worried about it. I swept and mopped the kitchen floor. I watered the half-dead houseplants. I drew the half-dead houseplants on a page from a notebook while I watched kids' TV. They came out quite well, wilting and thirsty and sad in spite of the water I'd just given them.

At ten forty-five, Freddie was still asleep. His coffee had gone cold and so had the replacement. I made a third, steeled myself, and touched his shoulder.

'Freddie.' I whispered it right into his ear. He usually liked that. He shouted and sat bolt upright.

'What the hell?' he said.

'Sorry!' I stepped back, trying to assess how angry he was. 'Sorry, darling.' The *darling* felt weird: I was trying it out.

He looked at me, his eyes wild. His breath smelled of last night's whisky and I tried to edge backwards without him noticing.

'What are you doing?'

'It's just . . . We're meeting Phoebe and Enzo in forty-five minutes. Sorry. I've been awake for ages.'

He was silent for a while. Then he pulled me to him and kissed me on the mouth. It was intense.

'The things I do for you, doll,' he said.

He went to the cafe while I met their train. They could easily have found the place themselves, as it was right under the platform boards, but I wanted to be in control. I was so desperate for this to work. I loved Freddie, and I loved Enzo and Phoebe. It should have been simple.

Freddie was calling it 'damage limitation', and had made me promise that it wouldn't take more than half an hour.

'I can't believe he's going to be there,' said Phoebe on the escalator down from their platform. 'I mean, if I was him, I probably wouldn't be up for this.'

'Same,' said Enzo. 'Haze, you're spinning out. It's going to be fine. *Calmez-vous.*'

'Promise?' I said.

'Course,' said Phoebe.

He was waiting exactly where he said he'd be, at a table for four. He had put his coat across two of the chairs and his bag on the other to stop people taking them. He hadn't bought drinks yet, but as soon as he saw us he stood up.

'Hey!' he said. 'There you are. Great. Hi! I'm Freddie. Good to see you.'

I looked at him through my eyes, and then through theirs. However I tried it, he was perfect. He was wearing his double denim again, which I now knew was what he did when he wanted to project off-duty rock star. His dark red T-shirt suited him, and he was the most handsome man in the station, and the world.

I did the introductions and Freddie went to get us all drinks. I said I'd go with him.

'Thanks so much for doing this, darling,' I said. The *darling* felt slightly less strange second time round.

'If it makes me your darling,' he said, 'then I'd do anything. You know that. Right, what are you having?'

'Oat flat white,' I said. 'Thanks.'

He turned to the barista to put the order in. 'One cappuccino, one black Americano, one skinny flat white, one oat latte. Cheers.'

I started to say I didn't want it *skinny*, that I hated skimmed milk and I wanted oat milk. That actually if an oat flat white was too fatty I'd rather have my coffee black. But I didn't. I just decided to order black coffee from now on. There were no calories in that at all, which meant it wouldn't be an issue. Then Freddie bought an array of cakes, so I thought the *skinny* thing had been a slip of the tongue.

Did he think I was fat? I looked down at myself. I was pretty sure I looked OK. I mean, I wasn't *thin*, but I was fine. Healthy.

Back at the table, Enzo and Phoebe were ready.

'Thanks for meeting us, Freddie,' said Phoebe in a formal voice. 'You know, Hazel didn't tell us she was seeing you until we busted her, so it's just good for us to see that she's OK. Not that we're her parents.'

Freddie grinned. 'It's great that you look out for her,' he said. 'Look, guys, while we're being formal, I'd like to say that I'm not the kind of guy who pursues teenage girls. I mean, of course I'm not. I've never done anything like this before.' I pushed Ollie's words out of my mind, though the name *Julianna* was irritatingly hard to dispel. 'But, shit, you don't need me to tell you that Hazel is special. She's different from anyone I've met before, and I love her. There you go. Love.'

I couldn't look at anyone but Freddie. I was gazing at him and I couldn't stop. He loved me! He put his hand on the inside of my thigh, under the table, and held my gaze.

'Love?' I said.

He stroked my cheek. 'Love,' he said.

I didn't care that my friends were here too. I didn't care that we were in public. A ten-year age gap was nothing. It was about to be eleven years again, but that would only last eight months, and then it would be back to ten. I saw, more clearly than I ever had before, that my future was with Freddie. The odds weren't that stacked against us.

Enzo coughed. 'That's all very adorable,' he said, and I wanted him to stop speaking, 'but Hazel's still at school. She's got GCSEs coming up. She's a lot younger than you, mate.'

I held my breath. This was too confrontational. Freddie would hate it. He took his hand away from my leg.

'As are you, *mate*,' he said. 'And I'm well aware of those facts, thanks. I support her in everything she does, including her studying.'

I kicked Enzo hard under the table, but he just moved his leg and carried on. 'Just treat her properly. You know? Hazel's ... well, she's someone who needs to be properly cherished. Not messed around. I'm always going to be looking out for her.'

'Enzo,' I said. 'Stop.' I knew how this would go later. It would be my fault. I could see it playing out: the shouting, the blame, the tears, all over again.

'Cherished?' Freddie finished the rest of his coffee in one gulp. 'Fuck's sake! What are you, the 1950s? Haze is independent, which seems to have escaped your notice. She can make her own decisions, as is pretty evident. Of course I cherish her, but that's because I care about her, not because some snotty kid who pretends to be her brother is instructing me to.'

Enzo leaned forward and said, 'Here's the thing –'

I had never heard him use that voice before. Phoebe stepped in to defuse things.

'Sorry,' she said, talking over him with a smile. 'What Enzo means is, she's our best friend and none of us have any experience of your world, and we're just glad she's happy and that you're clearly as besotted by her as she is by you.'

She cast me an anxious glance. I signalled back my thanks.

'Do not apologize for me, Pheebs,' said Enzo.

Freddie nodded. 'Yeah. My brother and Lina, our drummer – they took some convincing, I can tell you. But they love Haze, and my Hazel song is the first single from the new album.'

They looked at each other, then at me.

'You've got a *Hazel* song?' said Enzo.

'Oh – I thought she would have told you that when she was unburdening herself of everything else.' That stung. I was glad I hadn't. 'I wrote it after our first date.'

He hummed a bit, and I sang along. I looked at Enzo and then at Phoebe for understanding, approval.

Phoebe gave it at once. I knew she had reservations, but she was doing this the right way.

'That's amazing!' she said. 'You wrote a song about Hazel, and it's going to be, like, on the radio?'

Freddie grinned. 'That's the plan. Oh, the album's named after her too. It's called *Hazy*.'

'I can't believe that. So cool.'

'It's not so cool.'

I couldn't look at Enzo. I tried to kick him again, but he was keeping his legs well out of the way.

'It's not *so cool* because it's bullshit.' He stood up.

'Don't,' I said.

'H, I'm not blaming you. It's him. The low-level wannabe rock star sweeping you off your feet. A grown man with a schoolgirl for his girlfriend. Sleazy twat. And, by the way, that wasn't a proper gig. You were doing covers. Like a wedding band.'

Freddie stood up too. 'Go fuck yourself.'

People were turning to look at us and I wanted to die. A second ago I'd been happy. Enzo had set fire to everything. I knew what the repercussions would be. I put my face in my hands.

'*You* fuck *yourself*,' said Enzo.

Phoebe leapt to her feet and grabbed his upper arm.

'We'd better go,' she said. 'Sorry, Hazel. Sorry, Freddie, and thanks for the coffee and cake.'

I watched her dragging my brother away. My eyes locked with Enzo's.

'Come home,' he said. 'H, come with us, now.'

The world stopped moving. A part of me suddenly did want to go. I wanted to walk away from Freddie and his anger. From feeling uncomfortable. From dreading the upcoming argument. I wanted to go back to my old life. I wanted to go to school, to worry about Mum and Greg, to focus on my GCSEs and start thinking about A levels and what to do beyond them.

If I didn't do that, there would be a rift between me and Enzo and I didn't know how we'd fix it because this was new territory.

If I went, I'd lose Freddie.

If I stayed, I'd push Enzo away. Would I lose him entirely? Not forever. We'd make up.

I looked him in the eye. 'Later,' I said.

And then Enzo turned away and they were gone.

Freddie knocked back his coffee and looked at me. I knew what I would see in his eyes, and there it was. Fury. Cold white anger. I had to do everything I could to make this right again.

'Sorry.' My voice was tiny. His jaw was twitching. He looked away. 'I'm really sorry,' I said. I knew Enzo was looking out for me, but couldn't find the words to say it.

Enzo wasn't meant to be the sensible one. He was the reckless one who did the thing that felt good at the time, whether that meant eating a whole cake or sitting on a beach all night. Why wasn't I allowed to do something exciting for once?

Freddie smiled. It was a fake smile and a new hard thing was in his eyes.

'Your friend seemed OK,' he said, 'but that guy is a dick. You're better off without the pair of them in your life. You've outgrown them.'

He looked at me, daring me to disagree. I saw clearly that I could either have Phoebe and Enzo in my life or Freddie. Maybe he was right: perhaps I had outgrown them. The three of them were certainly never going to be friends.

Phoebe had said all the right things. This was Enzo's fault.

Enzo's fault.

So I'd stay away from Enzo.

Freddie shrugged. 'Up to you,' he said, and he picked up his bag. 'You can commit to us a bit more, prioritize us, or you can go back to your dull little life. Your choice. I'm not actually bothered.' He stood up. 'Don't follow me. Just remember: you made this happen by shooting your mouth off. If you hadn't done this, we'd be absolutely fine.' He walked away. I didn't follow.

I finished everyone's coffee. I started eating the cakes. My favourite was a chocolate brownie because they were, I thought, objectively the best cakes. I took a bite, and then another, but it didn't taste right.

What was I doing? I thought of the tasteless skinny coffee. I thought of Kate Moss on Freddie's bedroom wall. I looked down at my thighs in my jeans on the seat. I piled the unfinished cakes on to the tray and put it on a different table.

Enzo and Phoebe both messaged me a million times, but Freddie didn't. I called and he didn't answer, and I was glad because I hadn't actually planned what I was going to say. I stared at the people going past, particularly noticing the women and the way they looked. I studied the two paths in front of me.

I thought about the way Freddie made me feel. When he was happy with me, there was nothing in the world that was better. He was a drug. No boys of my own age came close. His hands on me. His lips. His intoxicating presence. The fun, the music, the joy of it all. I wasn't ready to give that up.

I didn't like the fact that two men were both telling me what to do. I needed to decide for myself.

I examined my feelings. I was angry with Enzo. I kept coming back to that.

Twenty minutes later I wrote a message.

I'm sorry, I wrote. Yes. I will commit to us. Nothing like this will happen again. Can I come to the flat?

He didn't answer for half an hour. I was still sitting at the table, staring at my phone, when his reply arrived.

It just said: if you mean it then yes

32

'Venice'

This isn't Venice.

Sotto Sotto.

I call it the Deep Down.

I clutch the side of the boat. Her words have winded me.

I remember myself saying to imaginary Enzo that it wasn't Venice. But then I decided that it was Venice, and it wasn't Enzo. Maybe it was neither. I look around, across the water, watching the skyline receding.

I remember Enzo's reply, or the reply I formulated for him, and I try to echo it.

'Kamila,' I say. I use my most confident voice. 'This place has canals. It has St Mark's Square. Gondolas. Loads and loads of bridges. We're literally in a boat right now. Behold. Venice.' I indicate its shrinking skyline with a sweep of my hand. I make myself sound a lot stronger than I feel.

I know, though, really. As soon as she said it, I let myself see the things I'd hidden from myself. A part of me has known this all along. This *is* Venice – surely it is, for all the reasons I just said – but it's not real Venice. It's Deep Down

Venice. It's something weird, something that is not a part of real life.

I can't let myself crumble. I cannot look this in the face, not now.

'Whereabouts in Australia are you from?' My voice sounds manic. 'Have you been to the UK? I live in Kent. It's pretty close to London. Have you been to London? Do you have any brothers or sisters? Are you travelling on your own?'

I pause and draw breath. I didn't mean to say that all at once. Kamila gives a little smile.

'Um,' she says. 'Do you want me to answer all those? Sure. One brother, one sister. Yeah, I've been to London. And as you can see I'm on my own. That it?'

I look around, wondering why we're the only people on this tourist boat. I want to get off it, but I can't because we're in the middle of the water. I look at the driver (what do you call someone who drives a boat? Pilot? Surely not) and think of the woman in yellow who didn't say anything when I told her I liked her dress. I feel my fear swirling inside me. I can't bear to face it.

'Do you *drive* a boat?' I am seizing on anything to say, to stave off reality. We're not sailing because there are no sails. So this must be driving, but that doesn't feel right.

Kamila smiles, though it's not aimed at me.

'Me?' she says. 'Nope. I grew up almost as far inland as you can get. Everyone thinks Australia is all beaches, but not where I'm from.'

I don't tell her I didn't mean that, because she's given us something to talk about. I look at her cheekbones, her collarbones. I could look at her for a long time.

'How far from the sea?'

'Well, for starters we would never call it the sea. Or seaside. It's the ocean.'

'Sorry. How far from the *ocean*?'

She nudges me with her shoulder, and it's such an Enzo gesture that I have to fight away all kinds of stuff that I don't want to feel.

'Driving, straight? Maybe fifteen hours?'

'Fifteen *hours*?'

'Yep.'

I try to take that in.

'I'm pretty sure if you drove for fifteen hours from my house, not counting the sea, which right there is definitely not the ocean, you'd end up somewhere like ...' I try to picture the map of Europe. 'Well. Maybe somewhere like Venice, I guess.'

We both look back at the skyline disappearing from our vision. Somewhere like Venice.

Kamila seems happy to talk about trivia, and we swap stories, like she said, for the time it takes to get to Torcello. I'm frantic, desperate not to face the situation. I make myself breathe. *In and count to eight. Hold it for six. Out and count to eight.* Is that how it goes? It seems to slow my panic down anyway, and I focus entirely on the immediate. I fire questions. I make a point of not noticing that there's fog instead of a horizon line.

She is eighteen. 'If it's next year now, though,' she says, 'I might be nineteen? Weird that I've missed my birthday. I must have lived through it without realizing. When's your birthday, Hazel?'

'December the first. You?'

'March the twenty-first. I like it because it's the autumn equinox.'

'Spring.'

'Not in Australia, babe.' I think about it and nod. Obviously she's right. *Duh.*

'What's the nearest city to where you live?' I say. I really can't bear to slow down.

'City? Technically, that would be Darwin, but it's not actually *near*. However, we have a town much closer. Alice. Alice Springs. A town like Alice, you know?'

'No way!'

I see her grinning at my reaction. 'Why's that interesting? Let me tell you something: it's not.'

'Because I guess I was thinking about Sydney Opera House and surf beaches. Are you from the Outback?'

She laughs. When I look at her, I do too. Our eyes meet and something passes between us. Not time glitching, but something that makes me tingle.

'Yeah,' she says. 'I guess I am. Bondi, Queensland, all that – those places are pretty much as foreign to me as they are to you. I'm practically Crocodile Dundee.'

'And your family are still there.'

She gives a tiny nod. 'Yeah. Parents and sister. Big brother moved to Bali, but my little sister's still home. But hey – let's not go there yet.' She pats my shoulder. 'You're not ready for that shit.'

I think of Mum, of real Enzo and Phoebe, wherever they might be. Whatever they're doing. I feel sick.

'What brought *you* here?' she says after a while.

I swallow. I do the breathing again.

'I needed to get away,' I say in the end. 'I was in a relationship that had become . . . Sorry. I can't talk about it. I'll tell you another time. But I needed to get away fast, and my brother Enzo – his mum has an apartment here so I think I asked her if I could stay in it and she said yes. I picked the key up from the hotel next door. I don't remember doing any of that. I think it was real Venice then. Maybe? But now it's . . .'

I'm floundering, so I'm intensely grateful when she picks up on the most mundane detail out of everything I just said.

'Your brother's mum isn't *your* mum? Half-brother?'

'Stepbrother, but also I guess half-brother because his dad's my adoptive dad.'

I spend ages explaining our family set-up, including the divorce. It takes a long time, and I feel myself calming as I speak. Just talking about it makes me feel normal. I miss them. I miss all of them. I wish Mum was here. I even miss Greg. I guess he's allowed to have a girlfriend over a year after he and Mum broke up. I suppose Enzo and I *have* given him a bit of a hard time.

Has he got a girlfriend, though? Surely I just made that up.

'You know, I thought you were Italian when I first saw you. It's your hair and eyes, I guess. You totally look like an Italian babe. You're a doll.'

The word *doll* stings. I push it aside. 'My real dad was half Greek,' I say. 'So I'm a quarter. I've got a Greek surname. Angelopoulos. People used to laugh at it at school, but I like it. Mum and Greg wanted me to change it to my stepdad's name, but that's Wilkinson, and I didn't want that. Partly because I liked being first in the alphabet and Wilkinson would have been a downgrade. Also because it's not my name.'

'Hazel Angelopoulos?' she says, and gives me a real smile for the first time.

I tense, waiting to hurtle through time and space. It doesn't happen. I return her smile. It makes things feel easier.

'That might just be the best name I've ever heard. Does your dad – I mean, it sounds a complicated situation, but does he, did he, speak Greek?'

'Yeah,' I say. 'I mean not lately. He died, hence the stepdad adoption and all that. I need to go to Greece to see his family, and his – well, the place where it happened. But it's weird.'

I'll do it, I decide. If – when – I get out of here, I'll go and visit my Greek family. I'll find people with my name. If I talk to other people who loved him, I might believe he's gone.

If I get out of here.

'Ahh, shit. I'm sorry.'

'I barely remember him, but I . . . well, I think about him more than you'd expect. I've never believed he was actually dead. Because I was there. But I don't remember it, and that feels too bizarre. When my mum remarried, I was ten, but I wasn't giving up that name even if she was. Angelopoulos has always been a part of me. It's who I am.'

It feels good to talk about this stuff. I've only ever said it to Freddie before, and I feel sure Kamila isn't going to weaponize it.

'Too right, girl! You tell them. I'm Aussie through and through, and my mum's family are Pakistani. So I have Kamila – K and one l, remember – as my first name, and my last name is King.'

'Kamila King is a cool name.'

'I guess we're both awesome then.' She looks out to sea. The wind ruffles her hair. I check out her cheekbones. They're perfect.

She spins back and I think she catches me looking. 'Oh God, Hazel. You're scaring me.'

'*Scaring* you? Sorry. What am I doing?' I shift up closer so I can hear before the wind carries her words away.

She looks away again. 'Don't apologize! It's just, you're too good to be true, Hazel Angelopoulos. Much too good to be true.'

'What?'

'I mean, I've been on my own here forever. Maybe over a year, if it's actually 2024. Sometimes someone comes along and we hang out for a bit, but I've never actually felt any kind of connection before.' Her eyes meet mine. 'If it's OK for me to say that. I've never felt that it's someone I'd be friends with in the other world. And you're going to leave. And I was rude to you when we met. But I'm not sure if I have it in me. To go all in, and then lose you like I lose everything.'

She curls in on herself, in a ball.

I pull back. 'Seriously?'

She nods. Neither of us speaks. The boat glides across the still water. I wait for her to flip back to the way she was before, but she doesn't.

33

Torcello is the greenest place I've ever seen. There are trees, and there's grass, and, unlike in Venice, hardly any buildings. It's green as if someone had painted it with watercolours. I step off the boat and on to the wide bank, which is paved with bricks.

The air is so clean that it makes my lungs feel different. There's a path ahead of me. Things are growing everywhere, and no one is here but us. Mist is hanging over the water and the grass. It's beautiful. It feels like the Garden of Eden. If we're going to find a route out of here, maybe this is the place. I start walking.

'What's here?' I say.

I look round but she's not there. She's a little way behind, and she's still ignoring me. I wait for her to catch up, then say it again. She huffs and looks away.

'Oh Jesus, Kamila!' I'm starting to shout. I can't help it. 'Look, fine. We won't be friends. Just – why did you bring me here if you're not going to talk to me? I could have stayed in Venice, where there are at least other people. Since we're here, you have to fucking talk to me.'

She flicks her eyes to me. 'You swore at me, Hazel Angelopoulos.'

'I fucking did.'

She shakes her head and carries on walking. I walk faster, overtaking her. I follow the wide path along the water's edge. The path's bricks are arranged diagonally, rather than straight, and I walk in zigzags because I keep following their lines. There is wild greenery on both sides of me, springing up all over the place, unimpeded by humans. It smells of life, of growing things.

In the inconvenient headspace, when Kamila wasn't talking to me, my mind has been whirring. It's harder and harder for me to shut this down.

This place smells of life, which I'm beginning to feel might be entirely inappropriate.

There's a little bridge up ahead of me, a small one. It has no railings or anything. Could I just step off the side? What would happen? I don't try. On the other side of the bridge there's a courtyard with buildings round it, and one of those buildings is an old church.

This one looks *very* old. I know nothing about it, nothing about Torcello, and I don't have imaginary Phoebe to fill me in with facts that I'm guessing might actually have been random things I pulled from nowhere. To be honest, I am done with old churches. If Kamila walks into that one, she might disappear like Phoebe. I don't want to go in there. I want to . . .

What? I want to keep myself busy. I can't face the thing that is in my head. I don't want to follow the train of thought that is edging its way to the front of my brain. I can't stop and let it catch up with me. I think I know what's going on, and I cannot let it in.

There's a cool wind in my face. The church door is open, but everything else is closed. I walk past the church and find a bell tower, which also has an open door. I go back to the church. There's a very old-looking stone chair just right there on the grass, so I sit on it. Nothing happens, but it's nice to sit down. A plaque next to it tells me that it's Attila's Throne. Why not?

I sit on the throne and pretend to myself that I'm Attila the Hun, but realize that I don't know much about him except that he was fierce, and that he lived a very long time ago. Is this even his chair in the first place? It probably isn't. I try to channel some terrorizing strength and spirit, but stop when my bum gets cold.

I decide to walk round the perimeter of the island, but there are trees in the way and little canals everywhere without bridges and I don't get far. The sun is warm on my arms and I get so bored, so lonely, and Kamila hasn't come after me like I wanted, so after a while I head over to the bell tower and set off upwards.

There are not actually many steps: the ascent is mainly a steep slope with steps at the corners. The climb makes my legs hurt and that actually cheers me up a bit because it's a concrete thing that I can hang on to. These must be real legs if they hurt: I'm less worried right now about whether Venice is real, and more worried about whether I am. It's taking every bit of mental energy I have not to contemplate what's going on beyond that, so the truth of the fact that I'm climbing a tower that's been here for maybe a thousand years and that the exercise is making me huff and puff is a comfort blanket and I wrap it round me. Physically, I am present. I'm on the island of Torcello with a strange and moody girl who's avoiding me. I'm climbing a tower because it's here. This feels as real as anything else that's ever happened to me.

I run and reach the top out of breath. There is a huge bell in a cage of wooden beams, and I step back, wondering whether it would hurt my ears if it rang. Then I think I could ring it. Was there a rope dangling down there at the bottom? What would happen if I pulled it?

If there is one when I get back down, then I will.

For now, though, I just lean on the ledge and take in the view. The walkway goes round the bell in a square and I edge my way along, staring out from all directions, wondering which side faces towards Kent.

For a second I'm somewhere else, looking out over a city. Pulled along by my wrist to lie about my age to a man with a dolphin on his T-shirt.

No. That's gone. Below me Torcello is sharp and real. I see Kamila walking along a path beside a field, the water on the other side of her. I wave but she's not looking. Beyond her Venice is silhouetted on the horizon. It's a distant skyline – churches, lines of ancient buildings against the sky, a bit blurred, like a painting. Behind it, and all round the rest of the horizon, there's fog.

I walk round the bell and look out from all four sides of the tower again and again. It's the same on every one. The close things are sharp and defined. Further away they're like a painting. I remember my first morning here, thinking it was so much like being in a Canaletto that you could practically see the brushstrokes. It's just like that here, except not Canaletto. I don't know who would have painted this marshy green scene because I'm not Phoebe, but I can see that if you put a frame round it you could stick it in a gallery.

Then, in the distance each time, there's fog. Just fog. I wonder what would happen if we took a boat and went out to it. What's on the other side?

I didn't ask Kamila why she hadn't tried to leave. There's a railway station. There's a vaporetto that goes to the airport. There are, obviously, boats everywhere, and people like the man who brought us here who drive/pilot/sail them.

I start to walk down.

At the bottom of the tower there is a rope for the bell, just hanging there. I pull it as hard as I can. Nothing happens. I know nothing about bell-ringing apart from a vague feeling that if you hang on to the rope you get pulled up into the air.

I don't hang on to the rope. I yank it down, again, but as far as I can this time, and let it slip through my hands as it flies back up. I do it again and again and eventually, in the end, the bell rings.

It's loud. I love it. I do it again and again.

'What the hell are you doing?'

I keep going. I don't know why I'm doing this. I do know. I'm doing it to keep busy, to stop me looking at the thing that, in spite of all my efforts, is taking shape in my head.

'Ringing the bell,' I say over my shoulder. I sense her watching and I just keep doing it. I like the way it makes my arms hurt. Just as I'm getting tired and preparing to stop, Kamila nudges me.

'Shift up then,' she says. 'Let's have a go.'

I pass her the rope and show her how to do it. She rings the bell too. When she's tired, she passes it back to me. We ring the bell on Torcello for a long time. The sound punctuates the still air. It feels as if we're summoning something, challenging something. But nothing arrives. Nothing changes.

'Of course I've tried to leave.' We're standing at the edge of the water, looking out at the fog. Kamila is talking to me again, it seems. 'The train station is there, sure, but the trains don't go. You can't get to the airport because it's on the mainland.'

'What if you take a boat?'

She hesitates. 'Steal one? Because I've obviously asked boat people to take me to the mainland, but they never do.'

'Yeah. Steal one.' I think of Enzo and Phoebe almost doing that, a few days and also a lifetime ago. Could I have got in with them? Would everything have been different?

Of course not. What am I thinking? They weren't even here.

'I haven't done that.' She stops and huffs. 'Why haven't I?' She grins. 'Guess I'm more honest than you, babe.'

I look out at the fog. I look back to her. I don't understand her: I feel a huge connection with this girl, and every single part of me is longing to spend all my time at her side. I've never been good at being alone, properly alone, because I don't like the way it makes me panic. I have always needed Enzo, Phoebe, my imaginary dad, Freddie. And now I've found someone who is as trapped in whatever this is as I am, and she's moody as hell.

'Shall we try it?' I say. I'm half expecting her to turn away again, to stomp off.

Finally, she meets my eye.

'I mean – yeah?'

It turns out that stealing a boat is easy. It's easy if there happens to be a little motorboat just there, and if someone has helpfully left the keys in the ignition, which they have. I check the name on its side. It's called *Uccello*. The same as the one Phoebe and Enzo messed around in, a million years ago, on our imaginary first day here.

Uccello. That doesn't bode well, reality-wise.

All the same, touching my little glass bird grounds me. She's connected to my dad and that knowledge makes me love her even more.

I climb in. The boat wobbles a bit but it seems fine. It's not the cleanest but it's just what we need. I sit on one side and Kamila climbs into the other. I feel a surge of optimism. This is going to work: I know it is. The *Uccello* boat is going to take us away from . . .

I don't let my mind finish the sentence. Instead I turn the key. The engine starts.

I look at Kamila. She mimes applause.

'That was easier than I thought it was going to be,' I say.

'Yeah. I thought you had to pull a . . .' She mimes yanking a cord and letting it go. I thought that too.

I try pushing a lever and the boat splutters and stops. I do the whole thing again, and it stalls again. Eventually, after a lot of trial and error, I move the lever slowly enough and we start to sail/drive. Kamila has untied the rope. We move away from land, slowly and then faster.

The wind blows our hair. I look at the bell tower sticking up into the sky. I turn the boat round and steer us away from land.

'Sorry!' She had to shout to be heard because now we're going fast and the wind is carrying our words away. I look at Kamila and try to slow down a bit, but I stall the boat again. Once we're moving, she tries again.

'Sorry,' she says, shifting closer. Her presence makes me feel new, hopeful in spite of everything. 'I hate myself for shutting you off. I'm going to try to stop that. I can't help it. It's happened so many times, I have my defences up.'

'Sure.' I look away, trying to pretend this is a casual thing, that I'm not really bothered either way.

'It's because you're too cool.'

'Right.' I give her a little smile. 'Yep. Sure. You can't bear to talk to me because I'm so cool.'

'I know! I know it sounds like shit but it's true. Honestly. I'm so happy you're here. I'm glad, for me but not for you, that you've turned up in my zone. But everyone I've met has left, and I know that you will too, and I'm scared.'

I don't reply. I see the Venetian skyline off to the right, and steer away from it, between smaller islands. If we keep going, sooner or later we'll reach the mainland. Somewhere out there, there's the real world. There must be.

I believe her. But all the same I cannot stick around with someone who treats me well or badly depending on their mood. I've done that and I'm never doing it again. I bite back the impulse to tell her that everything's definitely going to be fine, and steer the boat towards the fog.

Is this the actual boat that Enzo and Phoebe climbed in? Or another boat with the same name?

But they weren't even there.

'When you first saw me!' I shout as the clear air around us starts to fade into the mist. 'Through the window? You remember?' She nods. 'Was I on my own?'

Our eyes meet. We're coming into the fog now.

'No,' she says. 'You were with two people. One was Phoebe. Lovely Phoebe. The other I guess was your brother. And when I looked at you, everything kind of glitched.'

Shit.

Shit, shit, shit.

I'm going to have to rethink everything, again.

34

London

One morning, at the end of April, I crept into Freddie's room with wet hair and tiptoed around, collecting my things. I picked up my shoes and sat at his desk to write a note.

> Had to go and study. Sorry – I'm really behind. I'll call later. love you xxxxxx

I went over to the bed to put it next to him, where he would definitely see it. When his hand shot out and grabbed my wrist, I gasped. I tried to pull away but couldn't.

'Don't go,' he muttered. 'Hazy. I need you.'

I kissed his hair and tried again to extricate myself. Freddie did seem to be emotionally dependent on me now, which made me feel amazing and a bit unsettled. I was sure it was because we understood each other, because of our shared grief. Everything we'd both been through had drawn us close, close, close together, and it was exhilarating and brilliant, but I was really, really messing up the rest of my life.

'I have to, though,' I said.

I was feeling so sick about the exams that I couldn't ignore it any more. Mum was actually focused on me now, and, because I always used studying as an alibi when I was with Freddie, she thought I was amazing. She also thought Enzo and I were still the best of friends (he was blanking me, no matter what I tried to say to him, and he'd moved into the flat with Greg), and she thought I was staying over with Phoebe, or at Greg's, every weekend. She was more present now that a few months had gone by since the split, but she was still too distracted to see what was really going on. Too easily placated. She believed everything I said.

Freddie pulled me closer. 'You don't.'

I laughed and tried to pull away, but he gripped my wrist harder and I couldn't move.

'I really do need to,' I said, and the dread built in my stomach. 'I'm super behind. I should have done a ton of revision by now, but I haven't. I should have finished my art coursework, but there's one piece I've hardly started. I've been with you all the time. Lucky me, but I do actually have to pass my exams.'

He let go and shifted over, and I knew the bed was warm and that he wanted me with him, so I climbed back in for a second and kissed him. I had showered and brushed my teeth. Freddie was warm and gorgeous and I didn't mind the morning breath. I didn't mind anything about him: he was a drug to me and I knew that his pull was stronger than everything else.

I did have to go and work, though. Everyone said they'd done 'no revision'. It was the catchphrase among all my friends. 'Oh my God, I've done no revision and I'm going to fail everything.' A wild exaggeration for effect. But I really *had* done no revision, or almost none. I'd been to the revision classes at school because I had no choice, and that was it.

I was mainly at home during the week, but every time I sat in my bedroom and made a revision timetable, and got my books out, Freddie would call and I'd end up abandoning it to talk to him. Every time I caught a train to London, I'd try to do an hour's work on the way, but I would just stare at things I didn't know and spiral in panic. Every time I tried to get on top of my art, a message from Freddie would stop me. I had been on track for good grades. I'd chosen my A levels and got a place at sixth-form college. I wanted to go to uni, though I wasn't sure how I was going to juggle that with Freddie. It was a problem for two years from now. GCSEs, however, were a problem for today.

'Tell you what,' he said, 'brilliant idea alert! Do it here. Clear the desk over there and get your books out, or your sketchbook or whatever, and I'll bring you drinks and you can tell me about . . . oxbow lakes? Simultaneous equations? *Macbeth*? Whatever. Doll – as soon as you've done those exams, you forget that shit straight away.'

I looked at his desk. It had half-empty glasses on it and it didn't look like a place for studying. I looked at the prints of nineties Kate Moss, photographed in black and white, looking intimidating and beautiful and skinny. I didn't have any books with me. I didn't have a sketchbook.

Freddie set me up on his laptop and I did a token hour of history on BBC Bitesize with half my mind on other things. He didn't bring me drinks: he vanished into the living room while I stared at Kate Moss, who was better than me in every way. Then he came in and said, 'Come watch me on *Assassin's Creed* for a bit. You need a break.'

I resisted but I knew I was going to give in.

'Kate Moss has been staring at me,' I said.

'Ahhh, she's all right. Bet she didn't bother with her GCSEs.'

I looked at her. She looked back. I heard her challenging me. *You don't look like this, Hazel. Do you?*

'What is it about her?' I reached out and touched the picture. He had actually got these framed. He really loved them.

Freddie stopped and considered. 'It's just the look,' he said. 'I mean, all of it. Gorgeous. The whole aesthetic. Don't you think?'

I looked at her. She was so thin. 'I guess,' I said.

So, instead of studying, I watched Freddie's avatar running round Paris. I tried to work out how to make myself more like the photos in Freddie's room. I knew that I could do it and I decided, in that moment, that I would. I was going to become the sort of girl he considered 'gorgeous' – so gorgeous that he framed her photograph and looked at it every day.

I saw his digital self climbing, looking for collectibles. I concentrated because I knew Freddie loved it when I did that, but my mind was half on my studies and the sick feeling inside. After a while, I picked up a pencil and took a piece of paper from their broken printer and started drawing the strange avatar and the pixellated churches.

'You're not concentrating!' he said, motioning me to stop. 'Come on, doll. This means a lot to me.'

I sighed. It wasn't worth arguing.

So, when the exams began in May, I was woefully underprepared. It was made worse by the fact that Enzo wasn't speaking to me, had blanked me carefully at every turn since St Pancras. Once I'd made my decision, he'd ignored my messages, failed to answer my calls, and when we saw each other at school he turned his face away, and the whole thing made me feel shit. The enormous town house generally just contained Mum and me, and at weekends there was just Mum. She went out all the time, to work, to cycling club, to choir, so it was usually empty.

Phoebe called for me, unexpectedly, on the morning of our first exam. Mum had arranged to work from home so she could make sure I had breakfast (I'd taken to skipping it), and when she opened the door to her she was delighted.

'Phoebe!' she said. 'How lovely to see you. Good luck today. You girls have certainly been putting the hours in.'

'Thanks, Susie,' said Phoebe, and I ran to get out of the door before the conversation went any further. In spite of everything, I was happier to see Phoebe than she would ever know. I stepped forward and hugged her. She stiffened, and then relaxed and hugged me back.

Phoebe and I had been semi-talking. She would message every now and then, reminding me that she was always there if I needed her. I would say thanks. When I saw her at school, we'd exchange glances and tight smiles, but we weren't actually friends any more. I missed her. I wished I could have Phoebe, Enzo and Freddie in my life, but I was learning that the world didn't give you everything you wanted. So I was surprised to see her on the doorstep.

'Thanks for making breakfast, Mum,' I said, and I hoped she wouldn't find the half-croissant I'd shoved deep into the kitchen bin. 'See you later!'

Mum hugged me. 'Good luck, darling,' she said. 'You'll be fine. You've worked so hard.' She pulled me close and said quietly, into my hair: 'Your father would be so proud.'

I was dirty with guilt. I didn't hear my dad's voice any more. I hardly even thought about him these days because there was no space in my head because of Freddie. When I did think about Morris, he was bound up with poor little Harry Kennedy, lost in accidents.

'Thank you,' I said, and I got down the steps and on to the pavement as fast as I could.

'You OK?' said Phoebe. I nodded.

'You called for me.'

'Wanted to make sure you actually showed up.'

'Thanks, Pheebs. It's really nice of you.'

That first exam went badly. So did the second and third. The art portfolio had already gone badly because I just hadn't put the time in. I sat in exams, writing what I could, knowing that I was messing these right up, hoping to scrape through. I watched everyone else, the people who had prepared properly, scribbling away, writing it all down, and I wanted to cry. In fact, I often did cry. I just sat in exam rooms and cried. I learned to take tissues in with me, discovered that there was a rule that you weren't allowed to produce them from your pocket or teachers thought you had answers written on them. So at the start of each exam I would place a pack of tissues on the table, ready.

The only one that went OK was art because it was ten hours over two days and you could actually lose yourself in it. I hadn't done the prep work properly, but still that one, I felt, went fine. I did the storm picture that I'd started months ago. It went surprisingly well. Everything else was shit.

Just before half-term, I came home to find Mum agitated. She was sitting at the kitchen table, staring at her laptop screen. Her hair was in its usual at-home messy bun, and she was twirling a strand of it round and round her finger. I could tell from her face that it was something big and it stopped me in my tracks.

I was certain she'd found out about me and Freddie. I could see it. Someone had contacted her. Maybe there was a photo of us online (though we'd never put one anywhere). Someone might have recognized me and sent it to her.

Or perhaps Enzo had finally ratted me out. He could have told Greg and, despite the fact that Mum and Greg weren't speaking, Greg would have overcome that to email Mum because even though I never saw him he was technically my dad, and if my lies were exposed he would be on it. I knew he would, the bastard.

She would have said, '*But Hazel goes to yours every weekend.*'

And he would say, '*I haven't seen her for months.*'

When Mum looked up, though, her expression was slightly wrong.

'What?' My voice didn't really come out, so I said it again. 'What?'

'No,' she said. 'No, don't worry. Something's come up. I've been asked to do something. But I won't. I can't.'

It all lifted away from me and I grinned at her and put the kettle on. 'Don't be silly. Of course you can. What is it? Tea?'

She gave me a lovely look. 'Coffee? A nice one?'

'Of course.' I set about making her a coffee, using Greg's old espresso machine. While it was heating up, I forced myself to calm down. The dread, followed by relief: it was all too much. When I was on an evenish keel, I said: 'Go on then. What is it?'

She told me, looking embarrassed, that she had been invited to step in as a speaker at a conference in Oslo. 'The thing is,' she said, 'it's after half-term, during the last week of your exams. And we're in such a lovely groove here. I can't leave you.'

I handed her the coffee. 'Mother – of course you can.'

'There'll be other opportunities.' Her eyes kept darting towards the screen. 'No. I'll say no.'

'You will not! You have to go.'

A part of me, treacherously, was thinking about Freddie. He was fascinated by this house. He was desperate to come and look round my home, and since Enzo hadn't been here for weeks, probably months, it felt safe. If Mum was away, he could visit. Stay over. I snapped to an image of me telling him the house was empty for . . .

'How long?'

'Five days.'

That would work.

I instantly hated myself. Still: Mum could do her conference. Freddie and I could stay here. Win-win.

My last five exams, though. Win-win-lose.

Freddie arrived the day after Mum left. We passed Enzo as we walked home from the station and he gave me a look I couldn't bear, so I turned away and, when he'd passed, agreed with Freddie that he was a wanker, ignoring how dirty that made me feel. I messaged Phoebe and told her she didn't need to call for me before exams any more.

I led my boyfriend up the steps to the front door and fixed a huge smile on to my face.

I was working hard to hide the fact that I wasn't feeling brilliant. My head was pounding and my throat hurt, but Freddie found people being ill extremely boring, and he was right. It *was* boring. And he was here and I was excited. I wasn't going to be ill.

'Whoa.' He stood in the hallway, just inside the front door, looked around and laughed. I saw him take in the cream walls, the stained-glass window halfway up the stairs, the glass vase of dried flowers. The big mirror, the table that had keys and post on it.

'This is the famous Hazy household?' he said. 'I like all the beige. It's kind of Ikea double plus.'

It was always easier to agree.

'Yeah,' I said. 'I know.'

He followed me down to the kitchen in the basement.

'Fair play,' he said. He looked at the pans hanging from the ceiling rail, down at the checked tiles, around at the French windows out to the little garden. 'Cool kitchen.' He walked over to the stove, lit all six gas rings and pretended to warm his hands. 'Will you inherit this place, doll?'

'They're going to sell it,' I said. 'When Enzo and I go to uni. Divide the money, I guess.'

He turned and put an arm round my waist. 'What's all this talk?' he said with a wicked grin. 'Did I miss something? I think you meant to say *when I become a full-time muse and rock star's girlfriend.*'

I forced a smile, wondering whether I could take a couple of paracetamol without him noticing. If he went to the loo, I'd definitely do it.

I had talked before about going to uni. Last time Freddie had said, '*Go somewhere in London and you can live with me.*' Now he seemed to be telling me I shouldn't go at all.

'Sorry.' Still, I loved him wanting me, seeing a future with me. I'd worry about the actual future next year. 'I meant when Enzo goes to uni and I become a full-time muse and rock star's girlfriend.'

I turned off the gas rings.

'That's better. Shame you don't get to keep this place, though.' He paused and anger flickered into his eyes. 'Also, don't say that guy's name to me.'

'Sorry.'

'We'll live somewhere like this. I mean, without the beigey crap.'

I wanted to say, 'Don't say that.'

I wanted to say, 'It's not beige and it's not crap.' And I should be able to say Enzo's *name*.

I wanted to say, 'Shut up. If you don't like it, you can go away.'

But I didn't. Of course I didn't. If we argued, I would end up crying and apologizing. I was terrible in an argument. That was something I'd learned about myself.

All I said was, 'It's not *all* beige.'

'Close enough,' he said. 'So, yeah. A town house with a huge kitchen. Colour everywhere. One day a few kids to fill the place up.'

A few kids? That was new. I imagined our children. It was a bit much. I stepped towards him and kissed him so I didn't have to engage with the idea.

He kissed me back. 'Where's your bedroom?'

I went to the bathroom, locked the door and took some codeine I found in a basket of stuff under the basin.

Freddie stayed with me those first two nights and I had to work harder and harder to cover up the fact that I felt like shit. I faked everything, but when I tried to look over my biology notes the words swam in front of my eyes. I liked the domesticity between us, and Freddie loved the house.

'You know what, doll?' he said when I got home from a disastrous exam. 'This is really showing me what I need to do. Make some proper money, or get myself a rich girlfriend, and move out of the flat. I don't need my brother putting a downer on everything I do, and Lina's just as bad.'

It was a punch to the stomach. 'Get a rich girlfriend?'

'Don't be like that – I mean, hello? This is your house. I meant you.'

But he already had me. I wasn't rich. Greg was rich. I let it go.

By Wednesday, I couldn't ignore the fact that I was feeling truly shit. I coughed my way through the chemistry exam. People kept looking at me. I didn't know any of the answers and guessed most of them. My head was full of cotton wool. I felt that I was on the ceiling, looking down at myself floundering. By the time the exam was over, I was slumped at the desk, half asleep.

Enzo ignored me. Phoebe put an arm round me and supported me out of the exam room. Then she said the words I hadn't been articulating to myself.

'Have you done a Covid test?'

Covid was over, though. I wasn't meant to have it now.

Phoebe bought a test and I did it in the school toilets. The positive line came up stronger than the control one. Even with everything, Phoebe walked me home and straight into the living room, where she sat me down. I fell sideways on to the sofa and she put a cushion under my head. Freddie came bounding up from the kitchen.

'Hey, guess what?' He was excited, restless, full of energy. I watched him skidding to a halt, saw his mood changing. 'Oh,' he said. 'Phoebe.'

'Yeah,' she said. 'Hi, Freddie. Look, sorry to barge in. I know . . . Well, I brought Hazel home because she's ill. She has Covid.'

Freddie stared at me. I wasn't looking at his face, but I knew what it would be doing. He'd be annoyed with me for spoiling our week. He'd be furious when he realized that he was going to catch it too. Those things would have flickered across his face, and then he would have replaced it all with sympathy. I left enough time for that to happen, then looked up.

'No! Oh, Hazy. My poor darling. You have been a bit off colour, haven't you?' He turned to Phoebe. 'Don't worry. I've got this.'

'I'll message Susie. I'm sure she'll be able to come back a day early.'

'I can look after my girlfriend, thanks.' Then his voice changed. I heard him pulling himself back under control, making an effort to say whatever it took to make her go away. 'Don't worry. You look after yourself, Phoebe. You've got exams! I hope you don't catch it too.'

'Thanks! You too.'

'I'll be fine. How did today's exam go?'

I smiled. This was the Freddie I loved. I hoped this one was going to stay.

'Fine, thanks,' she said. 'Considering. We've only got one more. Physics, the day after tomorrow. I'm sure there's some paperwork to get you out of it, Hazel. I'll talk to school for you.'

'Thanks, doll,' said Freddie. 'Hazel, I'll get you some painkillers. In the bathroom, right?'

He called her *doll*. I told myself it was a slip of the tongue, that he had just said our special word to the wrong person by mistake. I felt sick, but then I closed my eyes. I felt lots of things. I would forget about it.

As soon as Freddie was out of the room, Phoebe leaned into me.

'Don't be angry,' she said. 'OK? But I'm going to make a group chat. You, me and Enzo. Because yeah, he worries about you too. It's called "Coursework Chat", and all you have to do is post anything in it, any time, and share your location. OK?'

I screwed up my face. Then Freddie was back. He handed me a huge glass of water and four tablets. I took them all.

'You said *guess what*?' I managed to say as soon as Phoebe had gone. He sat down and pulled my head on to his lap. I had a flicker of a realization that the reason I was surprised that he had just asked Phoebe how today's exam had gone was because he hadn't asked me, ever.

'It's good news.' He stroked my hair. 'The best. It's the single. "Hazy Girl". The thing we needed to happen. Has happened. Six Music have picked it up.'

I sat up. I felt the blood in my brain doing weird things. 'Oh my God!'

He grinned. 'Right? This is it. You see? You're my lucky charm. This song is going to actually get us somewhere. Launch us.' He extricated himself from underneath me and stood up. 'I'm going to take care of you until you're better. Fancy a drink? We have to celebrate this.'

'I fancy a drink of Lemsip,' I said.

'I'm off to the shop. I'll get you soup and stuff too. Sick person food, right?'

He came back with Lemsip, champagne and some Covent Garden soup, and gave me a mug of one, a glass of the other and a bowl of the third. I only wanted the Lemsip, but I had a sip of champagne to keep him happy, then poured half the rest into the yucca when he left the room. I ignored the soup because if I was going to be ill, I might as well take the easy opportunity to lose weight. I remembered Kate Moss, the challenge in her eyes.

I felt rubbish, but there was a song about me – a song that had my name in the title, from an album that also had my name on it – going on the radio. Kennedy were going to be properly famous, and I was in the middle of it.

I woke up in bed, feeling like I was dying of thirst. There was a mug next to me. I was on my own. I picked up the mug and took a gulp, but it wasn't water. It was white wine. I retched, then went back to sleep.

Later, Freddie was sitting on my bed. 'Come on,' he was saying. 'It's medicinal. Don't be boring.'

I took a sip and choked.

'Oh, Hazel,' he said. 'Come on. You're no fun at all.'

I woke up again because he was shouting.

'This isn't what I signed up for! I'm going back to London, doll. I can't do this any more.'

The next time I woke alone, opened my phone and trawled through everyone's exam experiences on social media. I read about their jubilation at the end of GCSEs. No one had messaged me apart from Phoebe, my mum and Greg. I checked Greg's, alarmed about being busted, but it just said, Congratulations on finishing your exams! Would be good to see you.

I tried to call for Freddie.

I woke again. I sat up in bed. I was thirsty and hungry and needed the loo and definitely wanted all the painkillers. Even though I was at the epicentre, I could tell that I smelled awful. The laptop was on the floor next to me and there was a book tucked under the duvet. I was hot, my hair sticking to my forehead. I coughed, and then kept coughing for a long time. I took a sip of the water beside my bed and it was stale, but at least it was water this time.

When the coughing passed, I called, 'Freddie?' but not loud enough for him to hear unless he happened to be on the landing. I looked for my phone, but couldn't see it, so I levered myself around and attempted to stand up. My head still pounded, there was a high-pitched ringing in my ears, and I sat back down with a bump.

OK. I needed to get to the bathroom, then find my phone. I crawled across the bedroom floor and noticed that all Freddie's stuff had gone.

Out on the landing I heard someone on the floor below. He was here! Of course he was. I took a deep breath, coughed and shouted his name as loudly as I could. There was silence, then footsteps on the stairs and there was Mum. I burst into heaving sobs when I saw her and she ran to catch me.

'Hazel! Hazel, oh, darling! What's happened? I thought you were at Greg's. You're sick? You should have said. Look how skinny you are! Who's Freddie?'

I closed my eyes. Freddie had left, but Mum was here. I lay back and let her take care of me. Even as miserable as I felt, the words *look how skinny you are* made me feel a tiny bit better.

A bit later, when I was clean and medicated and lying down in fresh sheets, she said, 'Hazel, darling. I don't want to worry you, but while you've been up here sick and out of it, do you think we could have been ... burgled?'

I didn't answer, but I felt it like dread in my stomach.

She carried on. 'It's just that there are a few things missing. I had some cash in a drawer. And a couple of smaller things – the vase, the Picasso print. God knows why anyone would want that. And a – a little glass ornament that was your father's. It was in my room. Do you know what's become of it?'

I shook my head. I couldn't tell her and she never mentioned it again.

35

'Venice'

We plough on, right into the fog. I'm half expecting to crash into the edge of the world like in *The Truman Show*, which Enzo and I watched a million years ago. It doesn't happen. We keep going through a tunnel of fog. There's nothing else: just the two of us in a world that doesn't seem to exist any more.

Me and a girl I want to cling to. Me and the only person in the universe who understands.

I'm focusing on this, on the moist air that surrounds me, on the engine thrumming and making the boat vibrate. On Kamila, my new unpredictable not-really-friend. On being here, now, wherever and whenever this is. I'm not focusing on the fact that Enzo and Phoebe were here after all because I don't want it to be true. It means everything I worked out about myself is wrong.

It means ... it means I have no idea what's been happening. And, oh God, it means that something awful did happen to Phoebe and Enzo. Phoebe did go into the tomb. Enzo did step off the roof.

No, no, no.

I take Kamila's hand. She lets me. With my other hand, I steer us into blankness.

The fog is all around. It becomes lighter, and I see the sun through it, and then we're emerging into bright light. I feel a grin spreading across my face. We've done it. We're somewhere else. This must be the real world, out of the Sotto Sotto thing. It has to be. I can go home. Kamila can go back to Australia. We'll keep in touch about our weird Italian experience, and I'll go and find real Enzo and Phoebe and check that they're OK and, no matter what, I'll make it up to them.

I look at Kamila with a big smile, but I don't see it reflected on her face. Then I follow her gaze.

We're heading towards one of those stripey wooden poles.

We're back in the middle of Venice.

We're back in the middle of Venice and I need to face this thing.

I stand on the bank of the canal and cry. I cry for my friends, my dad, my life. I can't get out. I want to go home and I can't get home because I think I'm . . .

'I'm so sorry.'

She has her arm round my shoulders. I shrug her off, but she hugs me tight and I like the way she smells and the way she feels, and I'm hiccuping on her shoulder and she's holding me.

'Sorry.' She whispers it this time, into my ear, which makes me shudder. This emotional mix is very confusing. 'I know how you're feeling, if that's any use. I've been feeling that way for . . . ages. I was having one of these moments when you met me.'

'I want to go home.' I whisper it. She hears because she's right there. 'I can't, can I?'

'I know, babe. I know. I wish I could take you there. But you'll be home, doll. You will. One day.'

I pull away. The word *doll* again is a sword to my guts.

'What? You will be home. I mean, we have to believe it, right?' says Kamila.

I look away. 'It's not that.' I close my eyes and my voice comes out quietly as I say, 'It's just that you called me *doll*. I was with someone who called me that and it was . . . It comes with bad memories. He'd always call me that, even when he was . . .' I can't say it. I stop.

'Oh God, I'm sorry! Right. Noted. No more doll, I promise. The word is henceforth banned. It's a weird thing to call someone anyway, right?'

I nod. I can't go there. I take her hand again. It's warm and comforting. Different from Freddie's. I came to see that Freddie held my hand to make sure I was always there, at his side. Kamila is holding it because she's my only human connection in this strange other universe. And she's hot.

We walk along the bank of the Grand Canal.

I remember feeling, before, that we could be in a game. That I might be an avatar, incapable of making my own decisions.

I realize, though, that I'm hungry, and that comforts me because it's a real, physical feeling. One that used to be complicated and which, in this weird world, isn't. A feeling that means I am, in fact, inhabiting my body.

'Can we get some food?'

She nods. 'Yeah. Starving. Good plan.'

We find a pizzeria in a square. The outside tables are covered in checked tablecloths. The building has a flowering creeper growing up it and pots of geraniums outside. When we sit at a table, the air around us smells gorgeous, and my stomach actually rumbles.

A waiter appears between us, but instead of bringing us menus he's brought us drinks we didn't ask for. A carafe of water, a carafe of what I think is white wine, and a glass of something fizzy and orange, complete with olive on stick, for me and something dark red for Kamila. He puts them all down carefully without looking to us or speaking to us.

This is weird.

'It's the fact that they never look at you,' says Kamila when he's gone, after ignoring our polite *grazie*s. 'When you're on your own. You just want one single person to look at you or talk to you, and they don't. That's the thing that kills me.'

The word *kills* rings out across the square. No one else looks round. I push it away, make an effort to ignore it. It's creeping closer, though. The suspicion.

'I was feeling that we were in a game,' I say. 'As if we were avatars. And people like that guy would be – what are they called? The people who are just there, but you can't interact with them?'

'NPCs,' she says. 'Non-player characters. You're right. It does feel like that.' She pours us both some wine. 'I hadn't thought about the fact that we could have fallen into a game. That's a new one. I mean, how would that even . . . ?'

'How would anything even?' Despite that sentence being grammatically horrible, she nods.

I drink the orange drink. It's Aperol Spritz: of course it is. I love it. I drink half of it in one go. I remember drinking one before, with Enzo.

I wonder when it all stopped being real. When Phoebe went into the tomb? Before? It's too tangled and I don't want to think about it. I just need to work out how to get away.

I close my eyes for a moment, half wondering if I'll open them and find I'm in Pizza Express with Greg and his new girlfriend, that I've imagined this whole thing to extricate myself from an awkward social situation. I open them, hoping for a Pizza Express pizza in front of me. Maybe my old order of the Veneziana, with its sultanas and capers, is the thing that made me imagine weird Venice. Though, by the time Greg was wanting to take us out for divorced-dad lunches, I'd have been asking for an undressed salad.

In fact, the food has appeared while my eyes were closed and there *is* a version of a Veneziana there, but it's bigger and has more things on it. I'm still with Kamila, still in Sotto Sotto Venice.

The food smells incredible. My stomach rumbles loudly, and Kamila laughs.

'Right?' she says. I look at her plate. Her pizza is covered in meat. She sees me looking and shrugs.

'Can't help myself,' she says. 'What can I say? Aussie farm girl.'

I drink the rest of my Spritz. It has three fast-melting ice cubes in it, and they clink together as I lift the glass.

The pizza is already cut into slices and I follow Kamila and eat it with my fingers, wiping them on my napkin when I need to, which is often. I let the food stay in my mouth and allow myself to savour the taste of it.

Food is amazing. Pizza is brilliant. I feel my eyes fill with tears at the truth of that, at things I lost sight of. I try to push the tears away, but it all crashes in on me again. The things I've thrown away. The things I can never get back. I sit and cry, and Kamila pats my hand, asking no questions, and then I wipe my face with my napkin and carry on eating and drinking.

I wish Phoebe and Enzo were here too. I'm sure Kamila would like them, and they'd like her. Then I remember what she said.

'Oh,' I say. 'You said *lovely Phoebe*. Why did you say that? Did you – did you meet her?'

'Oh yeah,' says Kamila. 'Yep. She was one of the ones who got away.'

'What do you mean?' This makes no sense.

She looks shifty suddenly. She turns away from me and picks up a piece of pizza crust.

'Oh, nothing. I mean, I saw Phoebe once or twice. Then she was gone. She got away. Lucky her.'

I look at her, knowing that she's holding something back.

'When did you see her?'

'I saw her in one of the big churches. Two or three times, and then she was gone.'

'What else?' I say.

'Nothing. There's nothing else. Come on.'

My mind is swirling like the horizon fog. I make an effort to let it go, for the moment. Phoebe jumped around in time like I did: she must have met Kamila on one of her trips. I remember Phoebe behind a pillar next to the Canova tomb, talking to a figure who slipped away. Was that Kamila? I rationalize it like hell, and then I let it go. I'm eating food with a girl I really like. A hot girl who was wary when we met, but who is my only human connection.

A hot girl who makes me feel I can be myself, even when she's moody. I feel calm with her. Relaxed. If she's snappy, I can snap back and she's not going to escalate it until I feel it's all my fault and apologize. For now, I decide, I will try to live in this moment, in this weird place, since there's nothing I can do to get away.

I will try to be happy.

36

For the next few days we just exist. Her barriers slowly come down. My barriers already seem to be down. With Kamila, I appear to have no barriers at all.

Vittoria's apartment is still there and I take Kamila to it. After that, we sleep in it every night, opening the window to let the cool air in, sleeping side by side in the double bed.

Sleeping closer and closer together.

Kamila allows me not to face this thing that I secretly know. With Kamila, I can live on the surface, feel happiness, look at the line of her neck and the high arches of her feet. I can watch her face as she sleeps and know that I'm not alone, and, even when she's not with me, I feel strong. We spend our days walking round the city, and talking about everything. Everything apart from what this place is, and what has happened to bring the two of us here.

One morning we're wandering around, talking, and I ask her more about growing up on 'the property', which I have found out is Australian for *massive, massive farm*.

'It wasn't so bad,' she says. 'I mean, we weren't that isolated. We could be in Alice Springs in a few hours, and at least there were pubs, cinemas, shops in Alice.'

'You had to drive a couple of hours to find a shop?'

'I know you've never been to Oz.' She grins and looks around. 'It's on a different scale from Europe, mate. When I came over, my first stop was London. It seemed the easiest, you know? I felt I knew London, from TV and movies and all that. I could not fucking believe it, H.'

I smile. Two pigeons land in front of us, and I wonder whether they're real pigeons, then tell myself to stop thinking about it. They are appearing in my mind as real and that's all that matters.

'Which bit of it couldn't you believe?'

'Well, first off the cold. So when I arrived in London it was early December. You know what I had in my head?'

'Snow? Movie snow?'

Kamila points at me. 'Correct. The famous White Christmas. Everyone knows you have them over there. I hadn't done much research: I just knew that it always snows in London at Christmas because I'd seen it on screen in the movies. Every. Single. Time. Snow and warm fires and roast chestnuts and goodwill. Yeah. It was pissing down and freezing, and I'd travelled in my shorts because I hadn't thought ahead to getting off the plane, and I'd bought skiing clothes for the winter because I genuinely thought they'd be useful, what with all that snow. I had to queue for over an hour just to show some grumpy twat my passport. After that, I was the girl getting changed in the Heathrow dunnies, pulling on my waterproof trousers, thinking of home, literally checking for the next flight to see if I could go back without even leaving the airport.'

I squeeze her arm with mine, as they're still interlinked. 'Was it OK, though? Christmas? In the end? I mean, did you have other clothes?'

'Yeah,' she says. 'It was actually fine. I went to stay with family friends, in a place called *Bristol*, and even though the weather was shit as heck it was fun. I stopped being homesick after a while.'

'Are you homesick now?'

She stops walking and thinks about it.

'Yes. I just tell myself that I'm going back one day. You'll get home too. Everyone else manages to leave the islands, so why not us, right? I mean, that's the attitude I try to have. As you've seen, I'm not always great at it.'

The idea that everyone leaves so we will too, to our separate lives on opposite sides of the world, immediately makes me feel better.

'Exactly. Why not us? Look, shall we – shall we just do that? Shall we just hang out together without thinking about the big things? We can help each other keep on and then see what happens. Sooner or later we'll go home.'

She gives me a side-eye. I do it back to her. Then we're both grinning.

'Yeah,' Kamila says, 'let's do it. I'd like that, Hazel. We can live in the moment.'

*

And so we walk and talk, endlessly, and she becomes the best company I could possibly have wished for. We talk about Venice. We talk about home. We talk about ourselves, our lives, our dreams. The only thing I don't talk about – the tiny enormous detail I leave out – is the relationship that has propelled me here. And she doesn't push me on it: she knows that there's something big, and she doesn't try to get me to tell her.

The thing with Kamila is, she doesn't pressure me at all.

We walk and walk. We talk and talk. She shows me things. I don't have much to show her since, compared to her, I've only just arrived.

'This is the railway station.' She gestures to a building next to us. When I look at it, I see that there are even trains there. 'Don't get excited. They don't go anywhere. This is where I arrived in the city, I think. Did you come by plane?'

'Yep. I don't remember it, though. Only vaguely. I'd – it had been difficult. A weird time.'

Am I ready to tell her? I might be coming close. Because she hasn't asked me, I think I might be able to say it.

And then we cross a bridge and it's there, right in front of us. I step back and look away.

'No way,' I say. There it is. I want to be sick. I can't go back there. I can't go close to it. 'Not that place. I'm not going anywhere near it.'

'Oh – Santa Maria glorious thing?'

She is looking at it with too much interest.

Phoebe, vanishing.

'Please don't go in.'

She looks round and smiles. 'I've been in loads of times. I didn't know its name. I spoke to Phoebe in here. She was cool. I saw *you* here. So this is where she went through a door into a monument and disappeared?'

I step back, and back again, and again. Kamila takes a step forward. I watch her getting closer to the church as I get further away from it.

'Don't!'

'Don't you think, though, that if there's a way out through here we should try it? Together? It's gotta be worth a go?'

While we've been walking, the sky has clouded over and now a drop of rain falls on my cheek. I brush it away. The tall doors are open, and Kamila takes another step across the paving stones towards them.

I know she's right. There's a way out, in here. But it's a bad one and we can't go there. I don't know how I know that, but I do.

I cannot lose Kamila like I lost Phoebe. Everything in me knows that she must not go anywhere near the door in that tomb. I run to her, through the rain that is starting to fall properly, and I grab her hand. She resists. We stand in the empty square and face off against each other. The rain drips down our faces.

'Why not, though?' she says. 'Don't you think it would be cool as heck to try it together? Whatever's in there – it might be the way home.' She pushes her hair back with her other hand. There are raindrops on her cheekbones.

'No. I mean, yes, but not there. Not through there, Kam. It was a bad place. We can't. You have to trust me.' I tug at her hand. She frowns at me. She is so hot: I could look at her face forever. We gaze into each other's eyes.

She softens. 'I do trust you.'

'Then please,' I say. 'Not in there. Please don't. It would be terrible.' I have no idea what I think is through there now, but every instinct I have is telling me to stay away.

After a moment, something changes in her eyes. She blinks and nods. We carry on looking at each other. We're still holding hands.

'OK then, Hazel,' she says. 'Since it means so much to you. Let's not. Let's stay here.'

I can see that she is saying this reluctantly and I pull her away from the church before she changes her mind. We walk across the bridge, round the corner, down an alley and come to another bridge, over a wider canal. We still seem to be holding hands. I stop on the middle of the bridge and lean on the railing to look at the raindrops falling into the water, spreading their concentric circles out. Kamila stoops to pick something up from the ground.

'You really follow your instincts, huh?' she says. She straightens up. 'I've lost that, I think. I've spent too long second-guessing everything. You're a bit of a – a breath of fresh air, Hazel Angelopoulos. So I'm going to follow an instinct of my own.'

She holds out something to me.

She's picked up a leaf. I can see the top of a tree, on the other side of a nearby wall. I take it from her. It's a wet leaf, but it's in the shape of a perfect heart.

'I just passed up investigating an exit from this place for you. Have my heart.'

Everything surges through me. Things I thought I would never feel again. Things I never have felt before, not properly, not like this.

The heart she gave me is wet. I fold it over and put it in my pocket with Cello. My two precious things.

'Thank you,' I say. I step towards her. The rain falls on us, around us, into the canal.

She leans towards me. I put a hand on her shoulder. She puts one on my waist. I tip my face up and she tips hers down and we kiss.

And nothing in any world
has ever been
like this.

37

Kent

1 December

It was my birthday. I woke alone in my top-floor bedroom, listening to the rain hitting my window. This was the first birthday I'd had in six years that wasn't going to start with Enzo jumping into the room and singing to me. I checked my phone. Nothing from Freddie: he wouldn't wake up for hours yet.

I stayed at Freddie's most of the time now, but I was here today because Mum was so desperate to see me on my birthday. It was easier to check in with her in the morning and go to London after college.

I hadn't seen Enzo properly for about nine months. We were doing different subjects at college, and if we happened to pass each other we would both look away. At times, I missed him with all my being, but I knew I had to get over it. Freddie was right: he wasn't my brother. He'd been a good companion when I was a lonely child, but now we had grown apart. He never came to the house: he was, as far as I knew, always at the flat with Greg.

Although it was nice, their place was small. This house was theirs. I sometimes wondered if they thought Mum and I had planned a long and brilliant eight-year heist to steal a house.

Hey, Dad, I said in my head. Then I said it aloud since there was no one here to witness it. 'Hey, Dad.' I waited for him to reply, but he didn't because he was dead. It was stupid, but I missed the version of Morris who used to hover around, watching over me in my head. I'd pushed him away to make space for Freddie, but now I wanted him back, just for a moment.

I forced his voice to say, *Happy birthday, Hazel.* Then he vanished.

Today I was going to go to college and concentrate in all my classes. That was, pathetically, my birthday present to myself. I would even go to extra maths and start to focus on the retake I had to do in a few months. Then I was heading to London.

Poor Mum still had no idea. Her thing in Oslo last summer had gone well and she was flying high at work. She barely came home from the office and we communicated mainly by text. I occasionally got away with pretending I was upstairs when I was fifty miles away in Kilburn, but I knew she'd actually be home on my birthday.

I jumped out of bed and headed to the shower, which was always clean now that Enzo wasn't here. I was seventeen today and I hadn't been this pleased about a birthday since I was six. It was Friday, which was perfect. I could see Mum this morning, then go and, for once, work hard at college for a few hours. I finished at two on a Friday anyway so I'd be in London by half three.

Freddie had made evening plans for us. We were less secret now, in his world, and with selected people in mine too. Freddie just told people I was nineteen and, as Enzo had once said, no one really cared. Even with the success Kennedy were having, no one seemed bothered about who, or how old, his girlfriend was.

I had a shower and went downstairs in my dressing gown with a towel turban on my head. For once Mum was waiting. She leaped up when she saw me.

'Happy birthday, darling!' she said, and she sang the song and it wasn't even embarrassing. We hugged.

'You feel very bony under there,' she said, stepping back. 'Are you eating enough?'

Bony. I loved that. I would savour it later.

'Yeah. Is there cake?'

'Oh, for a teenage metabolism. There is, but do you really want it for breakfast?'

She looked so happy. Mum was ready for work and I realized she was looking good. She'd had her hair cut into a sharp bob that made her look like Anna Wintour. She'd got the yoga and Pilates habit. She was, I saw, doing OK. I wondered whether she was going on dates. If she was, she hadn't mentioned it.

I realized what I was meant to be saying here.

'You look skinny yourself!' It was a few beats too late and she didn't look as pleased as I'd expected. I realized that *skinny* wasn't what she was after. 'Good, I mean. You're looking amazing, Mum.'

She grinned and touched her hair. 'Not too much? The trouble with having an actual haircut is that as soon as you've got used to it you have to go back and have it done again.'

'Not too much. Brilliant.'

She patted my shoulder as she went to the cupboard, coming back with a Colin the Caterpillar cake. She knew I loved them. I *did* want cake for breakfast. I also didn't. I had to eat it, partly to stop her worrying and also because I wasn't going to be back until Sunday night.

'Pass the knife,' I said, and Mum made tea, and I cut us both slices of cake for breakfast.

I put all thoughts of fat and sugar from my mind and savoured it. It was the best breakfast of my life. I had a second piece, a third. I couldn't stop. All of a sudden, I was starving. I looked at the rain splattering on to the French windows, and for a moment I wished I could just spend the day at home, with Mum. Going out in London tonight would take a massive amount of energy. At least I had sugar in my bloodstream now.

'Sorry this has happened,' she said, out of nowhere. It hung in the air, and for a second I didn't know what to say. I didn't bother to ask what she was talking about because I knew. I remembered my sixteenth birthday when I had only met Freddie twice, when Enzo had woken me up with a song, when Phoebe baked me a lemon meringue pie. Mum thought that stuff had stopped because of her divorce. I felt terrible for letting her think that, but honestly it made my life so much easier.

'It's fine,' I said. 'Really. Are you OK?'

I was seventeen and I felt very mature.

'Yeah,' she said. 'I suppose I wasn't, but I kind of am now.'

I wanted to ask what had happened between her and Greg. There was a lot we didn't talk about. We'd never discussed the things Freddie stole from the house after she mentioned them that first time. I knew he'd taken them. It made me sick with guilt. I'd tried to ask Freddie, but he'd just got angry that I'd accuse him of such a thing. I'd tried to steal them back, but they'd vanished.

'Shouldn't *we* be living in the flat?' I said.

'It's a guilt thing. Sooner or later he'll want to switch. Look, I feel terrible about you and Enzo. I thought he'd be back and forth, but he's not. I know you see each other at college and at Greg's, but I'm so sorry this has come between you.'

I knocked back the rest of my tea. 'Don't be. We're fine. We probably needed a break from each other. We're OK. Promise.'

'And . . . well, are you still seeing Lewis, darling? I mean, I know you stay out a lot and I'm not sure you're really always with Phoebe.'

She looked me in the eye. I looked away.

'I'm fine,' I said. 'It's not Lewis, no.'

'You don't have to tell me anything you don't want to. But just tell me you're safe and happy. You don't always seem . . . happy. You know?'

I forced myself to meet her gaze. 'I'm honestly fine, Mother,' I said. I heard the defensive edge in my voice, but couldn't stop it. 'I'm seventeen. You don't need to worry about me.' I thought of Freddie, of the way he slung an arm round my shoulders. The way he kissed me. The way he made me feel on a good day. And I grinned at her. 'Actually I'm really happy. I might – well, I might introduce you to someone at some point. He's a musician.'

Maybe I would! Maybe she'd be OK with it.

She stood up and kissed my head. 'A musician! What sort?'

I panicked. 'Classical.' That sounded safer.

'How fabulous. And he treats you well?'

I thought of the mood swings, the raised voice, the bruises on my arm where he grabbed me in the heat of the moment.

I thought of the moments that made it all worthwhile.

'Yes,' I said. My voice was shaky. I said it again. 'Yes.'

'What's his name?'

I panicked again. 'Harry.'

'I'd love to meet him, my darling. Just take care.'

Harry? Why had I said that? Why had I told Mum that I was going out with my boyfriend's dead brother? A brother we never spoke about, whose picture I still hadn't seen. I shuddered. I could never tell Freddie I'd said that, which meant I would never actually be able to introduce him to Mum.

Sixth form was different from school. Phoebe and I would have drifted apart anyway, even without Freddie. That's what I kept telling myself. As it was, she had ended up telling me to come to her any time I needed her and walked away. I'd never written in the 'Coursework Chat' that she'd set up for me. It lurked right down at the bottom of my chat list.

I got through lessons (art and resit maths) and opened various presents from my new friends. I'd managed to reinvent myself as someone cool, and the guys I hung out with here were different from my schoolfriends. They were people who, if you told them you had a twenty-seven-year-old musician boyfriend in London, said how brilliant that was and asked if I could introduce them to his friends (the answer was no: I was possessive over my London life). They were people who bought the Kennedy album, who hummed the single when they saw me coming, who made a big thing about being on the inside and not talking about me on social media. 'Hazy Girl' had done well, had been everywhere for a while, and although Kennedy weren't superstars yet they were on the way.

During the day, I kept thinking about the three slices of cake I'd had for breakfast. I would skip lunch but that wasn't enough. I needed to work it off.

I was walking towards my locker to get my weekend bag and run to the station when I saw something stuck to it. It was a card and a small package, attached with masking tape. I recognized the writing on the card and my first feeling was that I was glad I hadn't seen him. My second was more complicated, and I squashed it.

The card just said: *We love you H. Come back to us.* It was signed by Enzo and Phoebe. The package was a soft

Jellycat toy, a little bird with green and yellow wings and the cutest face I'd ever seen. I grinned at it in spite of myself and put it carefully into my bag. They knew I'd love it because they knew me. They knew me in a way that the people who had given me generic presents (albums I already had, chocolate I wouldn't eat) didn't.

A girl I didn't know well, Jade, had actually bought me the Kennedy single. 'It's called "Hazy Girl" and you nearly are too,' she said, smiling. She had no idea. I loved that, and I couldn't wait to tell Freddie. I did, however, miss my oldest friends.

I wanted to stick a thank you on their lockers, but I realized I didn't know where they were. I would text them later.

Freddie opened the door with a flourish. He looked like what he was: a successful musician. 'Hazy Girl' had been the hit they needed. It had changed everything. Well, not quite: they weren't planning on moving out of the Kilburn basement flat into anywhere nicer.

'*We'd move to* your *house*,' he'd said when I asked. '*But no, we're not. We need a lot more financial security before we can go anywhere. Sorry to make you carry on slumming it. I hadn't realized.*'

I'd tried to explain that wasn't what I'd meant at all, but he wasn't hearing me.

'Madam Birthday Girl!' he said now. He was hyper, happy, and I was relieved. I stepped into his arms. 'Look at you! Seventeen years old and slightly more socially acceptable for me. Happy birthday, doll.'

I followed him to the kitchen and he made me sit down while he opened a bottle of champagne. Their management had sent a case of it last week to celebrate the fact that 'Hazy Girl' was being used in two films and an advert. Someone had cleaned the kitchen, and it might even have been Freddie because, when he was in a good mood, those things occasionally happened.

'Cheers.' We clinked glasses. 'To my Hazy Girl. To us.' He paused. 'And, since no one else is here, to the people we miss. To Morris and Harry.'

I looked at him and my eyes filled with tears. 'Thank you.'

'Stay right there,' he said, and he disappeared and came back with a wrapped present. It was soft, clearly clothes, and I kissed him.

'Thank you so much!' I said. 'You didn't need to get me anything.'

'Ha. Imagine if I hadn't, though.'

I loved it when he was like this. His face looked different. It changed shape when he smiled. He sometimes said I was the only person who had ever made him feel happy. He once told me he hadn't been happy since Harry died, until he met me.

'What kind of a boyfriend would I be if I didn't get my gorgeous doll a birthday present?'

The most beautiful dress unfolded itself in my hands. It was dark red velvet, with an actual corset in it, and a slit up what I supposed would be the back.

'Oh my God,' I said. 'This is incredible!' I meant it.

But it was also tiny. Would I be able to get into it? I wasn't sure that zip would do up. I thought again about the three slices of cake.

'Lina helped me pick it out for you. Try it on!'

Lina came out of her room while I was passing the door, her new girlfriend Ulla with her.

'Hey,' said Lina. 'Happy birthday, Hazel! Hang on – stay right there.' She went back into her room.

'How old are you now?' said Ulla, when it was just the two of us. Ulla was much less glamorous than Lina and I thought Lina could do better. So did Freddie. 'Twelve?'

'Nearly.' I gave her a childish, insincere smile.

Then Lina was back, handing me a small package. 'From me and Ollie,' she said.

'Thank you!'

I opened it at once. It was a silver necklace with spikes on it, like barbed wire. I would never have thought to choose a thing like that, and I stared at it.

'It's for protection. It'll keep you safe.' She gave me a meaningful look and I looked away, feeling Freddie's eyes on us. 'I know it looks aggressive but it's not. Do you like it? I was going to get you art stuff, but then I saw this and I wanted you to have it.'

'I love it! Thank you so much!'

'Sounds like someone likes that present better than the one her boyfriend got her.' I looked round at Freddie. 'And art stuff, for God's sake? Hazel's not an artist.'

'That's not true,' I said. 'I mean, the first bit. I love the dress!'

'Fuck off, Freddie,' said Lina.

'Please,' Ulla suddenly added.

I hated myself as I squeezed into Freddie's dress. He stood in his bedroom and watched. I pulled it up and tried to compress myself into it, but the fact was it had an American size zero label in it and, despite all my efforts, I was not a size zero.

His voice rang round my head. *Hazel's not an artist.*

I turned round, miserable. 'Can you do it up?' I stared up at the ceiling, desperate and humiliated.

He had a go. I compressed my ribcage, but I was spilling over it. I knew I was.

'Not sure I can, actually. Sorry. I thought it would fit. Now I feel shit.' He stepped back. 'I feel *shit*!' He shouted the last bit.

I stared down at the floor and made a superhuman effort and pulled the zip up. I felt the seams stretching. Then I saw, poking out from under his bed, the edge of Mum's Picasso print.

He really had stolen it. I didn't even have the mental energy to be shocked.

I would get it into my bag and take it home with me, tell her I'd found it behind the sofa or something.

'There you go!' I jumped in front of him. 'It fits. And soon it'll fit better because I'll make sure it does.'

He was half mollified. 'You will?'

'Yeah. I promise.'

'Right. Good girl. I want to show you off. We're going out.'

I didn't want to go out. I wanted to stay at home, the two of us.

I didn't say so because I couldn't face the argument.

We were standing in a crowded bar. Freddie had found us a table round the corner at the back, but I couldn't sit down because of the too-small dress. So I was standing up, a full glass of vodka and Coke in my hand, while Freddie was at the bar getting more drinks.

The music was loud: it was too loud to talk really, and that was just as well because I didn't have anyone to talk to. I stayed in the shadows, silent, waiting.

I could see Freddie's back. I could tell from the shape of his cheek that he was smiling. I could see that he was chatting, but I didn't know who to.

I looked at the door. I could just leave. Though of course I couldn't. I had to stay. I took a sip of my drink and then another and another. It hit my empty stomach and made me feel better and better and better, and then I was texting Freddie to get me another one because the buzz the alcohol gave me made everything feel all right. I saw him take his phone out of his pocket and read the message. He turned to me, and gave me a huge smile.

'Good girl,' he said when he came back with my new drink.

I drank my way through the evening. It was easier like that.

38

'Venice'

Once we've kissed, I stop caring about anything else. This is everything I've ever wanted. I just didn't know it before.

She races through my bloodstream. Kissing is a different thing, with her, from anything it's ever been before. The past fades away to nothing. Kamila is soft, gentle, full of love. She is all I have, the constant in a weird world. I like her, I love her, I want her. We cling to each other.

And, whatever else is happening, this is real. These are kisses.

We walk to the next bridge and kiss again, and I can hear the rain falling in the canal, know that it's making its little circles there. When we pull away from each other and grin, I know now I have to tell her at least a bit about Freddie. I have to tell her, and then it will be gone.

When I let even a glimmer of him into my head, I feel the loveliness sour, just for a moment. I feel his hands going from soft to hard. The anger at myself for provoking him, for letting it happen. The possessive hands, the kisses that marked his territory.

'What?' says Kamila, and I feel like such an idiot, messing up something that is real because I was ambushed by a thing from a different universe.

I shake my head. 'Sorry. Nothing. You are amazing. I have a bit of baggage. Just realizing that I need to tell you if we're going to do this. If that's OK?'

She takes my hand. Our fingers interlace.

'Are you kidding me? I've been hoping you'd tell me your stuff forever. Go on. Hit me. I mean, I know it's the relationship with the guy you can't talk about. You've alluded to him a few times. I am well aware that it wasn't great for you, and weirdly, even from here, I want to track the bastard down and punch him.'

I grin at her. I wasn't expecting that.

'He ain't worth it.' I say it in an *EastEnders* voice, but of course it's a reference she won't get.

'Yeah, I'm sure he ain't but still. If anyone hurt you – and I can see that he hurt you a lot – they have me to answer to.'

We walk for a bit without talking. From time to time, I stop and kiss her because this is about her, and I do not appreciate Freddie's intrusion.

A while later she says: 'I already know, but humour me. You're bi, right?'

We're sitting on the edge of a canal, our feet dangling off the bank, not quite reaching the water. It's not raining any more. It smells of stone after rain. Our fingers are touching, the smooth stone beneath them.

'Yeah,' I say. 'But I've only had one real relationship, with the guy.'

'Honestly, H? That's one of the reasons why I was off with you a few times. I won't do it again, I promise. Never. But I thought you were straight. Thought I was going to spend eternity pining after you while you were getting over some guy who treated you like shit.'

Treated you like shit.

Yes. He did. For some reason her saying this out loud is so powerful.

'I always liked girls more. I had a massive crush on a girl in Year Ten.' I'm not sure if Australian school years are the same, so I clarify. 'When I was fourteen or so. Fifteen, before I met my ex. It was a bit much for me. Before that I'd fancied boys, and I thought it would be easier to be straight, you know? So I didn't go out with anyone for a while, and then I met Freddie. And that fucked my life right up.'

Much of the past is swirling and unreal, but I know the stuff that is inside me, and I see things, now, that I haven't thought about for a long time.

'I loved girls. But for a while the boy thing won out.'

'The rock guy?'

I wince. I thought I'd hardly told her anything about him, but I've clearly said that.

'If I did some crap psychoanalysis on myself?'

'Be my guest.' She leans over and kisses my cheek.

'I was fifteen when we met. Seventeen when we – well, when we broke up, although it wasn't a normal break-up.

282

It was less than two years of my life, and I think … well, you know about my dad.'

She looks confused and I realize I haven't told her about him either. I've held back so much of myself.

'OK, well, as you know my dad died when I was little and I don't think – I don't think I ever got to grips with it. So, sorry in advance for the biggest cliché ever, but I reckon a part of me was looking for an older guy and when this cool musician guy picked me out of the crowd that just won out over everything else.'

'You don't remember your dad dying, right? So you never believed it.'

I fill her in as best I can. 'Yeah. We were on a beach in Greece. He was pulled out to sea by a current, and I was right there, but yeah. I've got nothing. Just an occasional feeling of water on my legs. My mum has always tried really, really hard not to talk about him. I heard her once saying that if I knew the truth I'd blame myself.'

'Blame *yourself*?'

I shrug. 'Yeah. God knows what I did. And if she thinks I'd blame myself, it must mean there's a part of her that blames me too. I mean, it has to have traumatized her. Your life changing from one moment to the next because of something your little kid did.'

I stop and look this in the face for the first time.

'I mean, whatever I did, I took her husband away from her. She must have hated me.'

It hits me like a wrecking ball. It destroys me. This is the thing I've swerved away from for years. I probably started

283

going out with Freddie just so I wouldn't have to think about it.

Kamila is there. Arms round my shoulders, shifting me back from the canal, leaning me against a wall.

'Sweetie. You didn't *murder* him. You were a baby! Oh God, you poor thing.' She scoots right up to me and pulls me in so my head rests on her shoulder.

'Mum's great,' I say, savouring the closeness. 'But she's maybe not great at facing things. She keeps herself busy. I think I do that too. She's brilliant – a neuroscientist and totally obsessed with it.'

'Sounds like an awesome woman. Apart from the bit where she made you feel it's your fault.'

'She didn't make me feel that. I wasn't meant to hear. But motherhood wasn't the centre of her life. And I think I've always had an instinct, or memory or something, that fatherhood *was* central to my dad. He was the stay-at-home parent when I was little, and I love Mum so much and I respect her and all that, but I needed him too. And then he was gone, and it was like half of little-me went with him.'

'Do you think,' she says into my hair, 'that maybe that's why your mum remarried when she did? To give you that stability?'

'Yep.' My voice is muffled in her shoulder. 'Yeah. I bet you're right. That's why she married the single dad with the matching kid. So they could stick their half-families together to make a new one. Rather than because they actually loved each other.'

'And it sounds like it worked, Haz.'

I like her calling me Haz. It's new, and it has a hard edge to it that makes me feel cooler. It distances me from the stupid song and the horrible album. Not so long ago I thought those things made me the most special girl in the world. The memory makes me shudder.

'I mean, they did it for you and for Enzo, and it worked.'

'It did.'

We pull apart and I lean back on my hands. I look across the water. There is a bird on the other bank, staring at me. *Uccello*. Like my little bird, which is always with me.

'It worked, until I messed it up.'

Kamila shakes her head. 'Nope. It carried on working. You got into a relationship with someone who turned out to be a bastard, but you're allowed to make mistakes. Enzo will still be there for you, whether he was in Venice with you or not – and I saw him so I know he was. That means he's been in your corner all along, and, when we find a way out of here, you'll be in his when he needs you.'

I grin. 'How do you always manage to say the right thing?'

'I'm actually terrible for saying the wrong thing. Famous for it. Maybe I just get it right when I'm with you.'

Later we're sitting on the roof terrace of the hotel next to the apartment, the islands spread out below us. The sun is shining and we are eating afternoon tea because, when we came up here, it was just there, ready for us.

I'm wearing a dress I found in a cupboard in the studio. It's mustard yellow, the colour of the cardigan I wore on

285

my first date with Freddie. Kam looks beautiful in a bright blue trouser suit. She's like a dark-haired Tilda Swinton, tall and gorgeous. Although their colouring is so different, she is also like Lina. I think, *When it comes to women, I have a type*.

'When I look at you,' I say, 'I half think – more than half actually – that you're a healing thing my brain has invented. That it's my way of reminding myself that I was always drawn to girls more than boys. That actually the first person I noticed in the band at that gig was Lina, the drummer. I was watching her, and then Freddie caught my eye because he was pissed that I wasn't looking at him. And you and Lina – you're kind of alike.'

Kam puts a tiny cake into her mouth. 'I'm cool with that. I mean, I have no idea who this band are, but the drummer sounds like the only good one. I think the same about you, but for a different reason. You're on a self-discovery thing, and me – I was just really lonely, mate. Picture me.' She indicates herself with a sweep of her hand. 'Poor old me, sad and lonely, on my own for all eternity. Hanging out with people briefly before they left. In the gallery on my own, just overcome with loneliness. Trying to talk to people who all ignored me because they're NPCs. Losing the plot, sitting in that corner and just crying for my home, my family, for anyone to talk to. And there's a lightning flash and this gorgeous chick – the one I've been seeing around the place and trying to approach – suddenly she's there. Trying to comfort me. I worry that my Italian won't be up to it, and then when she starts talking it's in my own language. You were too good to be true. That was why I didn't dare go all in.'

I stare at her. 'Did that happen?'

'Not the lightning flash, though it should have done.'

We both look out at the huge sky over the water. It crackles with lightning and rain pours down on us. We stand up and run for the doorway. Kam shouts over the rain that's bouncing off the flat roof in front of us, that's destroying what's left of the food. 'Ha. Like that. But otherwise, yeah. I wished for you, and there you were.'

'There I was,' I echo.

I lean forward, pouting exaggeratedly for a kiss. She leans in and puts one, gentle as a butterfly, on my lips.

More days have passed and I think maybe this is it. Maybe, whatever is happening here, wherever I am, this is my happy ever after. Me and Kamila, in some version of Venice, the City of Love.

'Is Venice the City of Love?'

I have asked this before, I know I have, but I can't remember when or to whom. We are lying in bed in the studio. It's been raining all night and we have the window open. It smells of the morning-after rain. I am lazy, ready to spend today doing absolutely nothing.

'That's Paris, babe,' she says. 'I think. Isn't it?'

'Oh yeah. Maybe. Well, Venice is mine.'

'You know it.' She props herself up on an elbow. 'How long do you think it's been, since we met?'

It's hazy in my head. I have no idea. I've lost track of everything.

I try to come up with an answer. 'Maybe a week? Month?'

'You're not bored of me?'

'Are you kidding?'

She grins. 'Just checking. Come on, Haz. Let's go and get breakfast. How about this: we take it out on the boat and have a picnic, maybe back on Torcello? Under the sun. After the rain. With Venice in the distance. What do you think?'

'I think yeah.' I don't mind what we do.

I should have said no.

39

We speed across to Torcello in our little *Uccello* boat. I still have my Uccello bird: I showed her to Kamila and told her that she was from an old photo of my dad, and she was as delighted as me, so now the bird is ours together. Cello is the symbol of the happiness we've made in this weird place.

I feel that Kam and I are two parts of a whole. We fit together in every way. I don't have to second-guess anything with her. I don't have to pretend, or to work round her feelings. Sometimes we mildly argue, and then we get over it. I kind of knew that this was the way things were meant to be, but I had no idea that it would feel so easy when you found the right person.

And my happiness with her means that I've been able to shove the problem of *what this place is* and *why we are here* right to the back of my mind, where it belongs. I don't miss Mum so much. I don't miss Phoebe and Enzo so much. I never look at my phone because there's no point. There's nothing I can do but hope that I'll see them again one day.

A woman at a cafe gave us two cups of coffee and a paper bag, which I'm hoping contains breakfast. I hope the coffee's staying hot because I'm too busy concentrating on driving the boat to drink it. I always do the driving. I like being that person. I haven't felt capable for ages. Ever.

Kamila is watching me and I like her expression.

'What?' I push my hair back off my face.

'Just you. You're different. I love it. Will you show me how to do that later?'

'How to do what?'

'The boat.'

'Sure. It's easy.'

She leans over and kisses me. My hair whips around in the breeze. The boat zigzags while my focus is elsewhere and we both laugh at it.

'I want to zip round the lagoon like you do, Haz,' she says.

After a moment, I say, 'If we go back to our old lives – what if we don't see each other again? What if we don't live in the same . . . universe?'

Kamila reaches for my hand and says: 'This is why we live in the moment.'

She sits beside me and I show her how to steer the boat.

I have no idea how I know which of the many, many islands in the lagoon is Torcello, but I do. I drive past the cemetery island, the one where they grow vegetables, a ruined house on its own little island, and Murano and Burano and then we're there. Kamila leaps out and ties the boat up, then holds my hand as I jump on to the bank.

'How do you do the knot?'

She shows me. 'I'm used to tying up animals.'

We sit on Attila's Throne, together this time, squeezing in side by side. We go up the bell tower, and then we go down and ring its bell. We sit on the grass beside the church and have our picnic. The coffee has gone cold, which is weird. Normally things stay the way you need them to be. The croissants are a little bit stale, and the fruit is overripe.

That's unsettling.

We go into the church and look at the mosaics.

I didn't do that last time and I wasn't expecting the centrepiece to be the Last Judgement. It startles me. It's huge, with a golden backdrop. The idea of people constructing it piece by piece, a thousand years ago, blows my mind. Worse, though, is the subject matter.

Death, death, death. I can't look away. The bottom right shows hell, with flames consuming sinners, and skulls with worms in their eyes. It's much more interesting than the heaven part. I stare and stare at it until Kamila pulls me away, and I'm glad that she does.

I feel different today. Something is wrong.

It's a relief to get outside again, and I push the strange feeling away and tell myself I'm exhilarated to be back in the sunshine. We treat the rest of the island as our playground because it is. We kiss up against a tree. We lie on the grass. I climb a tree and Kamila worries that I'm going to fall out, but I don't. Then, when the sun is starting to slip down the sky, we wander back to the boat.

'Right,' she says, climbing in, 'my turn to drive. What do I do?'

I stay on the bank and start to untie the rope.

'Turn the key,' I say, and the engine roars to life. I unwind the rope. 'You're going to need to pull that lever there, and then, when it starts moving, you'll get a sense as to how to make it go faster or slower. It's really straightforward actually.'

Before I can jump in, she pulls the lever and the boat moves off. We both laugh.

'Come back!'

'I'm trying, babe. Hang on, I can't go backwards. I'm going to do a loop around and come back for you. How do you steer it again?'

'Turn it to the right. There. That's it!'

I throw her the rope and she catches it and drops it into the bottom of the boat. She steers away from the bank, and I watch the boat zigzagging around as she works out how to steer it.

'Got it!' she shouts. 'This is fun. Coming for you.'

But she doesn't. I see her trying to pull the boat back, and see it resisting. She lets go altogether and flaps her hands at me. She waves her arms above her head, needing help. I don't know what to do.

'Hazel!' she shouts. 'What's happening?'

I jump into the water and start to swim after her. I swim faster than I've ever gone before. I've never been much of a swimmer and I can't get close. I wish I'd learned to swim properly, to do a fast front crawl. Because of Morris, I had never enjoyed being in water.

The boat straightens up and carries her away from me, even though she's not touching it. I look around, frantic. There's another boat a little way off. I climb, dripping, out of the water, and jump into it and start the engine. My heart pounds as I follow her. I watch *Uccello* going into the mist, and I hear Kamila's voice on the still air, and I point my new boat towards her and follow. I shout, 'Kam! I'm coming! I love you!'

I drive into the mist and through it for a long, long time. When I come out, I'm in the Grand Canal, exactly as we were before. I see the striped poles ahead, the flat faces of the buildings. I see our apartment and the hotel next door. I see everything that looks like home to me these days.

Everything except one thing.

Our boat isn't here. I tie mine up as best I can and sit on the bank of the canal and wait. We always end up back here: she'll come.

Then I remember the things that have been different about today. The coffee that went cold. The stale pastries, the squishy fruit. The Last Judgement.

After a while, I go to the studio, but she's not there. I remember Phoebe disappearing. I feel the same but worse. I run up to the roof and remember Enzo flying away. I look out of the window. I walk up the entire length of the Grand Canal and down the other side. I go back to my boat and sit and wait, and wait, and wait. It gets dark. It gets cold. I sit there all night because I cannot face the truth. I can't give up. She's going to arrive, I know it. She is.

But it gets light again. I stare at the misty horizon, but she doesn't emerge. I take the boat back over to Torcello, but she's not there either.

*

Three days later I can't hide from it any longer. Kamila has done the thing that she always said I would do to her. She's left me.

First Phoebe

then Enzo

and now Kam.

Kamila is the love of my life. She healed me.

I hear her voice in my head: *People always leave.*

They always leave.

I have been so happy and now I'm on my own, and everything turns to shit. I didn't need to be with Kamila all the time. She made me see that I was all right as I was, that I was capable, and I wish I could hang on to that feeling now that I'm alone. We had a magic world that existed outside of space and time. I think of the people in the mosaic of the Last Judgement being cast one way or the other. I had been in the lucky section, and now I'm thrown down to the flames.

Winter descends on Venice overnight. Winter clothes appear in Vittoria's apartment, and I wear them. Big jumpers, warm boots. I don't care. Sometimes I go out in summer things just so I feel the cold.

I sense myself losing my grip on reality, and I didn't have one to begin with because the place where I'm living isn't reality, and I can't do it on my own and I know really, but I just can't think it because, if I do, every single thing is going to unravel. I let the city around me do what it wants. I don't care.

I set off from Torcello every day, trying to follow Kam. I always steer the boat into the mist to the exact spot I last saw her, but it never works. I always end up back in the same place: on the Grand Canal, by the apartment, alone.

I don't know how many times it's got dark and light again. Maybe five, maybe ten or more. I stop going back to the studio and just walk around. Every time I'm exhausted and need to sleep, a place appears. One night I sleep on a boat, a thick blanket pulled over me. I wake up moored in a different part of the city. Another night I sleep in a house: I'm walking past, so tired I could fall over, and there's an open door with a light shining out, and, when I get in, there's a mattress on the floor and a pile of bedding. I sleep in the places the city offers me, and I don't question a thing. I don't give a shit what's happening or why I'm here because I know I can't look it in the face. Everyone else has got out and I'm the only one left. I lost Phoebe, then Enzo and then Kam. *Everyone always leaves.*

I realize I don't even see passers-by any more. There are none of the NPCs, the non-player characters who would either ignore us or give us something we needed. Even they don't exist any more. I'm completely on my own.

The city gives me food and drink when I need them, but there's no pleasure in any of it any more. The one thing it won't let me have is the thing I crave: company.

One morning I go into a restaurant. There's a bowl of porridge, so I eat it, drink the coffee and water that are next to it and leave the empties on the table. I look around for someone, for anyone, even if they're not real, but the whole place is empty and I am so lonely, so scared. I want to give up but I can't, because if I give up nothing will change.

If I give up, I will still be here.

If I give up, I'll be here, miserable and hopeless.

On the other hand, if I keep looking for a way out, then sooner or later I'll find one. *People always leave.* I am a person. I will leave. And the more I keep looking, the sooner I'll find my way out of here.

I dig deep inside myself and find some strength I didn't know I had. I think of Kamila encouraging me to drive the boat. She made me happy to be strong, to be myself.

I grab a piece of paper and a pen, and I make a plan.

I have divided up the city into zones and I'm trying to be methodical about this. I decide to start with the obvious exits and head back to the train station: there are trains at the platforms and I sit on each of them in turn, for as long as I can bear it. The seats scratch the back of my legs. The engines don't start. Eventually, after hours, I get off again, and when I've done that with every train I leave. On my way through the streets, I stop when I see a blue T-shirt flapping on a washing line. I get as close as I can and see that it's a Doctor Who branded one.

It's what the souvenir guy was wearing. The one that Morris might have worn in an old photo.

I get as close as I can. I have to climb up the outside of a building to get to it. I stand on a window sill, reach to the top of a shutter, haul myself up. I don't care if I fall. I get to the next window up, and the one above that, teetering, not even scared of the height. In fact, I welcome the danger.

When I get to the line itself, I yank it so hard that it snaps. The T-shirt falls into the canal and I climb down, wade into the water (which is only up to my thighs) and fish it out. When I've dried it in the sun, I put it on.

I climb into my boat and head towards the horizon, but I just end up back where I started. I try a different bit of horizon each day, but it never works. I try to channel Kamila's voice, telling me I can do anything.

I try to talk to my Cello, but she's just a glass bird and I feel stupid. Even though I'm wearing the same T-shirt as the guy who sold her to me, I feel our connection fraying. I want to see that guy. I think he would understand.

Mostly I want Kam, but I want Mum too. I want everyone. I would take any company right now.

This, I think, is my personal hell. This is as bad as it gets.

After it's been going on for what might be weeks or months, I know that I can't do it any more. One wintry morning, I run up all the steps (there are 323) to the top of the bell tower at St Mark's. When I get to the top, I look down at the stone pavements below, and I pull the safety barrier aside and sit on the window ledge. Maybe, like Enzo, I'll escape this way.

I look out. I feel like a fly in this city's web, but it's still beautiful. The huge square. The rooftops. The glistening water. City of Love.

I can't be here.

I shuffle forward and push myself off.

I'm standing on the ground.

I try again: I try to follow Enzo off the apartment roof, but it doesn't work. I try to escape by boat again and again and again, but I always end up back where I started.

I stop caring what I look like. Sometimes there are clothes in the sleeping places and, when there are, I put them on.

I go to the Frari and walk into it because the other horrors have long overtaken this one. I try again and again to go into Canova's tomb, but most days I can't even find the church, and when I can I climb the railings and walk into the tomb like Phoebe did, but it's just a cold, dark room with a locked box that I guess contains a sculptor's heart, and no exit. I give up, and realize that giving up is exactly the same thing as trying to get out. They both look the same.

I've got nothing. I've lost my friends, my family.

A bad relationship and a wonderful one.

My father, my mother, my stepfather.

My future.

I messed up my exams, which messed up my future plans, and then I messed up Year Twelve and now I'll never go to university. I think of the people in the Last Judgement mosaic and know that I'd prefer the flames and the worms to this. At least the burning people had company.

I'm alone, and I'm crap at being alone, and I think I'm going to be here forever.

Is this it?

Something moves next to my leg. I gasp, thinking it's a rat, but it's not and even if it was a rat I'd welcome it. I'd ask it to be my best friend. That's how pathetic I am. I feel it squirming and wriggling, working its way free, and then there's my bird, my Cello, hovering in front of my face. I reach out for her and she lands on my fingertip.

This makes me laugh out loud because it means I've lost my mind completely. I need company so much that I've brought my bird to life. And that's fine. Right now it feels like the best thing I've ever done.

'Hey – can you talk?' My voice feels weird. I don't think I've used it for a long time.

She flutters away. I try to make her talk, but it doesn't work. The light shines through her and makes rainbows on the diamond flagstones. I stand up, and I follow her out of the church.

40

London

March

I was sitting at the basement kitchen table in Kilburn with three drinks in front of me, waiting.

One was peppermint tea. One was water because I'd needed it for a headache tablet. The third was vodka, to perk me up. My head was pounding, but I kept sipping my drinks. One, then the other, then the other. I was fine. This was fine.

'Does he hurt you, babe?'

I jumped and looked up. Lina was in the kitchen doorway, looking at me. I didn't like the fact that her eyes saw everything, and I turned away.

'No,' I said.

I rubbed my arm. He didn't hurt me. He just held me too tightly sometimes. He was strong, and he was emotional. It wasn't his fault. I loved the fact that he was strong. I loved it that he was emotional. He wouldn't be Freddie if he wasn't.

'Babe,' said Lina. My head was fuzzy, but even so I knew that once I would have loved her calling me that. Now I wanted her to leave me alone. 'Babe, I can't do this any more. Look at you. Ollie and Ulla and I can't sit back and watch this happening to you. Please get away from him. Look what he's done to you.'

I shook my head. 'He hasn't! He didn't do this to me.'

'Whatever. The relationship is bad for you, if that's easier to hear. Look at yourself, Hazel! What are you doing right now?'

She walked over to the cupboard, took out some slices of sourdough and dropped them into the toaster. It was OK for her. She sweated it all off when she was drumming, or stretched it all away doing yoga.

I realized she was waiting for me to answer.

'Like, nothing? Drinking peppermint tea, waiting for Freddie?'

'Drinking peppermint tea, plus whatever is in those other two cups.'

I picked one up. 'Water.'

The toast started to smell amazing. It turned my stomach.

'You know this can't last? You know he's not your future. You can do a million times better.'

'You don't understand, Lina.' I looked away. I heard the scrape of a knife on toast and I knew it would be peanut butter. I wanted to be sick. 'We have a really deep thing. No one else gets it.'

She sighed. 'Sorry to be cynical, babe, but *you* might have a really deep thing going on. I like you, Hazel. I hope that one day, when you're out of this, we'll stay in touch.

We could be friends. But yeah, *you* have a deep thing or whatever. He doesn't.'

'But it's Harry, Lina. It's Harry that started it.'

She paused. 'Really?'

'Yes. That's the –'

I stopped because I heard a key in the door. It was either Ollie or Freddie, and if it was Freddie there was no way he could find me in the kitchen talking to Lina about Harry. That would be a massive betrayal. My heart beat faster. We both waited, though I knew it was Freddie as soon as he slammed the door, and I knew from the strength of the slam that he wasn't happy. My stomach turned.

Lina put a plate on the table and pushed it towards me.

'Always here for you,' she said. 'Him? Not so much.'

She vanished and I had a sudden moment of insight: I knew that she was going to leave the band. I could sense it in her. Kennedy would break up just when they'd had a hit, and it would be because of me.

'Hey,' said Freddie. His eyes were wild. 'What's this? Toast?' He picked it up and ate it.

'Hey,' I said. I stood up and went to kiss him, but he recoiled.

'You been drinking?'

I grinned and gestured at my three drinks. 'This one's peppermint tea. This one's water. This one might be vodka.'

Freddie, who had clearly been drinking too, made a face at me. 'Drinking on your own? That's not cool, doll. Not sure you need the buttery toast either.'

I heard the front door close. Lina was out, and that meant that only Freddie and I were home. That was good.

He left the room. I followed.

'I didn't make the toast. Lina did.'

He turned to me. 'Right. Look, I'm going back out because you're a mess. I don't care about the toast. It's the vodka – really not a good look for you, doll. You'd better sleep it off.'

His face was hard and he wasn't looking at me. He picked up a few things and strode to the front door. I followed him, hating being this person, but somehow unable to stop. He opened it. I tried to leave with him.

It happened fast. He said, 'Get away from me, Hazel. You're an embarrassment.'

He turned and shoved me back inside. I wasn't expecting it at all, and I fell over, landing hard on my hip. Then the door was closed and I heard him double-locking it.

I sat on the floor. I shifted over so I was slumped against the wall. I looked at the posters and drawings that papered it. They were dirty and scuffed.

Had he just shoved me?

Right over?

He had, and even I couldn't rationalize it away this time. I rubbed my hip. It really hurt.

I saw the reviews of the single that had been added to the wall since I first came here. I saw the words *catchy*, *fresh*, *ubiquitous*. I saw my name, a version of my name. I couldn't pull my thoughts together. I tried to find my dad's ghost to help me because, after all this time, I needed him.

He was nowhere. I even tried to summon Harry, but he wasn't there either. I was on my own.

After a while, I managed to stand up, wincing. I found a pen and, in a corner of a tour poster, I wrote, in very small letters, I hate you. In another space, I wrote Freddie. I remembered how I used to love drawing, and I found a blank space and drew a picture of the sea. Big waves, a stormy sky. The picture that I always used to draw, that I had never made into a painting.

I added a little child walking into the water. A man running after her.

I stood back and looked at it. He'd never notice any of it. I wanted to draw more. I wanted to scrawl all over everything. He had pushed me over. I was drunk. I couldn't do this any more. I hated him. *Hated, hated, hated.*

I looked through his room for the photo of his brother that he'd never shown me, and in the end I found a picture of a little boy under a pile of paperwork. It didn't say anything on it, but I knew it was Harry.

A little boy of maybe ten or so looked at me, out of the past. He was blond and cute, wearing jeans and a too-big sweatshirt, standing leaning against a tree. This boy looked a bit like Freddie and a bit like Ollie. This was Harry. I stared at him for a long time, until I started to cry. I put the photo back exactly where I'd found it. I felt bad for going through Freddie's things, but probably not as bad as he'd like me to feel.

I put my boots on, tucking the laces inside because doing them up was too fiddly for my clumsy fingers, and decided to go home. But I couldn't because I couldn't open the door, because he'd locked me in.

I tried all the windows, but none of them opened wide enough for me to get through, even though I had made myself into the smallest person I could be.

I sat on his bed and wailed.

41

'Venice'

The little bird takes me straight to the Frari church. I don't care about anything now, so I follow her in. I was in that church when the first of the people I love left me. The tomb with the heart in it has powers, and I don't know what they are, but anything that takes me away from here will be fine by me. No new place could be worse.

I stop on the threshold, remembering Phoebe and the tomb, but Cello flaps round my face, darting in and out of the slightly open door. It's different because it's bright in there. Then I hear very quiet music, and the idea that there might be someone inside playing it is too much for me. The music is Vivaldi or something, and even if it's a recording someone must have pressed play on it. I haven't heard music for far too long.

I walk in. The church is lit up. There is (of course) no one in there. I follow the bird to Canova's tomb, not scared of this stuff any more. I climb the railing, walk up the steps and through the door. The moment I'm through, the door slams behind me and the light changes. It's as if someone turns it on, except that it's not that. I'm in a different place.

Phoebe said: '*It was dark and then light, like the sun was starting to rise. Something was about to happen. There was something stretched out in front of me and it didn't have an end. It was weird but it felt ... good.*' And I know at once that that's where I am. I look for Cello, but she's gone. No, I put a hand in my pocket and there she is. Still, smooth, a cheap souvenir. Not alive any more.

It's hot. The sun is bright. This is where Phoebe came. I yell her name. I shout it into the wide blue sky.

'Phoebe! PHOEBE!' Then, just in case, I shout, 'Kamila?'

I look down and see that my clothes have changed. I've been wearing the Doctor Who T-shirt for days, weeks, and I still am, but now it's clean, and I'm wearing it over the yellow dress I wore with Kamila once, for tea on the roof. My legs are bare, and so are my arms.

Does this mean Kamila's here somewhere?

I turn back to the door, but there's nothing there. I look down at my feet. I'm wearing sandals, but underneath them it's sand. I'm on a beach.

I see a figure in the distance, standing on the sand. It must be Phoebe: it has to be. I start to run, but my sandals trip me up and I fall flat on my face. I kick them off, scramble back to my feet and run to her, yelling her name as I go. I want to hear everything that's happened, to tell her my story, my revelations. I want to tell her that I am entirely over Freddie, that I can say his name and think about him without cracking up. That I hate him. That I have fallen in love properly, that I understand now, and that I've lost everyone.

If I can find Phoebe, I can find Kamila too.

I run and run and run. My legs hurt and my breathing is weird, but nothing matters.

'Phoebe!' I shout. The wind takes my voice and blows it away.

As I get closer, I see that it's not Phoebe at all.

It's a man. I slow down and stop while I'm far enough away to escape if I need to. He's older than me, and he's not Enzo. I'm almost sure he's not Freddie. He's older than that.

He could be Freddie, though, and that stops me in my tracks. What would be worse than being stuck on my own for the whole of eternity? Being stuck here with Freddie, that's what. I'm ready to run back, back to the church, back to my miserable life of craving company and trying to get out.

But I don't run.

He's looking at me. He's not Freddie. He's someone completely different.

I know his face. And I watch him working me out at the same moment. Then he runs towards me and I run at him as hard as I can.

The first person I lost. The original. The thing that was my fault – the man I've missed every single day of my life.

'Dad,' I say, and I'm not sure whether I've said it out loud or in my head. I look at him and I say it again. 'Dad.' I've always called him Morris. Or 'my dad' or 'my real dad'. I don't think I've called him Dad since I was a tiny kid.

He's in front of me now. He looks into my face and I look into his.

'Hazel,' he says. 'My Hazel? Is it you?'

I reach out and touch his arm. He feels real. But he's dead.

It overwhelms me.

I'm in a weird place with my dad. He feels real but he's dead.

I feel real.

I've been in a weird space for a very long time.

It falls into place.

I've known it for a long time really. I just managed not to face it.

The man in front of me is Morris Angelopoulos. His hair is black, his beard is big and dark, and he has my eyes. My nose.

It's him. I'm with my dead dad, in the place where he lives now, which is a beach. I step forward and hug him, and he's still there. He's solid: he doesn't melt away. He holds me close and I've missed this so much for the past fourteen years that I never want to let go. I remember the smell of him. Everything about Freddie, Mum, Greg – everything that happened at home – fades away. All I need is my dad. Morris Angelopoulos.

He sits on the sand and I sit beside him. We look out at the sea, which is right there.

'Where is this?' I say.

'The beach,' he says.

I realize which beach and I don't want to ask so I don't. When I look at him, he's staring at me, taking me in. I smile at him.

'It's you. Oh, Hazel. My baby. Look at you! What's happened? Why are you here?'

'Dad?' I want to say that word forever. I smile at the way that tiny word has changed the whole universe. 'I mean, I have some questions.'

'Yeah. I can imagine.'

I take a deep breath and I say it.

'OK, so – am I dead?'

He doesn't answer. I listen to the waves lapping at the sand. I feel the sun on my bare arms and I wait for him to talk.

'You might be.'

'I thought I was on holiday,' I say. 'And then everyone left. I met someone and I fell in love with her. And I was so happy. And then she disappeared and since then I've been . . .'

He shifts up and puts an arm round my shoulders.

'You've been what?'

I inhale deeply. 'On my own. It's been hell, Dad.' I feel it bubbling up inside me. 'Did I go to hell because it was my fault? It was my fault that you died? That's why I've been on my own all this time?'

'What?'

It was hard enough to say it the first time and I know he heard. Instead I stare at my arm. It looks like my arm. I touch it. It feels like my arm. I sense the touch both with my fingertips and on my arm.

I turn it over. There had been a couple of bruises there, where Freddie grabbed me. There are no bruises now. The hairs on my arm, the Greek hairs that spoke to the heritage that I'd lost when I lost Morris, that I shaved off when I was with Freddie, they were back, and I was glad.

'You think it was your fault?' He is looking me in the eye. 'Please tell me you don't think that.'

I gaze out at the flat horizon of the ocean in front of us. 'If this is the afterlife, when did I die?'

'Hazel, baby?'

I turn to him. 'Mum never told me exactly what happened. It became a thing we didn't talk about. She said you'd died when we were on holiday, taken by the current, and that was it: no more details. And then I heard her telling – telling someone that if I knew the full story I'd blame myself. And so, I guess, I do blame myself. And then – well, I was seeing someone who made me feel bad about myself. And I know that hasn't helped.'

'Who?'

'A guy called Freddie. The worst thing that ever happened to me.'

'What did he do?'

I look out at the water. 'Bad things. But I got away. Let's not talk about that. Mum's doing OK, considering, you know.'

'Oh, how I miss Susie. I've missed the two of you. Did she never tell you the whole story?'

'Never.'

'My Hazel. One of the great disappointments in being dead is that you don't get to go and hang around as a ghost. I've wondered about you all the time.'

I raise my voice. 'I talked to you a lot. I imagined you were there. It would have been so great to find out you really were.' I stop, think about how I acted over the past couple of years and reconsider. 'Actually I'd be pretty horrified if you witnessed anything.'

'Well, I tried but it's not possible. You can see how far this is from that kind of world. How many levels you go through to get here. But I did – I did manage to see you, I think, in an in-between place. I sold you Susie's little bird.'

'That was *you*?' An in-between place, he called it.

'In a way. I know he didn't look like me. It's complicated.'

I think about the levels. The one that felt normal with time glitches. The one without Phoebe and Enzo, when I thought I was on holiday on my own. The one with Kamila. The one without Kamila. I have so many questions about the in-between.

I'm opening my mouth to ask them, when Dad says: 'I'm not sure how long we've got, darling, and we need to talk about what happened when you were three. That's the most important thing. For you to know the true story.' He strokes my hair, tucks it back from my face.

'You drowned.' I realize I haven't said that to anyone, ever. I've always stopped at 'he died'. Sometimes people pressed me on it because if someone dies young everyone wants to know what happened, but then I just say 'a current took him at the beach'. The word *drowned* has always been too much for me.

'Do you remember any of it?'

My breath catches in my throat. 'Sometimes . . . ?'

I don't want to say it. Then I do because I'm on some afterlife beach with my dead dad and a part of me is expecting to wake up any time.

'Sometimes I have the feeling of seawater.'

'Oh, darling. I'm not surprised that Susie's sheltered you from it. We were happy, you know? When you find the right person, you know it, and Susie was my perfect other half. And we had you, and you were everything I ever wanted, Hazel. You and your mum. The three of us. We might have had another child. We were talking about it. But we were perfect just the three of us.'

I can't speak. I just nod.

He takes a deep breath. 'We were on holiday, in Greece, as you know. One of the islands.'

'I'd been wondering if it was actually Venice.'

'No, baby. I think it'd actually be pretty hard to drown in Venice. Someone would fish you out. There are no waves and you'd never be far from the bank. This was back home. We were staying with my father's family on Syros. Have you and Suze been back?'

I shake my head. I think of the birthday cards that arrived from Greece, of the polite messages I occasionally sent in return.

'Yeah, it would have been hard for her. So there was a storm, and we were staying out of the water because the waves were huge, which is unusual down there. Susie and I were chatting away while you made sandcastles, and suddenly we realized you weren't there. You'd put down your bucket and spade and gone for a paddle, and we hadn't seen. So I did what any parent would have done.'

'You went after me.'

I look deep into my memories. Seawater on my legs. Big waves.

For a second it's there. Excitement at the huge waves, then water crashing on my head, forcing me down. A shout. A hand round my wrist.

It dissolves and there's just blankness.

'You saved me,' I whisper. 'You saved my life, and . . .'

He moves over, turns his back on the ocean, crouches in front of me so that I have to look him in the eye.

'And I would do it again tomorrow,' he says. 'And every day, over and over again, for every lifetime. Hazel? I have no regrets about that at all. I saved you. Best thing I've ever done.'

I let him hold me. I collapse on to him. I realize that Mum was right. Freddie was right. It *was* my fault. My dad died, and everything fell apart, and it was my fault.

'It *wasn't*,' he says softly. He's reading my thoughts. How is he doing that? 'Hazel? I need you to understand this. It wasn't your fault that this happened. And Susie has never told you it was either. She would never have said that. Three-year-olds have no idea. It was our fault. Mine and your mum's. Can you imagine? A stormy sea, no lifeguards, definitely not safe to go into the water. And we just sit there, drinking wine, laughing, and we don't notice our precious tiny child putting down her toys, standing up, walking all the way down the beach to the waves. You were the person who couldn't read the warnings, darling. You weren't meant to be sensible. We were. It was our fault.' He pauses. Then he says, 'Are you and Susie OK?'

'Not really.' I think about Mum now, if we're both dead, and I want to run back to her. 'Things have been ... well, I've been awful. She's doing OK. I mean, kind of OK, I think. She and I have never had that kind of bond that ... well, this sounds mad since you've been dead for most of my life, but that I've always felt with you. I mean – she married again.'

He nods, and breathes in and out deeply. 'Good,' he says after a while. 'If she's happy, then that's good. Is she happy? Does he take care of you both?' I can see how painful this is for him and now it's my turn to comfort him.

'Dad! We can take care of ourselves. And he was great.' I realize that this is true. Greg was great for us. And he's tried to be there for me and I've never let him. 'They're not together any more. She married him to get some stability for me, I think, and he did the same for his son.'

I tell him about Enzo, and he smiles because I'm smiling so much. God, I miss Enzo. I've missed him so much. I wish I could make up with the real Enzo like I did with that imaginary one.

'So you got a brother, after all? And a ... a dad.'

'No! You're my dad.'

He looks at me for a long time. 'Let Greg be your dad, Hazel. He's there. Susie chose him and she's good at people. Don't push him away because he's not me.'

I fill him in on my life, but I don't go into much detail about Freddie. I tell him that I messed up my GCSEs, but that I scraped into college. I tell him I want either to go to art college or do an English degree at a university far from home, though I'll have to pass a lot of retakes to get any offers (and also I seem to be dead). I run out of chat, and I know I need to address the other thing. The real one.

'So . . .' I don't want to say it, but look into his eyes and see the love, and they give me the strength to carry on talking. 'So, you're dead, and I'm with you, and that means I'm . . . dead too.'

He holds me close. I smell the dad smell again, the one I'd forgotten I'd forgotten.

'You might be, darling,' he says.

I pull back. '*Might* be? Seriously? What happened?' This makes me feel strange. I'd been so busy avoiding articulating it that now he's said it's not necessarily true I don't know how to feel. 'I mean, I don't feel massively alive, I guess.'

'I think you were in an accident,' he says, and it all comes flooding back.

42

Cambridge

May

Lina and I were standing by the stage, waiting for Freddie and Ollie. We were hardly ever alone together.

'I'll give you a lesson if you like,' she said. 'Not now, but whenever you're free?'

'I'd love that,' I said, and I would, but I knew it wouldn't happen.

'You'd be a good drummer, I think.'

She looked around, then carried on, talking fast, dropping her voice.

'Hazel,' she said, 'we're so worried about you. All three of us. Me, Ulla and Ollie. You're not happy. You have options.'

I turned my face away. I had been feeling good: I was wearing the dress Freddie got me for my birthday five months ago, and it fitted me perfectly. I was wearing the barbed-wire necklace with it because Lina had given it to me and I loved it. Because it would protect me. Freddie didn't like the necklace and I only risked wearing it when he was in a good mood, which he was tonight.

'I'm fine,' I said. 'I love him.'

'Why, though?' Lina was on edge, exasperated with me. I heard someone approaching and looked round, but it was Ollie. 'What the hell is there for you to love about him?'

I lowered my voice, almost to a whisper.

'It goes too deep for me to walk away. I lost my dad and he lost . . . Harry, and so we understand things about each other that no one else ever could.'

'Yeah,' said Lina. 'You said that before. I don't get it. Do you mean Harry their cousin? Because he's hardly *lost*, is he? I thought he moved to Thailand.'

'Cousin?'

We stared at each other. Since Ollie was there, I broke Freddie's rules and turned to him.

'Ollie, you know Harry?'

Ollie had hardly been listening. 'What?' he said. 'Harry, our cousin? What are you on about?'

Yeah. Ollie had never liked me and he didn't like me now. I was starting to have a bad feeling about this.

'I mean Harry your brother. He – he died. When you were all kids, in an . . .' My voice trailed off as I saw Ollie's face. I looked at Lina. I looked back at Ollie. I had all his attention now.

'My brother told you *what*?'

'Harry. He was two years older than you . . .' I stopped. I could see the truth on his face and I was not ready to confront what that meant.

And then Freddie was there. It was time for the gig to start.

*

I watched from the wings, but my mind was racing. I had never doubted Freddie's story about his lost brother because why would I? You'd be a monster to question a story like that. But I saw, now, that he had told me that story and then I'd kissed him. He'd offered me a tragedy that mirrored my own.

I stood in a daze, staring at my boyfriend. He kept glancing over at me: Freddie always knew when something was wrong. The song they were playing finished. Everyone clapped but they didn't love it. They liked it, but really they were waiting for 'Hazy Girl'. Freddie walked off the stage, over to me, and kissed me.

'You look beautiful,' he said. He stood back and inspected me. 'Gorgeous. I just had to tell you, doll. You OK?'

I nodded.

Then he was back on the stage, leaving me staring at him. I felt Lina's eyes on me and glanced over. She held eye contact for a long time and nodded, jerked her head towards the exit, then turned away.

What had I done? I stared at the band, looked out at the part of the crowd I could see, and tried to find my real self. Which parts of me were Hazel and which were a girl who was forcing herself into the shape of Freddie's ideal girlfriend?

I had convinced myself that I liked being skinny, even though I knew it wasn't good for me. I had liked it because Freddie adored it. I barely went home any more. Mum had a new boyfriend and she was distracted enough to believe me when I said I was fine and busy. I'd told her I had that fictional classical musician boyfriend who was a few years older than me, and she'd asked me to bring him home, and I'd said that I would. I was careful to reply to her messages and she didn't push it. A part of me wished she would: couldn't she see?

I needed her. Had he lied to me about everything? Had he tricked me into falling in love?

Freddie said I didn't need A levels and I should forget about my art because it was childish. I had reasoned that I could take exams afterwards if I wanted to. I had my whole life ahead of me.

When I did go into college, I wore wide-legged jeans and baggy hoodies. On the few occasions when I went home, I swamped myself in pyjamas and pretended to eat. I knew that this was wrong, but I'd chosen it because I had chosen Freddie, and Freddie loved 'heroin chic'. When I was with Freddie, I wore skimpy things, vest tops that showed my hard-won upper arms, shorts that showed the willpower that had given me those thighs.

My hair wasn't as thick and shiny as it used to be, and it took me longer to get it looking good, but I was better at make-up these days, and my hair usually got there in the end.

Freddie and I were together almost all the time. In my case, it was because if I went off and did my own thing he got jealous and ended up sending terrible messages and blocking me, so it was easier not to. I'd never given him one single reason not to trust me, but he didn't. Part of me liked it that he got jealous over me. If he went to an industry thing, I had to stay in the flat, and I did because I knew it made his life easier if he didn't have to worry.

Deep down I knew that this wasn't right. The realization was creeping up on me, and now, after that conversation, I saw that I couldn't do it any more.

My song was coming up. It was Kennedy's only hit, the thing that had launched them into the career they'd always wanted, but, although we didn't talk about it, the *Hazy* album wasn't selling on. It was just the single. Often Freddie would pull me on to the stage and sing it to me, even though Lina and Ollie had told him to stop, that it had been OK to do it once, but that actually it was weird. They didn't say this to him because he was too tempestuous, but they hated the fact that it drew attention to the fact that he, pushing thirty, had a teenage girlfriend. He had once been paranoid about anyone knowing about me, but now he didn't give a shit, about this or about anything. Freddie was out of control. I knew that really, but I also knew I was the only one who could sometimes talk sense into him.

After Radio 1 had picked the single up too, it had gone into the top ten, which was huge for a band like Kennedy. The venues they played were getting bigger. Everything was changing, except that the phrase 'one-hit wonder' was starting to appear in their coverage.

Freddie was changing.

He was becoming famous. He had been in magazines and then on their covers. Girls wanted to talk to him and I remembered that I'd once been one of them too. (Had I, though? Not really.) They waited for him outside the stage door, as I had accidentally done. I came to their shows because I didn't want him to slip someone else his phone number, someone older than me, someone cooler and stronger. He'd done it to me, and now I remembered that there had been someone else there, another girl, a woman, waiting by the van while he pushed his number into my palm and closed my fingers round it.

Maybe, now that I would be eighteen next birthday, he wanted someone younger.

I watched him swig from a bottle of vodka disguised as water. He glanced over at me. I looked away.

I stood there in my clumpy boots and red dress and hummed along with the intro. *Hazy gazey girl.* Everyone knew it, and the crowd started joining in. I watched Freddie. He was singing intensely, emotionally, but out to the crowd, even though it was my song.

Then I saw what he was doing.

He was singing my song to another girl.

No. He wouldn't.

I could see her: she was the opposite of me in every way. She was blonde and healthy, wearing, as far as I could see, a ripped T-shirt. She was staring at him and he was singing my song to her. I could see it all.

I stepped back.

What was I doing?

I took another step back.

I looked at Lina. She had noticed. She glanced at me and missed a couple of beats: I only spotted it because I knew the song so well. Our eyes met and I saw it: confirmation. *Yes, he is singing your song to someone else. Yes, he invented and killed a brother to reel you in. Yes, you need to go.*

I looked round. I could just leave now.

I had spent months being hungry so I would be the sort of girl Freddie liked. I had let him lock me in the flat because he said he couldn't trust other men around me. I had given up the future I actually wanted, walked away from everyone who really loved me. I had changed everything about myself and my life to suit Freddie Kennedy because I loved him, because I'd do anything for him, because I had, in fact, done everything for him.

And, knowing I was watching, he was singing my song to another girl who was also about ten years younger than he was.

He'd done this before, I was pretty sure of it. He'd done it before, but not right in front of me. Not blatantly like this.

And he'd invented a dead brother.

I looked at Lina again. She felt me looking and our eyes met. At last, I could sense my real self coming back. Something inside me snapped. I admitted that actually I wasn't happy. That Freddie was bad. That he had pretended not to trust me, but actually I should never have trusted him.

I knew that he didn't love me.

I knew that he had lied and lied and lied.

He was ready to take another girl for pizza. I didn't eat pizza any more: somehow I had become one of the boring girls who ate lettuce leaves, the ones he'd sneered at on our first date.

I'd turned him down on that date, and now I wondered whether he'd done all this to me out of revenge. I turned him down, so he had pursued me, lied to me and destroyed me. And now I was done. I'd hung on far too long, and here I was, watching him make promises with his eyes to another girl. A girl who I hoped, for her sake, would not wait at the stage door.

I had lost my friends, my brother, my mother, my future, my ability to fuel my body.

I looked back at Lina. I nodded. She raised her drumsticks in triumph.

Freddie was singing the final lines of the song, and as he did this he put his fingertips to his lips and blew the girl a kiss.

I turned and ran.

In the dressing room, I pulled a hoodie over the stupid dress and grabbed my bag. I couldn't see much through my tears, but I could tell that the dressing room was a tip. The ashtrays were full of cigarette butts, even though there was a NO SMOKING sign on the wall. There were clothes strewn about the place, millions of empty beer cans, and the smell was so strong that I felt someone had opened a can of DISGUSTING and sprayed it round the room. I'd become so used to all this that I'd stopped noticing it.

I'd loved Freddie for so long, so overwhelmingly, that I'd shut out everything else. Now I felt it pouring back in, all of it. Even though I loved Freddie – even though a part of me might love him forever – I hated him and I couldn't do this any more.

I knew the 'Hazy Girl' song was their finale, and I knew there'd be two encores. I was miles from home. I'd have to get on a train or something, fast.

I wiped my eyes with my sleeve. It came away with a smear of mascara. I knew I must look monstrously awful, but I grabbed my phone and forced myself to focus. I found the 'Coursework Chat' group and tried to type something, but all that came out was Hdjdhr, which I sent. Then I made an effort to calm down and focus. I clicked the + symbol. I found the word *location*. I shared my live location. I set it to keep sharing for eight hours.

As I was running down the stairs, I heard his voice.

'Hazel!'

They should still have been playing the first encore.

'Hazel? Get back here!'

This was how he talked to me. I'd let it happen. I'd set boundaries on our first date, and he'd reeled me in and broken down every barrier I'd ever had, one by one, so slowly I hadn't noticed things changing. Revenge for my turning him down, back when I was fifteen.

Ollie was at the stage door. He must have come straight there from the stage. I recoiled from the sight of him.

'You're leaving?' he said. I nodded. 'Good.' He gestured to me to go, then grabbed my hand and pulled me back. I looked at his steely eyes.

'Look, I'm sorry, Hazel. Ulla's angry with Lina and me because we've watched this happen. Do I have this right? He faked a dead brother?'

I stared at our feet, his and mine. I needed to go. 'If there's not a dead brother? Then yes, he did. But I saw a photo. In his room.'

Ollie half laughed. 'That? That's him as a kid. He keeps it because he thinks he looks soulful and cute. His one true love: Freddie Kennedy. Right, fuck off, Hazel. In the nicest way, I hope we don't see each other again. And – sorry.'

I needed to run, but I couldn't move.

43

Afterlife

I'm lying on my back on the sand, listening to my dad telling me that I might be dead, but that I haven't been here long enough yet to know for sure. I realize that Kamila was in the in-between place for ages, and so she is probably dead too. Even though I'd never known her alive, that breaks my heart.

I'm pushing away the memories that have come flooding in from Cambridge. There's plenty of time for me to piece that together. The whole of eternity. I try to push it away because this is my dad.

'It doesn't come with an instruction manual,' he says, 'but we're basically floating consciousnesses. I've been floating here a while now.'

I think of those time glitches. The blue place. The sky shouting my name.

'Do you hear your name?' I say. I gesture upwards. 'From up there, I mean. I used to hear voices saying my name a lot. Then it stopped.'

I prop myself up on my elbows and look at him. I need to focus. I ignore the memories that are edging back into my brain. I'm with Morris. The thing I've always wanted, though I didn't want to have to die to get here.

'You hear your name?'

I nod.

'And what do you do? Do you answer?'

I think back to all the times it happened.

'No. It never occurred to me to answer, I don't think.'

'Oh God, Hazel. If they say your name, answer them. Fight for it. Fight to get back.'

'What else happens?'

'At first you go to an in-between place. It's a space between life and death, I think. Somewhere in your brain. For me, it was London. I was trapped in a version of London that I thought was real.'

I think of my time in Venice.

'Were you on your own?'

'No, my darling. You were there.'

'Me?' I'm sitting up immediately. 'What?'

'Little three-year-old Hazel. You nearly died too, remember? You came to London with me and then you were gone. Jeez, I don't want to revisit that. The worst time. Running all over London looking for you and Susie.'

'Poor Mum!'

'Yes. Now in particular. Since we're both . . .'

He stops because there's a noise. We look at the sky. It sounds like thunder, but it's not. It's thunder that forms into a word.

Hazel.

It's thunder that is calling my name. I don't want to go because I'm here with my dad. I edge up closer to him, but he shakes his head.

'Go. You still have a chance. Go, Hazel. *Go.*'

I cling on. 'I don't want to. I can't go back, Dad. I can't lose you again.'

He hugs me. 'You won't lose me because I'll still be here, my darling girl. I'll still be here. I'll be waiting for you. And, one day, you'll be back. I don't want it to be now. You have your whole life to live. I'll wait.'

I shake my head. I'm scared to go back. I resist it and the voice becomes quieter.

'Go,' says Dad.

'No,' I say.

We look at each other.

'Fine,' he says, and just when I think he's agreed with me he carries on speaking. 'In that case, I guess I need to do the emotional blackmail. I can't live my life, Hazel. You still have a chance. As your dead father, I am imploring you to go back and give it everything you have. I am begging you to live for both of us. I can tell that things have been difficult for you, but you can go and make it better. Give Susie a message from me. Tell her we're OK. If nothing else, do it for Susie.'

I look away. I don't want to.

The voice in the sky is becoming fainter.

I don't want to but I have to.

I still have a chance of life.

'What do you want me to tell her?' I mutter it, annoyed.

He puts an arm round my shoulders and I feel better, more substantial, more myself again now.

'Thank you, baby. Tell Susie I'm waiting. I've always loved her. Tell her she's my little bird. Will you tell her that? She'll know.'

I think of my bird Cello. In that old photo and in my pocket. The bird that led me here. She has been part of Dad all along, and part of Mum.

'Of course. I promise. Dad, when I fall in love with people, they're mainly girls.'

'I know. You said that. You said you fell in love with a girl in in-between Venice.'

I want to tell him all about Kamila, but the sky is calling my name again, and then my vision goes blank and I can still hear my name, but everything else changes.

The sound of the ocean fades. I hear a whooshing noise rushing towards me, but then it moves away. The voice comes again, but this time it's different. It's a human voice, close to my face. The world is pulsating blue like it did when I glitched and I wonder where I'm going next.

'Hazel? Hazel, love – can you hear me? She's back! She's back with us.'

My surroundings fill themselves in. I'm lying down. There's a hard surface beneath my back. A blue light comes and goes behind my eyelids.

Everything hurts. I hate it here. I try as hard as I can to get back to Morris.

44

Cambridge

I couldn't move because my head was full of Harry: the big thing I had that bonded me to Freddie.

Harry and Morris. Our shared losses. The stories that brought us close, just before our first kiss. The men who should have been there, but weren't. I had made so many allowances for Freddie, because of Harry.

Harry who, I saw in a flash, had never existed. Freddie had made it up, the whole story, the dead brother, to reel me in. He had played me. I remembered a thing that had slightly bothered me for a while: on our first date, he'd said his parents had taken him and Ollie to Italy every year since he was a baby. *Two parents, two kids, a villa in Tuscany.* That hadn't seemed to fit with Harry, but I'd ignored it.

'Here,' said Ollie. He handed me something. A twenty-pound note. I took it. I wanted to run but I turned back. I had to know for sure.

'There was never another brother? He didn't die? In an accident, as a child?'

'Hazel – no. That's a lie. I'm going to fucking kill him. Now go!'

Freddie burst through a fire door, so I guessed there was a short cut from the stage. He was upon me, and Ollie was pushing him away, fighting him off. I ran through the door but Freddie did too. The night air was cool on my face and I took deep breaths, trying to calm myself.

I could have been round the corner by now if I hadn't just stopped to find out for definite about Harry. If the answer hadn't knocked the wind out of me. I was wobbling, stumbling. I should have gone when Ollie told me to fuck off.

Freddie grabbed my arm, held it tight. I tried to pull away. There were a couple of people standing nearby waiting for autographs. I saw their phones going up. I shouted to them for help, but they just filmed me.

How had I fallen into this? What was I doing with an out-of-control, lying drunk? Why had I done everything he told me to do?

'You come back,' he said.

His voice was cold, quiet, and it would have been better if he'd been shouting. I was so scared I was shaking all over. My whole body was moving and I didn't know how much longer my stupid legs were going to hold me up.

He yanked me to him and spoke into my ear. 'You don't get to leave me, Hazel.' He turned to the onlookers. 'Hey, guys! Great to see you. I'll be with you in a moment. Please – no photos.'

Freddie had never been properly violent to me. He'd held me down sometimes. Pushed me. Grabbed me so tightly that it left bruises. Now I was sure that the moment there wasn't an audience he was going to hurt me properly. Seriously.

'She *does* get to leave,' said Ollie, and Freddie turned on him and shouted a lot of swear words. I tried to pull my arm away, but I couldn't. He was gripping it too tightly. The people carried on filming.

'I do,' I whispered.

'Let her go,' said Ollie. 'Come inside. We'll talk about it after the encores.'

Freddie gripped me tighter. My heart was pounding. I needed to run away but I couldn't. This was fight or flight and I couldn't fight. He had taken all my strength.

'You can fuck off,' he said to Ollie. Keeping his grip on my arm, he punched him with his other arm. Ollie stumbled. Freddie didn't seem to care about the onlookers.

I knew what was coming. I closed my eyes and said: 'I know about Harry. I know you lied.'

'So what if I did?' said Freddie. He didn't even pretend.

And then I felt him stumbling and I was free and Ollie's voice was shouting, 'Run!' and I didn't look back. I just went. I ran to the corner and round it, and I kept going until I'd gone down so many random streets that he surely wouldn't find me.

I had make-up streaked down my face, a stupid velvet dress on and an oversized hoodie. If Freddie came looking for me, people would remember seeing me.

I ducked into a doorway and checked my phone. *Please have replied. Please have replied.*

Both Enzo and Phoebe had, and Phoebe's latest message said: We're in the car. Enzo driving. We'll be an hour and a half. Sorry we can't get there sooner. Are you safe?

I stared at it for ages. I didn't deserve them. Was I safe? No, but I wasn't in danger right this second. I reminded myself again that he'd never been violent. Violence was punching, and Freddie hadn't punched me.

He would do, though, when he found me.

I walked a bit further, my legs trembling, and found myself in front of one of those old colleges with grass in front and a gatehouse with a doorman inside. I stared at it for a moment. The building was honey-coloured stone, lit up by street lights. If I hadn't met Freddie, I'd have been applying to places like this in a few months. Now I was wondering whether I could use it as a hiding place. If I could persuade them I was a student, maybe they'd let me in. I leaned on the iron railings and dug around in my bag for a make-up wipe, then, when I found one, used it to clean my whole face. I was breathing hard, hyperventilating.

'You OK?'

I almost screamed. When I looked round, it was just a boy. He looked nothing like Freddie. He wasn't Freddie. I tried to calm down.

'Sorry,' I said. 'Yeah. Just – weird night. Can you take me in here? Would that be OK? I'm a bit wobbly.'

'Sure,' he said. 'Be my guest.'

I followed him in, with no idea at all of where I was going. He said, 'She's with me,' to the security people.

One of them said, 'What's her name then?' and, without missing a beat, my new friend said, 'Lucy.'

I nodded and they let us pass, laughing.

'I'm Josh,' said my saviour. 'Are you OK?'

'Yeah,' I said. 'I mean, no, but yes. I'm . . .' I cast around for a lie, failed to find one, so told the truth. 'I've left my boyfriend. I had to run away. He's . . .'

I thought back over the past year. I felt disloyal saying it. But then I saw a thing I'd never noticed before: Freddie had never actually hit me, but that was because I'd never gone against anything he wanted. Ever. That was why.

I took a deep breath. 'I'm scared of him.'

'Right,' said Josh, and his eyes darted around. 'OK. Look, you're safe here. Maybe we should call the police? Have to say, this stuff isn't in my comfort zone, but I'll go and get my friend Arianna. She'll know what to do.'

I followed him under an archway and into a grassy courtyard. The buildings around it were weathered stone. It was like the set of an old film.

'Where even are we?'

He smiled. 'Nice, right? This is Caius. Gonville and Caius College.' He pointed around. 'King's is over there. The famous one? But this place has been here since, like, the thirteenth century or whatever.'

'I had no idea Cambridge was actually like this. I'm going to have to start working harder.'

I was coming out with the kinds of things I thought people should say in this situation. Keep it trivial. Pretend to be normal.

'You're not a student?'

'Not yet.'

We went through a door into a hallway and it was like one of those movies. The tiled floor, the panelled walls. I followed him round a corner, past a row of pigeonholes with letters and flyers in them, and then we were in a bar.

'Right. Let's wait here and I'll get Ari to come. Have a seat. Look – if you're scared of someone, I think we need to get you some help. Maybe I should ask the bar staff.'

The room was wooden. It had a wooden floor and wooden walls. It smelled like polished wood, not like a student bar. There were several free tables, and I followed my new friend over to one of them. I knew that I was shaking. I couldn't walk away from Freddie. He wouldn't let me.

A voice in my head was screaming at me to go back and work things out. It was so loud I couldn't hear the sounds of the bar at all. I didn't even know if there was music playing.

The voice in my head changed. It became Freddie's voice, and it was shouting.

Get the fuck back here. Come back, Hazel Angelopoulos. Come the fuck back now or you'll regret it. I promise you'll regret it.

'. . . here then?' said Josh. He had black hair and dimples in his cheeks.

'Sorry?' I forced a smile. 'I mean, I'm really sorry. I'm not very together.'

'That's OK. I just said, you don't live here then? In Cambridge.'

'No. I live in Kent. I'm –'

He looked at his phone. 'Arianna will be about twenty minutes. Is that OK? She went to a gig this evening, but it's finished and she's on her way. Can I get you a drink?'

The room blurred, then became perfectly defined, then changed so it wasn't a room but a trap, then changed back into the Gonville and Caius College bar.

'No. I mean, what gig?' I saw the words as a speech bubble coming out of my mouth. I looked at them. *What gig what gig what gig.* I knew the answer. I knew it before he said it.

'You know Kennedy? With that "Hazy Girl" song that was everywhere? Yeah, them. I didn't fancy it but she loves them. Shall I get you some crisps?'

Josh, whoever he was, whyever he was doing this, was so kind. I imagined his friend Ari at the gig. I wondered whether she was the girl Freddie had blown the kiss to. I knew she wasn't, but at the same time she *might* have been and I knew I couldn't stay around to find out.

'I'll talk to the staff. They'll be able to help you.'

I couldn't confide in someone who had paid forty pounds to watch Freddie sing my song. I knew she'd think he was gorgeous, that I was lucky, that I was mad.

'Could I have a lemonade?' I didn't want any alcohol ever again.

'Sure?'

'Thanks.'

I watched him at the bar. He was speaking to the barman, and they both looked at me. The barman picked up a phone.

NO.

As soon as they weren't looking at me, I left. I ran past the pigeonholes and out into the grassy courtyard, and out through the gatehouse and on to the street. I wasn't safe here, but I couldn't meet Arianna straight from that gig. I just couldn't.

I couldn't let the police come. Freddie had lied to me, but he hadn't broken the law.

I walked towards King's College. Josh had said it was 'the famous one' and he was right: everyone had heard of it. It stood there in the dark. Mum used to listen to the carol service from here every Christmas Eve. There was something a bit comforting in it. I wondered if I could go in there, but it was guarded by porters too, and I knew they wouldn't let me through.

I saw a side street and headed down it. This seemed like a hiding place. I called Phoebe as I walked.

'Hazel! Oh my God. Are you OK? What's happened?'

I took a deep breath and said the words, to see how they would sound.

'I left him.' I wanted to say the rest of it, but nothing came out. Just that. It was enough.

'Are you safe?'

'Kind of?'

'You're in the middle of Cambridge?'

'Yeah.'

'We won't be long. Sit down somewhere. Go into a library or something. They must have cafes open in the evening. For the students. Find somewhere, sit round a corner out of sight

338

and wait. We're forty-five minutes away now. Wherever you are, we'll find you.'

'OK.'

'Haze – what happened?'

I forced myself to reply because I knew she would be imagining something worse.

'It's OK, Pheebs. I just realized I hate him. That he's been lying to me. He sang my song to a girl in the audience. I kind of saw myself from a distance, standing there, watching. I was at the side of the stage because he didn't want me talking to any other men. I know I look awful, Pheebs. I feel like shit. I'm hungry all the time. I've lost all my real friends. I've fucked up college. And he lied and pretended he had a brother who died. Just because of my –'

I had to stop because I was sobbing. I leaned on a wall and felt myself sliding down it. Cars went past. Even though I could smell that the bit of ground where I was sitting was used by dogs and probably drunks as a urinal, I didn't care. My stupid legs wouldn't hold me up any more. I just sat there.

Half an hour later a van pulled up, its wheels on the pavement.

45

'Come on. Let's go.'

Freddie was standing over me. The van's engine was still running.

Not Phoebe. Not Enzo. Freddie.

I looked up and down the street. I'd just been sitting here. Had I fallen asleep? Time had been doing weird things. I thought I'd had my eyes closed for most of it. Someone had put a sandwich next to me, and there were two pound coins beside me.

People had thought I was homeless. And now Freddie was here.

He was reaching out a hand. I reached back. I let him pull me up. Then I remembered and I yanked my hand away, propelling myself backwards into the wall behind me. He stepped closer and there was nowhere for me to go.

'What was that about, doll?' His voice was gentle again. He was my Freddie.

I felt the bulk of him against me, and in spite of everything I pressed my cheek into his chest and felt his arms encircling me, and everything was, for a fraction of a second, better. He smelled of Freddie, and even though that was mostly sweat, cigarettes and alcohol, it was the smell of home.

It would be so much easier to do what he wanted. It had always been easier to do that.

He stroked my hair. 'Silly girl. Come on. Let's get you in the van and take you home.'

Silly girl. *Silly girl.*

No. I was not a silly girl.

I was not a silly girl and he was a liar and a bastard. I was not a silly girl. He had taken everything from me and I was not a silly girl.

I thought of kind Josh and Caius College. People my own age, in a bar. Maybe a few teachers, or whatever they were called at Cambridge, scattered around. Before Freddie, I'd been working towards something like that. I had to fill in a UCAS form later this year, but I'd ruined it. My predicted grades wouldn't be high enough to let me apply to the places I wanted to go. And Freddie had made it clear, from the earliest days of our relationship, that he didn't want me to go to uni, didn't want me to be an artist, didn't want me to do anything except be the girlfriend he wanted.

I let the words roll around my head. Edinburgh. Sheffield. Exeter. New places, places I didn't know. Places that were just words. A new life as a student. New friends. Freedom. I didn't know what I'd study: maybe English, maybe art, maybe history of art. That way I could do it with Phoebe.

I thought of Harry. The imaginary dead brother I had never been allowed to mention to anyone. Of course I hadn't because it had been a huge cynical lie. Freddie had told me about Harry at the Tate, and then I'd kissed him. I thought we had so much in common. Throughout, I had made allowances for him because of Harry. Harry who had never existed. Freddie had been laughing at my grief all along.

I pulled away.

'No, Freddie.' My voice was so quiet that I hoped it wasn't just in my head. 'I can't do this. You pretended you had a brother because of my dad. And I want to do my A levels. I want to see my friends. I want to go to uni.' I looked up at the night sky. 'I want to be . . . single.'

Single! As I said the word, I knew he would hate it.

He pulled me back, clamped me to him and stroked my hair with a heavier grip.

'Shhh,' he said. 'Haze, you're going to be fine. Harry was real, I promise. Lina doesn't know shit. Come home and I'll tell you everything. If you want to do things differently, then yeah. Sure. We can talk about it. I'm not some monster who's going to stop you. I thought you loved our life together. I'm sorry. You're my Hazy Girl. Hey – without you, we wouldn't have been playing the Corn Exchange. That's for sure.'

I took a deep breath. Of course he was coming out with this stuff. It was exhausting. I knew what I had to say next. Did I dare?

A car pulled up in front of us, right behind Freddie's van. I hadn't known Enzo could drive. Greg had clearly bought him a car and I didn't know anything about that either, but this was a Mini with stripes down the side and it was exactly the vehicle Enzo and Greg would have chosen.

The passenger door opened. Phoebe got out on the pavement and opened the back door.

I took a deep breath. 'I don't love you. I want my life back.'

He gripped me by the tops of my arms. He drew his arm back and, before I could do anything, he'd slapped me across the face. My neck jerked. It hurt.

'Ungrateful bitch.'

I tried to pull away. He gripped me harder. I took a deep breath, kneed him hard where it would hurt most and ran. Phoebe bundled me into the back of the car, slammed the door and jumped into the front. Enzo was driving before she'd even closed her own door. We raced away, drunk people in the street parting to let us through.

'Pheebs,' said Enzo, his voice tight, 'I have no idea where I'm going.'

'Keep driving,' she said. 'Anywhere. I'll get directions up.'

'He hit her in the face!'

I was curled up, a hand to my cheek. He'd hit me hard. It hurt to touch it, but I couldn't take my hand away. He'd hit me because I was leaving him. He had been violent after all.

If my friends hadn't come to rescue me, I would have ended up in his van and he would have taken me back to his flat, and into his room, and closed the door. I saw it in flashes, stills from a film. He had been pretending to be nice to get me into the van.

This, my bruised face, was the good outcome.

'Turn right at the end,' said Phoebe. 'It's a one-way system. We need to get to the A11. Let's get out of Cambridge before we do anything else.'

'We should go to Venice,' said Enzo. 'Stay at my mum's place. Get her right away from that bastard.'

'Maybe we should,' said Phoebe. I felt a moment pass between them.

'Venice,' I said. That sounded like a haven.

'OK,' said Enzo. 'Message her and see if it's free? Her number's in my phone, under Vittoria.'

'Thank you,' I said. My voice sounded weird. 'Thanks for finding me. Sorry.'

'Hey,' said Enzo, his voice softer, and Phoebe reached back towards me. I grabbed her hand and clung to it. I still couldn't speak. I felt the tears at the back of my eyes, but they weren't falling.

I thought of Freddie appearing in front of me.

How had he found me?

I knew the answer. He had found me the same way Enzo and Phoebe had, except without my consent. He'd tracked my phone. He had probably been doing it for ages, but until now I'd always been exactly where I'd said I'd be. I'd followed all his rules.

Of course Freddie had got some sort of tracker on my phone without me knowing. Of course he had because that was exactly what he was about. He'd never have found me – slumped down a side street in a strange city, all out of energy with two pounds and a sandwich next to me – without help.

And, if he had managed it then, it meant that . . .

'Guys,' I said. 'Guys!'

Enzo said, 'There's a van behind us. Do you know his registration, H?'

I did because I'd often been sent across the car park to get a pay-and-display ticket. Those machines usually wanted your registration number. What was it?

'LM67 . . .' I couldn't remember the rest.

'Shit,' said Enzo. We speeded up.

'Don't go faster,' said Phoebe. 'Let me divert us to the police station. You passed your test three weeks ago, Enz. You can't get into some road-rage situation with an angry drunk guy. We'll all be killed.'

And we were.

46

I'm on the tarmac, trying with all my might to get back to the beach, to my dad. It was lovely there and nothing hurt. Here I'm terrified and everything, everything, everything feels horrific. My body is on fire. I can't feel my legs. I take a breath and it comes in with a whoosh, and I'm back in the real world, lying on some road outside Cambridge. Venice and the beach and Dad and Enzo and Phoebe have melted away.

And Kam. I feel Kamila being pulled away from me and nothing I do can bring her back.

I open my eyes and the person speaking is not God. It's a paramedic, and even though I've been in Venice for half an eternity with Phoebe and Enzo and Kamila, and on a Greek beach with my dad, I'm lying on the tarmac and there are blue lights flashing and cars shooting by on the other side of the road and my face hurts and my body hurts and I don't know what's happening and I understand that the blue lights in the in-between places were just from the police cars. I thought I was glitching and jumping around in time, but I've been here all along.

And no time has passed at all.

This is the time travel I didn't want to happen. This is not a micro time slip. It's a big one, a massive one, a horrible one.

I hear someone say, 'Hazel,' and they're talking to someone else, not to me.

The other person is there and they crouch beside me with the first person and say, 'Hazel – can you hear me? We're going to get you on to a stretcher, OK? And we'll move you into the ambulance.'

I want to say *Phoebe*. I want to say *Enzo*. I can't say a word and my head is hurting more than anything that's ever happened before, and I try to move and it works a bit. My arms but not my legs.

'That's great! Well done.'

I let myself fall away. This isn't real. It didn't happen. We're in Venice. We're on holiday in Venice. We went to Vittoria's flat. Enzo and Phoebe and me. Or was it just me? I fell in love with a girl. I met my dad. I bought a glass bird. I need to get back to that bit, but I can't because he sent me here to live. I fight and fight to get there. I fall away and away and away.

And there's nothing. I can't get out of this.

I'm walking along the Grand Canal. I buy a glass bird.

I'm in the hotel breakfast room and Enzo is saying, 'Let the fun times commence.'

I'm eating. I'm taking food up to my lips and chewing it because it's nice, because I need it, because it's breakfast time, because I've liked food all along and I only starved myself to please a messed-up control freak. I'm feeling my way to normality. We're laughing together.

Phoebe is there. I must stay in the times before Phoebe, and then Enzo, vanished. The times when Kam was my future. I must stay here, before the blue light and the voice in the sky started trying to pull me back.

I'm leaning out of the window, looking at Venice, and I'm telling them it's like a painting, and Enzo says he's changing his name to Giovanni Antonio Canal. We just woke up. We have the holiday ahead of us. It's the holiday Enzo and I have been planning since we were eleven. We're happy. I'm staying. It's the City of Love.

I do. I stay there, living it on a loop. Waking up in Vittoria's apartment, getting ready for the day, heading down five flights of stairs. I dress myself more appropriately because no one needs to wear an AllSaints dress to spend the day walking around, looking at churches. When I do it again, I wear jeans. I wear sweatshirts. I wear whatever the hell I want. I ignore my hair and tie it in a knot, out of the way. I relax into the moments, hang on to them.

I say sorry to my friends properly. I say thank you. I tell them I love them.

When I come back, it's because this time the voice belongs to my mother and there is something I have to tell her.

'Hazel. Darling Hazel. Please come back to me.'

She's saying the words from the 'Hazy Girl' song, even though she probably doesn't know it. In spite of that, I force myself back. I open my eyes and there's a whoosh of reality again and everything hurts, but I try to smile. She takes my hand and squeezes it. That hurts too.

'She's awake! Enzo!'

I stare at Mum. She looks different but all I see is Mum. I try to remember what Dad told me to say to her. Already it's fading. He's losing his edges. That must have been a dream. All of it must have been a dream.

The word comes to me and I whisper it. 'Bird.'

She says, 'What was that?' and then Enzo is there.

Real Enzo.

I thought he had gone, but he's right here, and I'm so happy I want to jump up and hug him, though of course I can't. He appears at my bedside with his arm in a sling. The side of his face is scarred. He puts his good hand on top of my head and stares at me.

I stare back. It's him. It's actually Enzo. I look at his face, the contours of it, the fact that it's here, looking at me. Real Enzo, not the Venice version.

And he doesn't seem to hate me, though he should.

'New glasses,' I say. At least I try to say it. It doesn't really come out.

'What's that, darling?' asks Mum.

I try harder. 'New glasses.'

He understands and touches them. 'Yeah. Old ones are in some bush by the road. Thought I'd go a bit bolder this time.'

No one speaks for a while. I want to ask about Phoebe, but I don't. I can't. I think of her disappearing into that tomb. Morris is through there too. I cannot deal with what that might mean.

'Do you want more painkillers?' says Mum. 'And can you say it again? What you were trying to tell me just now.'

I scan my body, checking for pain. It's only my head that hurts. I can hardly feel the rest of it. I lift the sheet and see both legs in plaster. *Shit.*

'Head,' I say, and then there's a nurse there, and I just let them do what they want to do. I don't have the energy for this. I don't have any energy at all. I need to go back to my dad.

But I have to say it to Mum first. I look at her hard until she turns back to me, and then, when I have her full attention, I say it. *Little bird.* I watch her face. I try again. *You're his little bird. Morris.* That was the full message.

And I see it means what Dad said it did. As she comes into focus, rather than being a presence of *Mum*, I can see that she looks terrible. She doesn't have her sharp haircut any more. She has bags under her eyes and she looks exhausted. I wonder how long she's been here. I still don't know what happened, but I know it's every mother's nightmare, particularly when she lost the love of her life fourteen years ago.

'Did you say *little bird*?' Her voice is a whisper.

'I saw Dad.'

I say it so quietly that my voice barely exists, but I know she hears. We look at each other. She believes me.

47

I get better. It takes time, and there are some very, very bad days, but I'm healing. I think constantly of my dad on the beach in some afterlife version of Greece, and even though the details are drifting away, a pencil drawing that someone is rubbing out, I have written it down and I know it's real. I know it's real because he told me something I couldn't have known, and Mum understood.

And I'm making my own pencil drawings now. I finally understand why I always drew stormy seas and beaches. I was trying to explain it to myself, the thing I didn't know I remembered. I draw that and I draw Venice, badly. I draw Torcello. Attila's Throne. The bell tower. I try and try and try to draw Kamila, but I can't get her right. In fact, all my pictures are terrible, but I keep every single one of them as a fuck you to the man who had said, '*Hazel's not an artist.*' The man who had chased our car out of Cambridge.

As well as drawing, I write it all down. I write about the hallucinatory Venice that started as a joyous holiday and went weird, that shifted to a solo trip after Phoebe, then Enzo left, the swirling through the days, the magic food that, even though it wasn't real, felt real. That reminded me that food is good and lovely and necessary.

I begin to face the fact that I have had an eating disorder for a long time, and that it's going to be a long process to recover from it. It's not, in fact, as straightforward as turning up in Venice and starting to eat Italian food: in this real world, I have a lot of work to do. Freddie took so much from me, and I just handed it to him. I'm discovering that to start to heal my relationship with my own body, I need to forgive myself. It's going to be a long haul.

I write the story of my relationship with Kam. How happy we were. How much I loved her. How much I wish she'd been real.

I write down every single moment that I spent with Phoebe because Phoebe hasn't come back. She was so badly injured that she died on the road just outside Cambridge. She came to rescue me and now she'll never do anything else ever again.

I look at photos of us. I cry forever.

I watch the funeral over Zoom from my hospital bed.

Over the weeks, I piece together the story of that evening. Phoebe and Enzo rushed to Cambridge to rescue me, though they should probably have told an adult. In fact, this whole story is about things we should have told an adult.

They got me away from Freddie, who was wild with anger and drink and probably drugs. We were driving home, but Freddie drunk-drove after us and, since Enzo was a new driver and not nearly as confident, Freddie managed to push us off the road. Phoebe was on the phone to 999 when the crash happened. That was how they were there so fast, with an ambulance, and it's probably how Enzo and I made it out alive.

Freddie was unhurt but arrested. Kennedy went to number one with my song after the story came out, which is gross, but they have, of course, broken up. I avoid Kennedy at all costs, all the time. At one point, Mum said, tentatively, that Ollie and Lina and Ulla had sent their love and wanted to know if they could come and visit me, but I said no. I just can't.

I've been talking and talking. I have a therapist because it's too much for me to get through on my own. Why did no one tell me that you could do this? That after confronting things, and talking about them, you start to make sense of them? I'm working on my eating. It's difficult – I still hear his voice in my head, still feel I don't deserve to be healthy – but I'm getting there. I want to be well for Mum and Greg and Enzo. I've come back, after all.

I don't feel it's my fault Morris died any more. But I will always feel responsible for Phoebe. I understand a bit about coercive control, and I'm starting to see why I tried to mould myself into the person I thought Freddie's perfect girlfriend would be.

I have a long way to go. I have to come to terms with the fact that my stupid poisonous relationship cost my best friend her life. Brilliant, wise, clever Phoebe has gone. Her family say it's not our fault, but I know it is. It's mine. Enzo blames himself because he was driving, but everyone else blames the drunk driver who pushed our car off the road, and that is fair enough. The person who really did it was Freddie. I even met Jakub, who is, impossibly, real, when he came to tell me not to blame myself. It was sweet of him, but I will never, ever, ever stop doing that, and I will never forget the look in his eyes.

I think every day about Phoebe walking into that tomb. Going through the door and being somewhere else forever.

A month after the accident, I'm in a hospital near home, getting better, even though I don't want to.

'How's my favourite patient?' says the nurse, Tony. He says that to almost everyone: I've heard him. If he doesn't tell someone they're his favourite patient, it must mean he really hates them.

I shrug. 'OK,' I mutter.

'Well, good news,' he says. 'They're only discharging you!'

I shake my head. 'No thanks.'

I can't go home. If I do that, I'll have to do things like go back to college and I just can't.

'Hey, it's meant to be good news. Most people are, like, pleased to get out of here?'

I shake my head again. I'd rather stay here, in another in-between place, forever than look at the tatters of my life. It's the guilt.

*

I've seen a lot of different doctors, but the one who comes round that afternoon is the one I like best. All the same, I don't want to see her because I know what she's going to say. I've forgotten her name (I forget a lot), but she's wearing a badge and so I see that she's called Dr Carlyle. Did I know that? I must have done.

'Sweetie,' she says, when we've argued for a while. Is her accent Scottish? I think so. 'Look, we need your bed. So I'm afraid you don't get to stage a sit-in. Your parents have made you a bedroom on the ground floor at home. You'll have a bathroom nearby. You're doing great and frankly other people need me now.'

I close my eyes, screwing them up like a child. 'I don't want to,' I say. 'I'm . . . I'm scared.'

She sits on the bed. 'I know you are. You've been traumatized and your mother has arranged more therapy for you, which I'm very pleased about. And look. Here's someone who's going to help you out.'

I look round and see Enzo standing on the other side of the bed. He and Dr Carlyle talk a bit and I tune out. I'm terrified. I can't go home. I can't go back to college. I can't do anything. I need to go back to my dream world, my afterlife, my Deep Down. Whatever it was.

Then the doctor has gone and there's just me and Enzo. He sits down and stares at me, and in the end I look back and he has my full attention.

'OK, Haze,' he says. 'Sorry: Haz. I'll remember that one day. Look, I know it's daunting, but we're really glad you're coming home. Greg's changed the living room into a bedroom for you, like Dr C just said, and it's going to be OK. I promise. You really can't hide here forever.'

'But I want to hide here forever.' However, something he just said caught my attention. 'Greg hasn't moved back in? Don't tell me we finally parent-trapped them?'

He gives a little smile. 'That would be a result. No, no chance. But they're speaking again now. They kinda had to. And everything is incredibly civilized. They're being really, really nice to each other. But Greg's still with Bella and I do believe Susie has a new gentleman caller on the scene too, though she's coy about it. But Greg's sorted the living room out for you.'

'OK,' I said. 'That's nice of him. What else?' I can see it in his face that he has more to say. He hesitates.

'Two things,' he says in the end. 'OK. First one – I wasn't going to tell you this because, well, like before I guess I didn't want to face it myself, but here we go. I can't seem to get it out of my head and I think I have to tell you.' He takes a deep breath. 'I remember. Hazel, I was there. Venice. I remember the things you remember, though I think they're fading away. I wasn't going to say it, but what the hell. I mean, why wouldn't I?'

'You . . .' I look into his eyes and I see that it's true. 'Do you? Seriously?' I'm smiling. It feels like my first smile for a long time.

'Yes. You, me and Pheebs. We took you on a gondola. Got you food. St Mark's Square. That – that Titian church. No one puts the T-man in a box, right?'

I stare at him. I'm smiling and crying at the same time.

356

'I mean, that's amazing.'

He nods. 'I guess there's a lot out there that we don't understand. Kinda thing. I've been reading about lucid dreaming, and it's maybe something like that. But seriously, we can't ever know, right? What happens after ... And now we know a bit. Fucks with my brain.'

'Same.' I take a deep breath and try to make sense of anything. 'I guess – all the things that happen to us happen in our brains. They're closed off, in a wall of skull. None of it is real-real. And that time in Venice, even though it happened in a fraction of a second or whatever, felt just as real as this. More real. This bit could be the dream.' I blink. 'I wish it was.'

'I'm glad you saw your dad,' he says quietly.

'I saw Phoebe too, just once. After she went. And she'll be on her version of my dad's beach. She will. She'll be in the right place that's hers for eternity, and one day we'll see her again.' I pause. 'And meanwhile we can remember her forever.'

In my head, she says, *Yes please.*

Phoebe is now the presence I feel around me, more than Morris. Now that I've talked to him, and now that I actually have Greg, I don't need the imagined father: I need the real one.

'Always,' says Enzo. 'And at least – when it does happen – we might have an idea of what to expect, right?'

I nod. 'I don't really get it because I didn't have enough time, so I don't know if Dad's always on that beach or if he went there to meet me because it's where we last saw each

357

other, or how many other people he talks to or anything – I've only seen a tiny, tiny moment. But yeah, it's something. It's not oblivion, and I always thought it was before. And hopefully he and Phoebe can see each other.'

Enzo holds out a tray of Ferrero Rocher. I take one. I look at it.

'I believe you, H,' he says. 'Sorry: Haz. I mean, I've believed you all along, of course, because I was there too.'

'Thanks.' I unwrap the chocolate.

'You bought a little bird, didn't you? Like that one.' He points to the other Cello, the one that Dad had bought for Mum years ago, the one Freddie stole. The one that Lina posted back to Mum after the accident. The one that's been beside my bed for weeks.

I nod and my eyes blur. Enzo hugs me and I'm crying so hard I don't think I'll ever do anything except cry for the rest of my life. He remembers it. We cling on to each other. He cries too.

Later, as he's about to go, when we've pulled ourselves together and had another chocolate and wiped our faces and started to smile again, I remember what he said.

'What was the other thing?' I say. 'You said two things.'

He turns and gives me a little smile.

'I'd just decided to tell you tomorrow, when you're home. I thought it might all be too much for one day.'

'Well, now you have to tell me right away. What is it?'

'Yeah, I know. OK. This might be a bad idea, but … fine. OK. Look, I did it. I looked up Kamila King. With a K and one l. I found her pretty easily, Haz. I mean, I think I did. Is this her?'

He turns his phone and shows me the screen.

And there she is.

I stare.

Everything changes.

When I speak, I can only ask one question.

48

Venice

Six months later

As I stand at the window and look across the water, I feel myself waking up. Because I'm here, in real Venice. Real Venice is also like being in a painting. It's almost exactly the same as the other one. I'm staying in Vittoria's studio, but it's not on the Grand Canal. Of course it's not. It's down a tiny alley with a little canal in front of it and it's nothing like the one I imagined. This one was furnished in the seventies and I love it. There's no rooftop terrace, no grand view of everything. I can see the building across the water and a line of washing.

The city still looks like a Canaletto, though it's winter now and everyone is wearing big coats and boots.

I'm eighteen, and I'm ready to do this. I know Phoebe is here. I've met my father on the beach in Greece, and somewhere Phoebe is in Venice. She's around me: I can feel her and I know where I need to go.

Enzo wanted to come, but I told him I have to do it on my own at first. He's coming out in a couple of days. Mum is so worried about me that she actually flew to Venice with me, then stayed on the mainland in a hotel, almost certainly staring at her phone screen the whole time, waiting to hear from me, because she knows I needed to do this myself.

I walk to the Grand Canal. I pass a souvenir seller and pause. I want him to be the same person, to be partly Morris, but he's not. He is, of course, his own person and he's not wearing a Doctor Who T-shirt. I want him to have the same bird for sale, but he doesn't. He looks up at me with a question on his face and I hold his gaze, smile and crouch down to check.

I pick up a bird that's nearly right but not quite.

'Do you have a green and yellow one?' I say, and he nods and rummages through a box of stuff. When he turns back to me, he's holding her. I take her. My bird. Cello, the twin of the real one at home, the one Freddie stole and Lina returned, along with the other things he took. I hand the man five euros and put her in my pocket.

I've been back at college since September, restarting my A levels, aiming high this time. I'm taking it slowly, and I know I don't want to go back to Cambridge, but I want to go somewhere good. Somewhere new and interesting, with new people and life experiences. I want to apply myself, to learn things. I don't care that I'm in the year below. I don't care that everyone talks about me. I don't care about that stupid song: Greg bought me some noise-cancelling headphones and I wear them any time it comes on. I blank it out completely, keep my head down and get things done.

I'm wearing my own clothes, eating my own food, living my life. My time with Freddie is over. He's in custody and there's a court case looming where I will have to speak, but I'm not thinking about that yet.

And I've let Greg in. Now that I've spent time with Morris, I see that Greg isn't a threat. He was never trying to erase my father. He was trying to look after me. And he does: I see him once a week, sometimes more. I've even, with Mum's blessing, met his girlfriend Bella, who is, indeed, real, and who has a cute little boy.

I walk to St Mark's Square. I don't duck down a random alley, because I've had enough of them. I'm happy to shuffle along with the crowds. I'm still not brilliant at walking, but I can get around as long as I stop quite often. I look at the people eating cake in Florian's, but because it's winter only the most intrepid are outside, and I don't want a cake. I see a man feeding the pigeons. I walk past the basilica, then turn back to look at it against the sky, dome after dome after dome.

It takes me a long time to reach Santa Maria Gloriosa dei Frari because I keep having to stop and rest. Also, I'd never have found it without the map on my phone. But I get there eventually. I walk over the little bridge and there it is in front of me. Huge, brick, less spectacular, from the outside, than the basilica. I remember random facts about it. It's in one of the *Assassin's Creed* games. They had to pretend Titian didn't die of the plague so he could be buried here. Are those things true? It turns out they are.

I bought expensive flowers on the way and a slice of *crostata al limone*, the closest I could find to the lemon meringue pie Phoebe made me on my sixteenth birthday. They're tucked into my backpack, the tart wrapped in a paper bag. I queue up and pay and have such a vivid flashback of being thrown out of this church that I'm not sure they'll let me in, but they do.

And inside it takes my breath away because it's exactly, precisely the same. The floor is red and white, worn old tiles. There is Titian's tomb, the one he's not inside. And there it is: Canova's monument. It contains his heart. I stand in front of it and all I can see is Phoebe.

It contains his heart and mine too.

I watch a shadow of her walking through that door. I stand still for a very long time. Then I put my flowers down and leave. I give the pie to a woman who is begging nearby because I know that's what Phoebe would have wanted.

The cafe opposite is the same as it was before. I can't sit in the window because a French couple is there with a small child. I smile at the kid. I'd been planning to write my name and Enzo's in the condensation and send him a picture, but actually we can come back here and do it ourselves. I order a frothy cappuccino and some chips and wait for my legs to stop hurting. I take some painkillers. I'm far from recovered, and my physio was very much against me doing any of this, but today is the only day I'm planning to do this much exercise and I have to finish it.

I eat a chip. I look at the rest of them. I'm doing OK.

I take out a pencil and draw a picture of the tomb. I write CANOVA above it, and make one of the sculpted figures into Phoebe. When I'm ready, I leave it on the table and set off, trying not to be scared.

I sit on a bench on the bank and look out at the Grand Canal. It smells of Venice – the canals, the damp, the wintery air. It looks like Venice. I lean down and touch the ground beneath my feet. I'm not sure what makes this city real and that one not, but anyway I'm here.

I sit still for a long time before the waterbus appears on the horizon. I watch it coming towards me and know that this is the one. Kamila left me by boat, and she's coming back in the same way.

Ever since Enzo found her, alive and recovering from an accident in Australia, we've been messaging. My first was tentative: I was aware that I was writing a social-media message to a stranger, that I was going to sound completely unhinged.

But she replied instantly, even though it was the middle of her night.

> Haz! Hazel Angelopoulos?
> You exist? Really????

She had been knocked down by a car in London, back in 2023, and when she'd recovered enough she'd been taken back to Australia, where she's been living with the memory of her weird dream for months. Like me, she had never been to real Venice.

I stand up and watch the boat dock from a distance. My heart is pounding. It's insane that a stranger has come halfway round the world because we met in some kind of between-world dream Venice, but it's happening. She might not be her real self. Real Kam might be a different person altogether.

Then I see her and I feel myself light up.

I feel the whole of my face smiling and I start to walk. Then, as best I can, I run towards her. She steps off the boat, puts her case down and squeezes me into a hug. I bury my face in her. I know her. Everything about her is familiar to me. She smells the same. She's everything. She's more real, even, than she was then.

I step back. We're both crying.

'So this is the real Hazel,' she says, and I look down at myself. Jeans, a hoodie, the barbed-wire necklace for protection, even though I will never see anyone from Kennedy ever again. Clumpy boots.

She is wearing black jeans, a black jumper, a pink coat, boots. Her hair has grown a bit, and it's almost down to her shoulders. I see my own wonder reflected in her face.

I take her hand. She grips mine tightly.

We walk together, through the streets of real Venice.

Acknowledgements

This book has been a journey that was, at times, as disorientating as Hazel's. Enormous thanks as always to my fabulous editor Ruth Knowles, who read drafts that were heading all over the place and showed me how to make this story make sense. Thank you, too, to everyone else involved at Penguin: I continue to be overawed at the fact that my books have a penguin on the cover. Thank you, Lowri Ribbons, Jane Tait, Josh Benn, Philippa Neville, Debs Warner, Jessica Read and everyone else involved. Also to the fabulous Stephanie Thwaites and Grace Robinson, and everybody else at Curtis Brown.

Thank you Mercy Brewer for beta reading: you are brilliant and exactly the person I want reading my books.

Craig Barr-Green: you selflessly accompanied me on a research trip to Venice and spent a huge amount of time in Santa Maria Gloriosa dei Frari without a word of complaint before we headed off to Torcello and general holiday times. Much appreciated!

On the home side of things, huge thanks to everyone around me for all the support. I'm lucky to have such supportive friends and family, as well as writing buddies. Thanks to Gabe, Seb, Lottie, Charlie and Alfie for being brilliant from near or far, and to all my family and friends, including the lovely Cornish creatives who are always around for solidarity and coffees. And to Craig, for bringing me drinks, reading early drafts, and telling me I can do it even when it doesn't feel that way.

About the Author

Emily Barr worked as a journalist in London, but always hankered after a quiet room and a book to write. She went travelling for a year, which gave her an idea for a novel set in the world of backpackers in Asia. This became *Backpack*, a thriller that won the WHSmith New Talent Award. Her first YA thriller, *The One Memory of Flora Banks*, has been published in twenty-seven countries and was shortlisted for the YA Book Prize. Emily's third YA thriller, *The Girl Who Came Out of the Woods*, was published in 2019 and nominated for the Carnegie Award. *A Girl Can Dream* is her seventh YA novel. Emily lives in Cornwall with her husband and their children.

Follow Emily Barr
on Twitter @emily_barr
and Instagram @emilybarrauthor
#AGirlCanDream

Helplines

If you or someone you know is experiencing coercive control, help is available:

National Domestic Abuse Helpline (UK): 0808 2000 247
This helpline is free of charge and open 24/7.
EU-wide domestic abuse helpline: 116 016

Womensaid.org.uk and **refuge.org.uk** signpost to multiple resources for anyone in an unhealthy relationship.

Women's Aid Ireland: 1800 341 900
The website www.toointoyou.ie is a resource for young people with concerns about coercive control.

The **Bright Sky app** is free to download, and offers support and information to anyone worried they, or someone they know, might be in an abusive relationship.

Samaritans (UK): 116123

For help with disordered eating:

Beat (UK): www.beateatingdisorders.org.uk
The website has a tool to find local help.
Youth helpline: 0808 801 0711
General helplines:
England: 0808 801 0677
Scotland: 0808 801 0432
Wales: 0808 801 0433
Northern Ireland: 0808 801 0434

Bodywhys (Republic of Ireland): 2107906, www.bodywhys.ie

READ MORE BY EMILY BARR

Senara has never been in love before. She's not done anything exciting before. Always the sidekick . . . until the summer that changes everything.

What do you do when – with every day that
passes – you're literally growing apart from the
best person you've ever known . . . ?

Flora has amnesia.
She can't remember
anything day-to-day.
But then she kisses
someone she shouldn't –
and the next day she
remembers it.
It's the first time she's
remembered anything
since she was ten.

But the boy is gone.

*I call her Bella because
she is the dark side of me.
It's Ella but not.
It's bad Ella.
Bella.*

Arty has lived in a hidden matriarchy in the hills of India all her life. But now a deadly plague is threatening her tiny commune, and she must go into the modern world for help, before it's too late . . .

The air is running out. We think there's less than a year of it. We are the last humans. What do we do? Make a list. Heal rifts. Do the things that scare us.

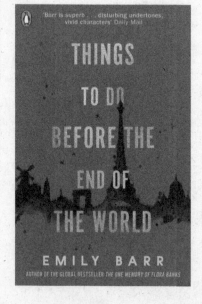